M

"I thought you were my friend,"

Alexandra said.

Her quiet statement drew Nolan's gaze up to meet hers in the mirror as he answered, "I *am* your friend."

She slowly shook her head. "A friend wouldn't look at me like—"

"Like what?" he demanded, starting to feel angry now. "Like a man looks at a beautiful woman?"

"Yes," Alexandra quietly stated.

"Wrong." Nolan took a deep breath and reined in his temper. "We *are* friends, Alexandra, but I am definitely *not* blind. I noticed you were gorgeous the first time I met you."

"But you never…"

"Tried to seduce you?" When she nodded, he shrugged. "You never gave me an invitation. Not even a subtle one. I valued your friendship too much to risk ruining it with an unwanted advance, but don't fool yourself into believing that I never thought you were a desirable woman."

❤ ❤ ❤

**HEARTS OF WYOMING:
Rugged and wild, the McBride family
has love to share…and Wyoming weddings
are on their minds!**

Dear Reader,

What would July be without fun in the sun, dazzling fireworks displays—or heartwarming love stories from the Special Edition line? Romance seems even more irresistible in the balmy days of summer, and our six books for this month are sure to provide hours of reading pleasure.

This July, Myrna Temte continues her HEARTS OF WYOMING series with an engaging story about best friends turned lovers. THAT SPECIAL WOMAN! Alexandra McBride Talbot is determined not to get involved with her handsome next-door neighbor, but he goes to extraordinary lengths to win this single mom's stubborn heart in *Urban Cowboy*.

Sometimes true love knows no rhyme or reason. Take for instance the headstrong heroine in *Hannah and the Hellion* by Christine Flynn. Everyone warned this sweetheart away from the resident outcast, but she refused to abandon the rogue of her dreams. Or check out the romance-minded rancher who's driven to claim the heart of his childhood crush in *The Cowboy's Ideal Wife* by bestselling author Victoria Pade—the next installment in her popular A RANCHING FAMILY series. And Martha Hix's transformation story proves how love can give a gruff, emotionally scarred hero a new lease on life in *Terrific Tom*.

Rounding off the month, we've got *The Sheik's Mistress* by Brittany Young—a forbidden-love saga about a soon-to-be betrothed sheik and a feisty American beauty. And pure, platonic friendship turns into something far greater in *Baby Starts the Wedding March* by Amy Frazier.

I hope you enjoy each and every story to come!

Sincerely,

Tara Gavin,
Editorial Manager

Please address questions and book requests to:
Silhouette Reader Service
U.S.: 3010 Walden Ave., P.O. Box 1325, Buffalo, NY 14269
Canadian: P.O. Box 609, Fort Erie, Ont. L2A 5X3

MYRNA TEMTE

URBAN COWBOY

Silhouette®

SPECIAL EDITION®

Published by Silhouette Books
America's Publisher of Contemporary Romance

This book is dedicated to the usual characters:
Kathie Hays, Terry Kanago and Mary Pat Kanaley.
Here's to girlfriends and slumber parties!

My thanks, as always, to Debra Sims of Douglas,
Wyoming, for help with information on ranching.

 SILHOUETTE BOOKS

ISBN 0-373-24183-6

URBAN COWBOY

Copyright © 1998 by Myrna Temte

Printed in U.S.A.

MYRNA TEMTE

grew up in Montana and attended college in Wyoming, where she met and married her husband. Marriage didn't necessarily mean settling down for the Temtes—they have lived in six different states, including Washington, where they currently reside. Moving so much is difficult, the author says, but it is also wonderful stimulation for a writer.

Though always a "readaholic," Myrna never dreamed of becoming an author. But while spending time at home to care for her first child, she began to seek an outlet from the never-ending duties of housekeeping and child rearing. She started reading romances and soon became hooked, both as a reader and a writer. Now Myrna appreciates the best of all possible worlds—a loving family and a challenging career that lets her set her own hours and turn her imagination loose.

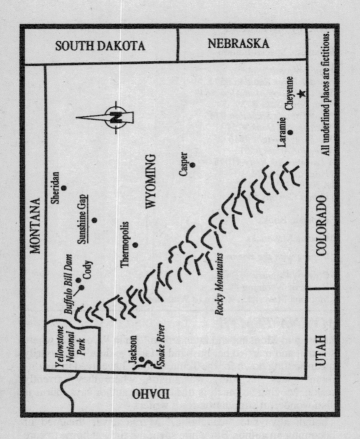

All underlined places are fictitious.

Chapter One

After a long, frustrating day in court, Nolan Larson carried a beer bottle onto his patio, settled into a padded swivel chair and leaned back, gazing up at the evening sky. Five years in Wyoming, and he still couldn't get over how much brighter and closer the stars looked here than they had in L.A. Watching them had become his favorite method of stress reduction. Already he could feel his pulse slowing, his nerves mellowing, the kinks in his psyche unkinking.

And then came the voice.

"He doesn't beat ya. He doesn't rape ya. He gives ya food to eat, clothes to wear and a roof over your head. Honey, what more do ya want in a man?"

Nolan choked on a swallow of beer and shot a surprised glance toward the five-foot hedge that separated his backyard from Alexandra Talbot's. The voice belonged to Alexandra, all right, but the words were completely at odds with the independent woman he knew her to be. What in the world was she up to now?

"Love. I want love, Belle." The voice was still Alex's, but now it sounded softer, sweeter, more...innocent. "And I don't love Bear Swanson. I don't reckon I ever will."

Nolan pushed himself to his feet and silently crossed to the gap in the hedge his son Rick, and Alex's daughter, Natasha, had created by continually squeezing through it to visit each other.

"Hah!" the Belle voice replied. "Love ain't all it's cracked up to be, Lizzie, and don't you forget it. You marry that Swanson fella, or you're gonna end up in some stinkin' saloon just like me. Believe you me, you don't want that."

Nolan looked through the opening and smiled. Alex's patio lights were on, illuminating the square of concrete like a stage. Though she wore jeans, a sweatshirt and battered brown loafers, he barely had to stretch his imagination to see Belle as a cynical, weary, dance-hall girl from the Old West.

Holding a large booklet in front of her, Alex pivoted and with subtle changes of posture, expression and diction, she "became" the person who owned the Lizzie voice.

"I know," she said. "But it don't seem right to marry a man just so he'll take care of me."

Alex pivoted again and Belle reappeared. "You'll be takin' care of him too, girl. Cookin' his meals, washin' his clothes, birthin' his babies. It ain't like he won't get nothin' out of the deal."

"Alexandra, I'm shocked. I thought you were a feminist," Nolan said, stepping into Alex's yard.

She screeched at the sound of his voice, then whirled around to face him, one palm pressed flat against her sternum. "Nolan, you wretch! You nearly gave me a heart attack."

Nolan grinned. Alex frequently caught him off balance, but he rarely managed to return the favor. "I'm sorry, Alex."

Raising an eyebrow at him, she snorted. "You don't look very sorry."

"What are you reading?" He pointed at the booklet. "A new play for your class?"

She glanced down at her hands as if she'd forgotten they held anything, then looked back up at him with her big dark eyes alight and a smile so full of pride and affection, it put a funny little ache in the center of his chest. He'd always thought Alexandra was a beautiful woman, but when she smiled that way, she was breathtaking. At times it made him wish their friendship could be more.

"It's the script for *Against the Wind*." She hugged the booklet to her breasts and hurried across the yard to join him.

"The movie they're going to film here this summer?" he asked. "At your family's ranch?"

"Yes, and it's wonderful. I can hardly believe my dopey cousin Marsh actually wrote this."

"I thought he wouldn't let you read it."

"He wouldn't, the big snot. For security reasons." Alex gave him her most dramatic eye roll, then hugged the script tighter. "And get this. Blair DuMaine asked little ol' *me*," she paused and thumped her chest with her index finger, "to help *her* learn her lines before they start shooting. Can you be*lieve* it?"

"When you're involved, I've learned to believe just about anything," Nolan said with a chuckle.

Alex's eyes glinted with fiendish delight. "That's not even the best part."

"Do I need to sit down for this?"

She took a swat at his shoulder. "Don't be silly. This is

just so-o-o cool. She's coming to play practice tomorrow night, and she's going to help me get my seniors to loosen up.''

"Blair DuMaine? Of the *Hollywood* DuMaines is coming to Sunshine Gap High School? For *play* practice?''

"Yup.'' Alex blew on her fingernails, polished them on her sweatshirt, then tossed aside her dignity and danced around in a brief, manic jig that made her short, glossy black curls bounce wildly around her face.

"How did you manage that?'' he asked. "Blackmail?''

"I didn't need to. She was incredibly gracious and generous. You'll really like her.''

"Me?''

"Yes, Nolan. You and Rick and Tasha are going to be our audience tomorrow night. Please?''

"Will I get to meet her?''

"Blair? Of course.''

"Will I get an autograph?''

"If you want one.'' Alex reached out and grasped his forearm. "You've got to help me out here, Nolan. Tasha wants to see the practice, but I can't leave her on her own that long without supervision. She'll get bored and dismantle the school while my back is turned.''

"Tasha's not that bad.''

"She's a teenager. I work with them every day, all day long, and a bored teenager is a dangerous teenager. Trust me on this, will you?''

"All right. We'll be there.'' Nolan held up his beer bottle. "Would you like to come over and have one?''

Alex glanced over her shoulder at Tasha's bedroom window. The light was out, the normally blaring boombox quiet. Then she turned back to him and grinned. "You're on. I'm too wired to sleep, anyway.''

He led the way through the hedge. The sky was crowded

with stars now, and the temperature had dropped ten degrees since he'd started talking to Alex. Bypassing the patio table, he climbed his back steps, confident that she would follow him into his kitchen.

While he took another beer from the refrigerator, she helped herself to a glass from the cupboard to the right of the sink. She carried it to the breakfast nook, kicked off her loafers, tucked her feet close to her bottom and curled into her favorite corner of the padded bench where she could still keep an eye on Tasha's bedroom window. Nolan sat on the adjacent side of the table, stretching his legs out on the seat. He listened for any sound overhead that would indicate Rick was still up, but heard only the hum of the fridge.

He couldn't count the number of evenings he and Alex had sat here after the kids had gone to bed, sipping and talking, sharing the joys and burdens of single parenthood, cementing the best friendship he had ever known. He'd been lost and more than a little confused after his wife's death and his subsequent move to Sunshine Gap, but Alex had taken pity on her new neighbor, cheerfully offering advice and assistance whenever he needed it. He didn't know what he or Rick would have done without her.

He hoped he had provided the same level of support for her. He liked to think he understood her better than most people, including certain members of her large, extended family. But Alex was so skilled at portraying whatever emotion she wanted others to see, sometimes it was hard to tell how she really felt.

"So, tell me the truth," Nolan said. "Is this play practice part of a nefarious plot to get yourself a role in the movie?"

Her mouth full of beer, Alex sputtered, swallowed and shot him a scowl. "Of course not."

"Why do you say that?" Nolan asked, surprised by the

vehemence of her answer. "You're a great actress. Why not use any connection you have to get your foot in Hollywood's door?"

"Oh, pu-lease," she drawled. "They're shooting a major motion picture, and I'm a high school English teacher who's done a little community theater. Big deal. I'm not even close to being in Blair's league."

"Not true," Nolan said. "You have a university degree in drama, my dear, which undoubtedly gives you considerable stage experience. I've also seen some of Blair DuMaine's movies, and I've seen you in community theater. You're every bit as good as she is."

Alex laughed at him. "That's terribly sweet of you, Nolan, but you're my best buddy. You're supposed to think I'm wonderful."

"Ha! I can be a mean, hard-nosed critic when I choose, and you are *really* good. I've always wondered what someone as talented as you are is doing teaching school in Sunshine Gap."

"Oh, yeah? Well, I'm not the only one who's wondered what a hotshot California criminal attorney is doing, practicing family law in Cody."

Nolan saluted her parry with his beer bottle. "Escaping California," he said with a chuckle. "It's hard enough raising a child by yourself without that kind of insanity going on around you all the time. At least here, I have half a prayer of keeping track of Rick."

"That's true." Alex propped up her chin with the heel of one hand and uttered a sad, or perhaps it was more of a nostalgic, sigh. "Nobody gets away with much of anything in Sunshine Gap. Not even the adults."

"How did we get off on this subject?" Nolan narrowed his eyes at her. "You wouldn't be trying to avoid discussing your acting abilities?"

She stiffened slightly but her gaze never faltered. "Of course not."

"Then tell me why you're teaching high school instead of pursuing a professional acting career."

If her back hadn't already been firmly planted against the bench seat, Nolan suspected she physically would have retreated from him. The sparkle faded from her eyes, and the animation he normally saw in her face drained away until she reminded him more of a mannequin than a living, breathing woman. The completeness of the transformation startled him. And intrigued him.

"Alexandra? What did I say?" He swung his feet to the floor and scooted around the curve in the bench until he was close enough to touch her hands, which were curled over her raised knees in a white-knuckled grip. "I'm sorry. You must know I would never intentionally upset you or—"

She cut him off with a quick shake of her head. "It's all right. Just some old...unfinished business."

"Do you want to talk about it?"

"Not really." She gave him a pathetic excuse for a smile. "It would bore you to tears."

Nolan took her right hand in his left and squeezed it. "Not a chance. You've listened to me talk about Jennifer at least a hundred times, but I don't know much about your allegedly torrid past. Except for the gossip I've picked up since we moved here, of course, seventy-five percent of which I don't believe."

Color flared in her cheeks, and her voice took on an indignant bite. "Only seventy-five? You mean you believe a *fourth* of all those stupid old stories about me?"

Knowing Alex, he actually believed most of them had at least some basis in fact, but he wasn't going to admit that at the moment. "If they're false, why don't you tell me the true story of Alexandra McBride Talbot? Start with why it upsets you to consider a professional acting career.''

She yanked her hand away. ''God, I really hate lawyers. They're so darn nosy.''

''Answer the question.''

''Oh, all right.'' She swung her feet to the floor, wrapped both hands around her glass and studied the contents as if there were secrets written in the beer bubbles. ''I did want an acting career. Since I was a little girl the only thing I ever really wanted to be was a movie star like Blair.''

''Did you ever go to Hollywood and—''

Alex sprang to her feet and paced across the room. ''Oh, come *on*. Get real. Do you know what percentage of the thousands of people who go to Hollywood ever succeed at finding work, much less becoming stars?''

''Excuse me?'' Nolan said with a surprised laugh. ''That doesn't even sound like you. Since when did the possibility of failure ever stop you from trying to get something you wanted?''

She waved his question aside. ''It doesn't matter. I gave up on that dream years ago. It's just that, seeing Blair and hearing about her production company...well, it's brought those old feelings back to the surface. But, give me a little time and I'll get over it.''

''Maybe you shouldn't get over it,'' Nolan said.

''I'm not good enough to be a professional.''

''Says who? How do you know if you've never tried?''

''I just do.'' Alex picked up a pencil from the cup by the telephone and pointed it at Nolan. ''And I'm not gorgeous enough, either, so stop grilling me. You're a lawyer, not a cop.''

''I'm only asking you to think rationally.''

She rearranged everything on top of the built-in desk,

then put everything back in its original spot. ''This isn't a real rational subject for me, okay?''

''Okay, but answer one more question for me. Why did you really give up on your dream, Alex?''

''My family wasn't exactly thrilled with the idea.'' She paced to the window over the sink and looked out at the darkness. ''You know how protective they all are. It's hard enough to break away from one set of parents you love, but with our weird family, I always felt as if I had two. Aunt Lucy and Uncle Harry were just as bad as Mom and Dad.''

Alexandra's family actually consisted of two McBride families. The relationships involved brothers, Gage and Harry McBride, who had married twin sisters, Mary and Lucy Parilli. The two couples jointly owned and lived together on the Flying M Ranch. Gage and Mary had produced Jake, Zack, Alexandra and Cal. Harry and Lucy had three children, Dillon, Marsh and Grace. The seven younger McBrides were actually double first cousins. They had been raised as if they were all siblings, however, and always treated each other as such.

''Your cousin Marsh went to Hollywood,'' Nolan said.

''He's a guy,'' Alex said. ''They didn't fight him as hard as they did me because they're really old-fashioned.''

''Or maybe he fought harder than you did because he was more confident of his talent.''

Alex frowned at him. ''What exactly are you implying?''

Nolan met her frown with a challenging smile. ''Maybe he was less...afraid to put his dream on the line.''

''You think I was chicken? That's a rotten thing to say.''

She marched back to the table, clamped her hands onto her hips and gave him the meanest high school teacher's glare in her arsenal. If he'd been sixteen, his eyebrows probably would have melted from the heat. But he wasn't sixteen. He was thirty-eight and far too experienced in handling hostility to be intimidated by it.

"You know what they say," he said. "The truth often hurts."

"That's *not* the truth. I was *never* afraid I couldn't act."

"That's what I thought," Nolan said with a grin. "And your entire family says you've been impossible to control since the day you were born, so stop using these pathetic excuses, will you? Why didn't you at least *try* to make it in Hollywood?"

Alex returned to the bench, lifted her feet onto the seat and curled up in "her" corner again. "All right, all right, here's the truth. My family insisted that I go to college first. I didn't really want to, but they refused to help me otherwise, so I finally gave in. I liked the profs in the theater department well enough to stay in school. Then I met Tasha's father, and you've probably heard the rest of the story from our friendly local gossipmongers."

"Tell me your side, anyway," Nolan said.

"It's hardly unique." She carefully peeled the label off her beer bottle, then folded it over and over until it became a little ball of paper. "Brad said I was exotic, or some such trashy line, which, like an idiot, I fell for. I got pregnant, we got married, and a year later we divorced. Suddenly I was a single mother with a baby to raise. End of acting career."

"You gave up a lifelong dream just like that?"

She flicked the little ball of paper she'd created back and forth on the table, using her index fingers. "Bradley Talbot was about as far from being a mature adult as it's possible for a man to be, and I didn't want his snooty mother to raise my baby. I realized that if I didn't want that to happen, I'd better do some fast growing up of my own. I used my share of the divorce settlement to go back to school and earn a teaching certificate.''

''I can understand you needed something secure to fall back on,'' Nolan said, ''but you could have used that teaching certificate in a lot of places that would have provided more opportunities for you to pick up acting jobs. Maybe even in L.A. Why did you come back here, Alex?''

She got up, grabbed a message pad and the pencil from the desk and brought them to the table. Doodling a series of circles, she said, ''I wanted Tasha to have the most stable, loving home I could give her, and that meant coming back to the Gap, so my family could pitch in when I needed a hand. Considering what a great kid she's been, I think I made the right decision.''

''You've done a wonderful job of raising her,'' Nolan said.

Alex raised one shoulder in a half shrug. ''So far, so good, anyway, for both Tasha and Rick. But it's way too early to start congratulating ourselves. They haven't even started dating or driving yet. God only knows what they'll get up to when they're in high school.''

Groaning, Nolan clutched at his chest. ''Don't remind me.''

''Too late,'' she said with a laugh. ''I already did.''

''Yes, thank you ever so much, pal.''

He sat back and watched her start a new page of doodles, boxes this time. He admired her willingness to sacrifice her big dream for her daughter's sake, especially since he knew that she hadn't become a martyr or taken out her disappointments on Tasha in any way. Tasha was a bright, funny, confident young woman who was very close to her mother, though they had the usual adolescent-versus-parent disagreements.

Still, it seemed a shame that Alex had been forced to

give up something so important to her. Bradley Talbot was now a state senator; he hadn't given up a thing but a few child-support checks. He hadn't even paid those on time or in full until Nolan had written the weasel a letter on office stationery, informing him of pending legal action if he didn't become current with his payments and stay current.

"You know, Alexandra," Nolan said, "you could still do it."

"Do what?"

"Become an actress."

She shot him a sideways glance, then uttered a rueful laugh. "Oh, it's too late. Way too late. Hollywood likes them young, and I'm on the wrong side of thirty."

Nolan made a point of studying her with a critical eye. "You still look about twenty. Twenty-five maximum."

"You're a terrible liar, Larson."

"I beg your pardon. The last time we went to a bar in Billings, you were carded, weren't you?"

"Aw, that guy was just trying to flirt with me."

Nolan gazed into her eyes and realized she wasn't fishing for compliments; she honestly didn't believe him. Nor would she believe him if he tried to tell her she was more than beautiful enough to be a movie star. He would simply have to show her.

Making shooing motions with his hands, he slid toward her until he crowded her right out of the booth. Then he grasped her elbow and marched her into the laundry room, where the previous owner of his house had hung a full-length mirror. Alex grumbled and fussed, refusing to stand in front of the mirror until he threatened to tell Tasha who had really decorated the high school principal's favorite pine tree with toilet paper during the recent spring break.

"I don't know what you think this will prove," she said.

"Do be quiet, Alexandra. And stand up straight. We're not starting until you stop this ridiculous sulking."

She sighed with what sounded like extreme aggravation. He stood to one side and stared at her, silently waiting her out.

"Oh, all right," she finally said. "Hurry up and do whatever it is you need to do. I should go home soon."

"Fine. Just listen to what I'm saying and look at yourself though my eyes for once. We'll start with your hair."

Her eyebrows shot up, disappearing under her bangs. "What's wrong with my hair?"

"Nothing. It's thick. It's shiny. It looks good no matter what you do or don't do to it. I even like it short, and I'm especially fond of long hair."

She turned her head this way and that, tugging self-consciously at a strand over her left ear. "I guess it's okay."

"Your figure is okay, too."

Her quick, indignant glare over her shoulder made him grin. Saying Alex's figure was okay was like saying Wyoming had a few antelope and a little sagebrush. A dedicated jogger and student of nutrition, she worked hard to maintain it.

She raised her rib cage and pulled her shoulders back, then put her hands on her waist, impatiently twisting to her left, then her right, as if trying to see herself from all directions. "My stomach's pretty flat. And my thighs aren't too big. My hips, though..."

"Alexandra, false modesty does not become you." That earned him another scowl.

"Give me a break, will you? I have given birth, you know. It's not like I have a perfect body."

"Believe me, it's close enough." He stepped behind her and brought his hands up on either side of her arms, determined to focus her attention where he wanted it. "Stop being so critical of yourself and really look. Your breasts are...well, they're nothing short of magnificent. And they're real, Alex. They're not even enhanced by silicone."

"No-o-o-lan."

Ignoring her shocked protest, he put his hands firmly on the sides of her waist. He'd never touched her in a way that had sexual overtones before, but now...well, he simply had to demonstrate his point. "Your waist is very small in comparison, see? And your hips have this delightful curve. It's a perfect invitation to a man's hand."

"Nolan Larson!" She turned halfway around and gaped at him. "I can't believe you—"

He released her hips, grasped her shoulders and turned her sideways to the mirror. Much as he wanted to demonstrate further, he didn't dare. "Your little rump is nice and round. And it's firm, Alexandra. Nothing is sagging or heading south. But, as great as everything else is, your legs are undoubtedly your best feature. I spent years ogling girls at the beach when I was growing up, and I have never seen a longer or sexier pair of legs than yours. Ever. They're really quite stunning."

"I thought you were my friend."

Her quiet statement drew his gaze up to meet hers in the mirror. If her eyes got any bigger they would blot out the rest of her face; the expression in them had moved beyond "surprised and shocked" to "absolutely appalled." Uh-oh. Maybe he'd let himself get a tad carried away.

"I *am* your friend."

She slowly, sadly shook her head. "A friend wouldn't look at me like..."

"Like what?" he demanded, starting to feel angry now. For God's sake, did she think he was completely sexless? "Like a man looks at a beautiful woman?"

"Yes."

"Wrong." Nolan took a deep breath and reined in his temper. The last thing she needed to deal with at the moment was his wounded ego. "We *are* friends, Alexandra, but I am definitely not gay, and I am not one of your brothers or cousins. I noticed you were gorgeous the first time I met you."

"But you never…"

"Tried to seduce you?" When she nodded, he shrugged, stepped away from her and shoved his hands into the front pockets of his slacks. "You never gave me an invitation. Not even a subtle one. I valued your friendship too much to risk ruining it with an unwanted advance, but don't fool yourself into believing that I never thought you were a desirable woman."

"Why didn't you ever say anything?"

"Such as? 'Oh, by the way, I think you're sexy as hell, Alexandra, and I'd love to take you to bed and have my way with you.' If I'd tried any kind of a line on you, you wouldn't have given me the time of day."

She looked down at her hands, and he thought he heard a sniffle.

"I…it was nothing personal. About you, I mean," she said. "You're a very attractive man, Nolan. Of course, I'm sure you know that. You *do* know that, don't you?"

"Relax, will you?" He tucked his index finger under her chin, lifting it for a better view of her eyes. "Oh, don't cry, Alexandra, please. I'm still your friend. I didn't say any of this to make you feel uncomfortable with me."

Sniffling again, she jerked out of his grasp. "Well, why did you say it then?"

"Because the odds of having a movie shot in Sunshine Gap, Wyoming, must be about a billion to one," he said. "This is a once-in-a-lifetime opportunity for you to fulfill a lifelong dream, and I'm trying to convince you to go for it.''

"Go for it? How?"

"Talk to Blair or to Marsh about getting a role."

"Oh, I couldn't."

"Why not? Tasha's thirteen years old. She can handle it if you spend some time on a movie set this summer. I'll even help you keep her entertained."

"It's not that easy, Nolan. They're going to start shooting the fifteenth of June. I'm sure they've already signed professional actors for all of the speaking roles by now."

"Perhaps, but things happen sometimes. It wouldn't hurt to let them know you're interested and available. At the very least, you could be an extra."

The sparkle reappeared in her eyes, but still she hesitated. "Oh, I don't know. Let me think about it."

"Life can be surprisingly short. You may not get to be a big star, but you can probably be in this one movie. Give it a shot, Alexandra. What have you got to lose?"

Chapter Two

Alex studied Nolan's challenging smile and felt the oddest curling sensation deep in the pit of her stomach. She knew what it was, of course. A thirty-three-year-old divorcée with a child knew what good-old, down-and-dirty sexual attraction felt like.

She'd simply never felt it toward Nolan before. She'd never allowed herself to feel it toward him.

Not that he was even remotely close to being homely. Tall and lean, and with features rugged enough to call interesting instead of merely handsome, he turned his share of female heads when he wore his conservative, gray-suit-white-shirt-blue-tie-and-wingtips lawyer outfits. Get him into a pair of casual slacks—the dear but stodgy man steadfastly refused to wear jeans—and a green polo shirt, however, ruffle his carefully styled, golden-brown hair and put a wicked grin like this one on his face, and he looked downright hunky.

But she really didn't think of him in sexual or romantic terms. She didn't want to, anyway. She wasn't supposed to, and she definitely could not afford to.

Nolan was simply…Nolan, which made him strictly off-limits. Calm, orderly and methodical, he was her exact opposite in temperament, but by some lucky quirk, they rarely irritated each other. Since he'd moved into the house next door, he'd become her best friend and ally in the child-raising wars that occupied the major part of both of their lives.

She wouldn't have traded him for any of the hottest actors in Hollywood. Well, if Mel Gibson should suddenly become available and offer to take Nolan's place in her life…she might possibly have to rethink her stance. But she doubted it.

Mel hadn't been there to hold her together when Tasha had nearly died from appendicitis. He hadn't helped her paint her house after he'd hired someone else to paint his own. He hadn't taken the time to teach her how to budget or nag her into starting an account in a mutual fund for Tasha's future college expenses and another for her own retirement, either.

Nolan had.

In hindsight, it seemed as if from the first day they had met, he'd supported her through every major and minor crisis in her life, offering help and advice when he had something to contribute, and a warm, solid shoulder to cry on when there was nothing else he could do. They had shared such a marvelous friendship, she really didn't want to risk damaging it with something as inconsequential as sex.

"Alex? Are you all right?"

She cleared her throat. Forced a smile. Backed a couple of feet away from him. "I'm fine, Nolan. Just fine."

He took a step toward her, then held up his palms and let out an impatient-sounding huff when she backed away again. "For God's sake, Alexandra, I'm not going to pounce on you."

That wasn't the problem, Alex thought with a gulp. The problem was that suddenly *she* wanted to pounce on *him.* In fact, she could hardly control a sudden fierce impulse to grab him and kiss the daylights out of him. Only the certain knowledge that their relationship would forever change if she did—in ways she couldn't predict and probably wouldn't like—gave her the strength to resist.

"I know you wouldn't do that." She turned and fled to the kitchen. Picking up her glass of beer, she drained it in one swallow, then tucked the script under her arm, carried the glass to the sink and headed for the door. "Well, I've gotta go. Tomorrow's a school day."

He reached the back door before she did and planted himself directly in her path, crossing his arms over his chest. "You're not leaving until we straighten this out."

"There's nothing to straighten," she said, studying the ridge of muscles standing out in sharp relief along the side of his jaw. "Everything's cool, Nolan."

"Then why won't you look at me?"

Quaking inwardly and feeling like the worst kind of coward, she met his gaze. The green in his shirt made his hazel eyes look greener than usual and incredibly attractive. And had his lashes always been that long and lush? Oh, drat and damn. Once she'd had a chance to regroup, she would be fine again. For now, however, her hormones threatened to rage out of control, and there was only one sensible course of action in a situation like this—lie through her teeth and get the heck out of here.

"Everything's cool," she repeated, forcing a calm smile onto her lips. "I know you weren't hitting on me. Honest.

You were only trying to boost my self-confidence. It was sweet of you. Really.''

He unfolded his arms and wrapped his hands around her biceps, but didn't budge otherwise. The worst thing about close friends was that they usually knew when you were fibbing. The second worst thing was that they rarely let you get away with it.

Absently rubbing his thumbs across the sensitive skin of her inner arms, Nolan gave no sign of noticing the crazy leap of her pulse. He simply continued to study her face with the same unnerving intensity he undoubtedly used on his opponent's witnesses in court. The poor souls.

"I wasn't trying to be sweet, Alex. I meant everything I said." His voice was low and so controlled she wondered how hard he had to struggle to keep it that way. "But I don't want anything from you that you don't want to give me. I don't expect or want our friendship to change unless that's what you want, too."

"I understand," she said, though she didn't believe him for one blessed second.

The words had been said, and they could hardly be unsaid. How could she ever look at him again and not remember that he thought she had magnificent breasts and the sexiest legs he'd ever seen, for heaven's sake? Still, she appreciated his attempt to reassure her. If they both worked really hard at denial, they might even be able to bury this incident deeply enough in memory to pretend it had never happened.

"We can talk about it again later if you want." She lifted her hands to the sides of his waist and gave him a gentle squeeze, using the affectionate gesture to gain enough leverage to sidle past him through the doorway. "But I really do have to run now. I'll see you tomorrow."

He hesitated just long enough to let her know that he

knew she was actually running away, then slowly released her arms and moved aside. "All right, Alexandra. Tomorrow. And we *will* talk about this again. Depend on it."

Scooting out the door and down the steps before he could change his mind, she waved an acknowledgment. The night air brought a blessed wave of coolness to her hot face. Sensing the touch of his troubled gaze on her back, she hurried to the gap in the hedge and slipped through it without a backward glance.

She automatically wiggled the switch to her patio light when she stepped inside her back door; he would stand watching until he knew she'd made it safely home. Lord, what an evening. With an irritated shake of her head she went upstairs and rushed through her bedtime ritual. Still too wired to sleep, she crossed the room.

Hugging her arms tightly to her sides, she leaned one shoulder against the wall beside the window and peeked at Nolan's house through a gap in the miniblinds. Rick's light was out. Nolan's wasn't, and he hadn't closed his drapes. Mercy, there he was now, pulling off his polo shirt.

She turned her head away, feeling extremely virtuous for curbing an urge to spy on the poor unsuspecting man. Not that Nolan's bare chest was any big mystery to her. She'd seen it plenty of times when they had taken the kids swimming or when he worked in his yard. And in the summertime he frequently went jogging without a shirt.

He wasn't as brawny as some of the ranchers around Sunshine Gap, but for a guy who made his living with his head instead of his muscles, he had a darn good body. She sneaked another peek through the miniblinds. He stood at his own window now, arms raised, the heels of his palms braced on the casing above his head. His biceps stood out, and his torso tapered nicely from his wide chest to his hard, flat waist.

She'd seen him stand there in exactly that pose many nights before, seemingly lost in thought. She couldn't make out his expression from this distance, but there was a lonely air about him that had always led her to believe he was remembering his wife. But what if he wasn't thinking about Jennifer? What if he was thinking about...Alexandra?

The idea sparked another one of those odd, curling sensations deep inside her womb. An image flashed through her mind's eye, the picture as clear and sharp as any Technicolor shot on a movie screen. In it, she stood behind him, wearing one of the oversize T-shirts she used for a nightgown. Laying her cheek on the smooth, warm skin of his back, she brought her arms around him in a hug, pressing her breasts against him. Her hands roved over his chest and torso, palms sculpting themselves to his muscles, fingertips playfully twirling through the tufts of hair, tracing the arrow-shaped line down to the button at the top of his slacks. Then he would turn to her and...

She felt her throat muscles contract in a hard, involuntary swallow. While her heart pounded into a galloping rhythm, her lungs didn't want to work at all. Her skin suddenly felt hot and tight and itchy, and she wanted...

"Don't go there, Alex," she muttered, forcing herself to turn away from the window. "Don't even *think* about going there."

Her perennially rumpled bed had never looked less inviting. The little stacks of half-read magazines were no longer potential gold mines of fascinating information; they were messes. The tacky knickknacks her students were always giving her, the closet crammed so tightly with clothes it looked ready to explode, the dresser top strewn with costume jewelry and lotions, makeup and perfume, nail polish and hair accessories made her wince.

This was not—as she frequently tried to convince herself—the bedroom of a busy, energetic, free-spirited woman. It was the bedroom of a slob. It was the bedroom of a woman who had given up on ever again having an intimate relationship with a man.

Not just Nolan. Any man.

In the same way she had given up on her dream of becoming an actress, she obviously had given up on her other dream of falling in love again, perhaps even having another child someday. And why? Was it because she'd failed so miserably at marriage the first time, she was afraid of failing again?

As Nolan had said earlier, that really didn't sound like her style at all. True, she had come home from Laramie, desperately clutching her baby in her arms, with her pride dragging behind her in the dirt. But all of that had happened over a dozen years ago. More than likely it had been the responsibility of raising Tasha that had shifted her focus away from dreams and onto the more pressing issues at hand—such as making the mortgage payment and buying food.

Pushing herself away from the wall, she dodged a mound of dirty clothes and a pair of sneakers on her way to the bed. She crawled between the sheets and lay back with a ragged sigh, born partly of weariness, partly of frustration. Was Nolan right? Should she try to get a part, however small, in *Against the Wind?*

On the surface it seemed so...enticing. To be involved with the production and see the process of making movies up close, to work with a star like Blair, perhaps even to glimpse herself on a big screen in a darkened movie theater, what could be more exciting than that? She'd left the wild, rebellious teenager she had once been behind and become a loving mother to Tasha, a good teacher to her students, a responsible, upright, tax-paying member of the community for years and years now.

Couldn't she finally allow herself this one small taste of the most cherished dream she'd had since she was four years old? Other than receiving child-support checks, she hadn't heard from Bradley or his mother in a decade. He'd remarried and started a new family as well as a political career. What possible interest would they have in anything she did now? Probably none.

But what about Tasha? She didn't think the Talbots could or would try to touch Tasha now, but... Damn, she wished she could tell Nolan the whole story and ask for his professional advice. She'd tried to tell him on one occasion, but the feelings of shame had made the words stick in her throat like a fish bone that made a person cough and gag and choke, but wouldn't come out unless it was forcibly removed.

She rolled over and punched her pillow twice before flopping back down on it. It wasn't any more comfortable, but she felt better for having pounded on something. Much as she loved Nolan for trying to encourage her, he was wrong to do it.

After years of teaching school and struggling to control her impulsive streak, it wasn't good for her to fantasize about ditching her conventional life to pursue an acting career. The desire to rationalize all the reasons she wanted to do exactly that was strong, even fierce. But she couldn't afford to give in to it. It wasn't as if her present life was miserable.

If not exactly thrilling, it was pleasant enough. She had a secure, meaningful job she enjoyed. Though already entering the throes of adolescence, Tasha was doing well in school and sports, and she had a nice bunch of friends to hang out with. Only an irresponsible idiot would mess with her child's life now, especially for the sake of an old dream that couldn't possibly come true, anyway.

Whatever sins she still harbored in her soul, Alexandra McBride Talbot had finished being an irresponsible idiot the day Tasha was born. Until the day she left home, Tasha would always be Alex's first obligation. Her dreams had waited this long; they'd just have to wait a few years longer. If she never got to be a movie star, too bad. That was the price any good mother would pay to protect her child.

With that settled in her mind, she tugged the blankets up to her chin and closed her eyes. Big mistake. Her mind wasn't ready to let go of that shocking scene in front of the mirror in Nolan's laundry room. Alex grinned, then chuckled, then giggled like a one of Tasha's girlfriends when a cute boy walked by in the hallway at school.

Lifting the neckline of her nightshirt, she glanced at her breasts. "Hey girls," she whispered, "did you know Nolan thinks you're m-m-magnificent?"

A most unladylike snort ripped out of her nose. "And he l-l-likes my n-nice, r-round, little r-r-rump, too." She inhaled a shaky breath. "And don't forget my stunning, s-s-sexy l-l-legs!"

She grabbed the extra pillow, buried her face in it and laughed until she finally regained control of herself. Then she snuggled deeper into the covers and closed her eyes again, murmuring, "Just you wait, Nolan Larson. I'll get you for this if it's the last thing I ever do."

The next evening Blair DuMaine arrived at the high school on time and ready to go to work. Alex welcomed her and, with no small sense of pride, presented her to the stunned members of the cast and stage crew of the senior class play. To Alex's delight, Blair talked to the teenagers as if they were simply fellow students in an acting class. How could the kids help but respond with enthusiasm?

In a matter of minutes they had put themselves under Blair's capable direction. To Alex, who for weeks had struggled to get her cast to express any of the deep, personal emotions required by their roles in Tennessee Williams's *The Glass Menagerie,* it was mind-boggling to see the kids practically swaggering through one improvisation after another. And they were good. Much better, in fact, than when they were limited to the lines the playwright had written.

During a break, she took Blair aside and asked if they should dump the play in favor of an evening of improv. Blair considered the question, then slowly shook her head.

"I don't think you have to go that far," she said. "If you and I run through a couple of scenes for them, they'll see how universal the emotions are, even though the dialogue seems pretty outdated to them. That's really all they need to capture the spirit of the play."

"Well, I guess it's worth a try," Alex said.

After making sure the audience, Nolan, Rick and Tasha, met Blair, Alex called the group back to order. Any flutters of nerves she'd suffered at the prospect of performing with such a famous actress quickly vanished. Blair DuMaine was a professional, inside and out; as such, she was perfectly capable of carrying her own weight on stage.

Alex actually found her easier to work with than the amateurs she normally encountered in community theater. Since she was used to being the most knowledgeable and experienced actor present, Alex always had felt uniquely responsible for the success or failure of any production in which she appeared. Blair's vast knowledge and experience freed Alex to concentrate on her own delivery for a change.

It felt wonderful.

When they came to the end of the first scene, there was a moment of silence, followed by a thunderous wave of applause, whistles and stomping feet. The sound was pure symphony to any actor's ears, and it tickled Alex to see the same flush of pleasure on Blair's face as must surely be coloring her own. By the time they finished the second scene, the kids were eager to get back on stage and take another shot at interpreting the characters.

Nolan took Tasha and Rick home. Alex hugged all three of them and thanked them for coming to the rehearsal, then went back to work. Blair coached the young actors to the most delightfully improved performances Alex had ever seen. When it was time to send the students home, none of them wanted to leave.

They finally did, however, and Alex invited Blair out for a drink. Blair hesitated, a part-sad, part-angry expression crossing her face. Alex's stomach contracted as if a fist had closed around it and squeezed.

"Have I offended you somehow?" she asked. "Or did one of the kids?"

Blair started, shook her head as if ridding it of some particularly unpleasant thought, then smiled at Alex. "Oh, no, Alex. I haven't had this much fun in a long time. It's just, um…getting a little late."

"Late?" Alex glanced at her watch. "It's barely nine o'clock."

"Dillon likes to start torturing me early in the morning," Blair said with a grimace.

Alex frowned. Her cousin Dillon was teaching Blair how to ride and do ranch chores to prepare her for her role in the movie. He hadn't been a bit happy about taking on the job, and Alex suspected his reluctance involved his feelings for Blair. Anyone with eyes could see that he wanted her like hell on fire, but knowing Dillon, he'd probably work both of them into a grave before he would admit it. When it came to stubbornness, the big dope could make the rankest mule look positively compliant.

"Is he still giving you a hard time?" Alex asked.

"Does Wyoming have wind?" Blair retorted. "Does it have mountains? Or jackrabbits?"

"Oh, you poor darling." Alex wrapped an arm around Blair's shoulders and gave her quick hug. "Well, in that case, you really need more of a break from the wretched beast. Why don't you come to my house, and we'll drink tea and you can cuss him out to your heart's content?"

"That sounds...lovely," Blair said.

They talked for hours. Alex enjoyed every moment. When Blair finally climbed into her little red car and drove away, Alex stood at the curb, watching the taillights shrink until they vanished. How long had it been since she'd talked to someone who understood her love of acting? Someone who didn't think she was strange? Someone who liked her, at least in part, *because* of her abilities and aspirations, rather than *in spite* of them?

The only other person she knew who even came close to being such a kindred spirit was Nolan. Too bad their relationship was so weird now. Darn him, she appreciated his caring about her happiness, but she really wished he'd never made those remarks about her body.

She doubted there was enough denial in the whole world to make her forget the things he'd said or the lusty look in his eyes when he'd said them. She wasn't even sure a fullblown case of amnesia would have accomplished that for her. Well, she'd have to get over it somehow. She needed him too much as a friend to risk losing him over a failed love affair. The thought made her shiver. Hugging herself, she hurried back into her house.

* * *

Early the next morning Nolan dressed in running clothes, hustled out his back door and stepped through the gap in the hedge. Already busy stretching out her left calf muscle, Alex turned her head and gave him a wary smile. Hell. Was she going to act weird around him forever?

He went into his own warm-up routine, pretending not to notice her skittish behavior. Unless one of them had a scheduling conflict, they jogged together every weekday morning, and he was not going to give up his exercise buddy over something so ridiculous. For God's sake, it wasn't as if he'd actually made a pass at her.

She crossed one foot in front of the other, bent over at the waist and pressed her palms to the grass. Since the temperature in Sunshine Gap was too cool to wear shorts in mid-April, especially this early in the morning, both he and Alex wore running tights. He'd seen her wear them hundreds of times before, but this morning…

Oh, man, they called them *tights* for a reason. That clingy, skin-hugging material outlined every firm muscle from her heels to her round little rear end with the faithfulness of a plaster mold. Nolan felt his mouth dry out as if a dental assistant had just vacuumed every drop of his saliva.

He wanted to touch her. Without any conscious orders from his brain, his fingers were already curving themselves to the approximate contours of her bottom. And he didn't feel the slightest urge to be noble. No, at the moment all of his urges were completely and unapologetically carnal.

Maybe Alex shouldn't trust him after all.

The idea shocked him. He dragged his gaze from her luscious behind and inhaled a deep breath. When he looked her way again, he found himself the target of a pair of beautiful, but extremely angry, eyes.

"Dammit, Nolan, cut it out," she said.

He forced an oh-so-innocent smile onto his face, straightened his shoulders, cleared his throat. "Cut what out?"

She pointedly lowered her gaze to the front of his running tights. Oops. They didn't hide any details of his anatomy, either. His anatomy was tattling on him big-time. So to speak.

His face and neck suddenly felt hot, and he shrugged with a nonchalance he didn't feel. "You were married once. It's just one of those...morning things. Men have them all the time."

"You never have around me before."

"I'm only human, Alex. What do you want me to do about it? Poke my own eyes out?"

"No, but you could stop looking at my tush that way."

Could he? Nolan wondered. Could he *really* stop looking at any part of Alex and noticing that she was sexy and desirable and gorgeous? Could he force himself to go back to treating her as a delightful younger sister the way he used to?

No. In fact, *hell, no* came much closer to the truth. Every drop of testosterone he possessed rebelled outright at the thought of it. The wicked sex genie had escaped from the lamp, and he had no intention of returning. Not now, not ever.

He could hardly tell Alex that, however. She wasn't ready to hear it. The betrayed expression in her eyes told him more clearly than words that he had better find a way to get them back onto a more comfortable footing with each other, and he'd better find it fast.

The question was how to go about it. Absolute honesty and straightforwardness with each other had always been the basis of their relationship, which had been possible only because they had never allowed the issue of sexual attraction to enter the arena. Most of that had been Alex's doing, but at the time, he'd willingly gone along with it. After the pain and confusion surrounding Jennifer's death and the move from L.A. to Wyoming, Alex's offer of an uncomplicated friendship had been as welcome as a lifeline thrown to a man swimming in shark-infested waters.

But he was over the worst of that now. If he was honest with himself, he would have to admit he'd been ready to move forward in his relationship with Alex for at least a couple of years. He'd simply been too comfortable with her and too hesitant to try to change the rules when he knew she wouldn't like the idea.

For all of her outward show of sophistication to the folks of Sunshine Gap, Alex had a wide streak of apprehension when it came to dealing with men. He suspected that she had chosen him to be her friend and escort of choice, mainly because she regarded him as "safe." Damn. None of this was uncomplicated now.

As a man and as a lawyer, he considered his integrity to be sacred. He didn't believe in the so-called ends justifying any means. He despised liars and spin doctors who twisted and shaded the truth to a point where it often ceased to exist.

That was why he thoroughly enjoyed his often-blunt and blustering Wyoming clients. Though he occasionally wished they could be a bit more tactful when stating their views in court, one never had to guess where one stood with them. He'd always respected that. He'd always treasured that aspect of his relationship with Alex, as well.

He didn't want to start being devious with her, but if he told her what he really wanted right now, she was going bolt like one of her brother Zack's Arabian horses. The feminine wariness—hell, the age-old, atavistic fear of a female scenting a male who wants to mate with her was right there in her eyes.

What else could a man do in these circumstances but try to lull her into a sense of security? It wouldn't be a false sense of security. Not really.

Alex was his best friend, for God's sake. He would never intentionally hurt her. He wouldn't have sex with her and then abandon her for a new conquest. He wasn't sure that he ever would want to marry again, but if he ever decided he did, he couldn't imagine taking that step with anyone but Alex.

So where was the harm in giving her a little more time to get used to the idea of expanding the present boundaries of their friendship? There wasn't any that he could see. If he was rationalizing a bit, well…sue him.

As lawyer jokes went, it was a feeble attempt, but it was the best he could do with Alex still standing there, looking at him as if he were a traitor and expecting a response to her ridiculous demand that he stop looking at her tush "like that."

"All right," he said, "but only if you promise to stop looking at my, uh—" he glanced down at the telltale bulge in his tights, then grinned and wiggled his eyebrows at her "—you know, like that."

"I never did that," she said, her cheeks flaming.

"Did, too."

"Did not."

"Did, too."

Laughing, he took off around the side of her house to the driveway and headed for their regular route along an unpaved county road. Still protesting her innocence, Alex charged after him. Neither of them spoke when she caught up.

There was a prickly tension between them for the first mile, but as they settled into their strides, and the sunshine grew brighter, Alex gradually relaxed and told him about her evening with Blair DuMaine after he'd taken Tasha and Rick home.

"So, did you talk to her about a part in the movie?" Nolan asked.

"No."

"You wanted to, though, didn't you?"

Alex shrugged, then nodded with obvious reluctance. "Maybe I did. It was fun acting with her. A lot of fun."

"She enjoyed it, too. Everyone saw you were both really getting into it."

"I know. Did it look as cool as it felt?"

"Yes, it did. And you should have asked her for a part."

"No way," Alex said. "It wouldn't have been right to hit her up for another favor after she'd already been so generous to the kids."

"Well, what about signing up to be an extra?"

"Oh, I don't know. That might be kind of boring."

"You could at least see how movies are made. I can't believe you'd pass up such an incredible opportunity to—"

Alex elbowed him in the ribs. "Nag, nag, nag, Larson. Give it a rest, will you? Now, just shut up and run."

She turned around and sprinted for home, forcing him to speed up enough to make talking impossible if he wanted to breathe. He decided to let her get away with it this time, but he had no intention of permanently dropping the subject. Alex had a huge talent for acting and she did a lot of good things for other people. He considered it his duty as her friend to nag her into doing good things for herself once in a while.

They slowed to a walk at the pavement, catching their breath and cooling down before they reached her house and separated to start their respective workdays. When he would have left her at her door, she tapped his shoulder.

He stopped and turned back to her, and found himself engulfed in a warm, sweet smile.

Her hair was windblown. Perspiration dripped down the sides of her face and neck, but her bright eyes and glowing skin gave her a natural, healthy beauty that made him want to— He cut that thought off before it could get him into trouble with Alex again. There would be time for such thoughts later. He would see to it.

"I forgot to thank you last night," she said.

"No, you didn't," he said, "and no 'thanks' were necessary. You certainly cart Rick around more than your share."

"I didn't mean about taking care of Tasha for me," she said, "although I did appreciate it."

"Then what?"

"After Blair left last night, I realized you're the only person outside of my college drama department who ever encouraged me to act professionally. I don't plan to do anything with Marsh's movie, but it means a lot to me that you had enough faith in my ability to nag me about it. It really was awfully nice of you to care that much."

Raising one hand to the side of his jaw, she leaned forward and pressed a whisper-soft kiss on his lips. It didn't come close to being a sexy kiss; it wasn't even in the same time zone. But that sisterly little smooch still managed to make his heart thump. She pulled back and gave him an impish grin that was pure Alex.

"Thanks, pal," she said.

"You're welcome, Alexandra." He wanted to argue about her decision, but knew this was not the time. Instead he reached out and ruffled her hair, then forced himself to turn away and head for home, calling over his shoulder, "Have a good one."

"You, too," she said. When he reached the gap in the hedge, she added, "Oh, and Nolan?"

He paused and looked back at her. "What?"

"You know, you really should wear those tights more often. You've got a fantastic behind, and your legs aren't bad for such an old guy, either."

"Old guy?" he demanded, hoping a show of indignation would hide his embarrassment at the idea of her studying his backside.

She made a pretend gun with her thumb and index finger and fired it at him. "Gotcha, Larson!"

Laughing, she ran up her back steps and into her house. He sighed, then chuckled and stepped through the bushes into his own yard. She'd only been teasing him, of course, but when he reached his bathroom, took out his shaving equipment and looked in the mirror, he made a discovery. A thirty-eight-year-old man was still capable of grinning like a thirteen-year-old boy whose favorite girl has just batted her eyelashes at him for the very first time.

Chapter Three

Alex dropped Tasha off at the junior high, then sped around the corner to the high school. Mentally bracing herself, she hurried inside. At this time of the morning, it always felt as if she were walking head-on into a wall of noise. Locker doors slammed, kids laughed and shrieked, trumpet blasts erupted from the band room, the volume rising and thickening, building to the deafening crescendo of the first bell. Alex had always found that hideous grating sound to be about as pleasant as that of a cell door clanging shut.

Thanks to an efficient small-town grapevine, her first-hour class had already heard about Blair's appearance at the seniors' play practice. Of course, none of the students wanted to talk about homework or tests or American literature when they could talk about a real, honest-to-gosh movie star. Alex spent the entire class period repeatedly dragging the kids back on task.

The rest of her classes followed the same pattern. Alex wasn't certain whether it was spring fever or her own distraction causing the kids to grasp any excuse to goof off. The truth was, after spending the previous evening with Blair DuMaine, the last place Alex wanted to be was in a classroom. When she should have been discussing assignments or planning lessons, she continually found herself thinking about acting.

Was she never going to get over it? It was like a bad case of malaria; just when she thought she had all of those dreams and yearnings safely tucked out of sight and out of mind, something would trigger another episode. It had never been this bad before, but then, she'd never had to watch someone else living out her dream in her own hometown before, either.

When her seniors came in, bubbling with excitement left over from their brush with stardom, Alex gave up trying to teach anything and threw her lesson plans for the day onto the desk. Tina Murphy, a serious, dark-haired girl raised her hand.

"Ms. Talbot, after watching you last night, I think you could have been a professional actress. So—" Tina hesitated, as if searching for exactly the right words "—why are you a teacher?"

The question hit Alex like a body blow, but she tried hard not to show it. "I like teaching."

Tina frowned. "Yes, I can see that. And I think you're a good teacher, but…"

"But what?" Alex asked.

"Well, you must have really wanted to be an actress if you took classes and everything. And you're always telling us to dream big dreams and go after them. So, why didn't you go after yours?"

Ah, the joys of teaching, Alex thought with a rueful sigh.

She loved her students' youthful idealism and hated it when they caught her, or at least thought they had caught her, committing an act of adult hypocrisy. She didn't mind talking with them about some aspects of her personal life, however, and she always tried to shoot straight with them.

"I married awfully young," she said. "I had other responsibilities that made pursuing a professional acting career very difficult."

"Does that mean you regret your decision to get married so young?" Casie Winston asked.

Regret marrying Brad Talbot? Yes. Regret having Tasha? Alex shook her head. "No, it was the best decision I could have made for myself at the time."

"Yeah, but—" Casie let out a dreamy sigh "—think about all the great movies you could've been in by now. And all the hot actors you could have kissed."

The bell rang while Alex was still chuckling at that remark. From that point on, however, her day went strictly downhill. Her last two classes were unbelievably restless. The principal, Mr. Sorenson, gave her a lecture on school policies regarding teachers inviting volunteers to work with the students without the principal's consent. Alex doubted any such policies existed; "Horace the Moron" was just ticked off because he hadn't been invited to meet Blair DuMaine.

By the time the final bell rang there was only one thought in Alex's brain—escape. She trudged out to her car with ninety essays to grade before morning, tossed her satchel into the passenger seat and peeled out of the teachers' parking lot. This was exactly how she'd often felt as a teenager, edgy and so full of energy that she was afraid she might explode if she didn't get out of this suffocating little town.

Five minutes later she screeched into her driveway, ran into her house and charged all the way up two flights of stairs to the attic. If it was crazy to do this, she didn't give a damn. Tasha wouldn't be home from track practice for a couple of hours. No one need ever know that Alex had gone a little bonkers.

She *had* to find her old trunk from college. She *had* to see and touch the pieces of her dream that she actually had achieved. She *had* to remember what it had felt like to be young and full of hope and ambition.

Flipping on the naked lightbulb hanging in the center of the room, Alex paused to catch her breath, then hurried to the dusty stack of aging treasures she'd collected since moving into this old wreck of a house ten years earlier. Heedless of possible damage to her sensible skirt and blazer, she moved boxes of books and baby clothes, craft projects and supplies she'd forgotten she owned, toys she was saving for nonexistent grandchildren, a lamp with a pretty shade she planned to have fixed someday when she had the time to deal with it.

At last she spotted the battered army green trunk, covered with peeling stickers intended to make it look as if it had been around the world. Heart in her throat, she sank onto the rough wooden floor beside it, undid the latches and slowly raised the lid. The overpowering smell of mothballs nearly made her gag, but after a moment she barely noticed it.

It was all still here. Her costumes. Scrapbooks. Photo albums. Scripts. Journals and notebooks from acting classes. A videotape of her last performance in a starring role. The production had been *Oklahoma!* and she had loved every grueling minute of the dance classes and singing lessons she'd had to take for that part.

Good grief, she'd even saved her ratty old leotards, tights and the audio cassettes she'd used to practice on her own. The impulse to see if she could still wear them was irresistible. Once she'd stripped off her school clothes and discovered she could indeed still wear the workout gear, she had to see if she could remember the dance steps.

Grabbing the tapes, she raced down the stairs to the living room, popped one of the cassettes into the stereo and shoved as much furniture out of the way as possible. The music came up, and she stood there a moment, scarcely daring to breathe until gradually her feet knew where to go and her voice found the notes and the lyrics. Energy roared through her body and a gigantic sense of fun filled her mind and her heart and her soul.

Her living room became a brightly lit stage, her furniture an enraptured audience. Other than moving her from one song to the next, time held no meaning. She lived only to dance and to sing and to act.

Oh, God, yes, to act. To act was to feel alive, perhaps even to *be* alive. It wasn't a disease like malaria at all. For her, at least, it was an addictive substance. It was her personal drug of choice. How had she lived so long without it?

The joy and the adrenaline were still pumping through her system when the music abruptly ended in the middle of the last song. Alex started at the silence, then turned around to find Tasha standing beside the stereo with one hand on the volume control and a horrible scowl on her face. Panting to catch her breath, Alex swiped one hand across her sweaty forehead and smiled at Tasha.

"Hi, sweetie."

Tasha ignored the greeting. "Mother, what the hell are you doing?"

Suddenly realizing this wasn't a stage after all, Alex glanced around the room. Uh-oh. If Tasha was home, it must be after five, which meant she'd been doing *Oklahoma!* for too long.

"Nothing important," Alex said. "Just getting a little exercise. Blowing off some stress."

"What's for supper?" Tasha asked.

"Supper? Um...I don't know. I haven't thought about it yet."

"Mo-o-om!" Tasha stretched the word into a three-note whine. "I'm starving to death now. I've been running and stuff for over two hours."

"Let's go see what's in the fridge." Alex headed for the kitchen. Tasha followed, grumbling all the way.

"You haven't been to the store yet, have you?"

"Well, no, but I'm sure we'll find something."

"That's what you said last night." Tasha slammed a half-opened cupboard door shut.

"Last night I had play practice."

"Why couldn't I have a normal mother?"

"I'm normal most of the time," Alex said, chuckling to hide how much that remark had hurt. Cripes, if the kid only knew how hard she had to work to appear as normal as she did...

"Oh, huh," Tasha said. "We never have meals on time unless we eat with Nolan and Rick. And you're always doing some weird thing nobody else's mom would do. Can't you just grow up and act like a real mom for a change?"

"Probably not, but you can always wish." After a quick glance at the inside of the refrigerator, Alex reached the conclusion that she could no longer put off buying groceries. Grabbing her purse from the counter, she dug out her car keys and headed for the back door.

"Make a peanut butter sandwich to tide you over and start your homework. I'll make a run to the store, and we'll have supper as soon as possible, okay?"

"Mo-o-om!" Tasha whined again. "I don't believe you.

You can't go downtown wearing that. And what is that awful smell? Mothballs?''

Alex glanced down at her leotard and tights, then sighed and hurried back upstairs. So much for her lovely dreams. At the moment they seemed like delusions of grandeur. Dressed more appropriately in jeans and a light sweater, she moved into her "normal mother" mode and rushed downtown.

She was home with the groceries in forty-five minutes. Vainly searching her cluttered counters for a place to deposit the first load, she finally gave up and plunked the sacks down before she dropped them. Something tipped over and made a splattering sound on the floor below. Ugh. It was probably a glass of juice left over from breakfast. Tromping back outside, she tucked her school satchel under one arm, grabbed the last two sacks and banged the car door shut with her hip.

Realizing she hadn't remembered to clear off a space for this load, she swore under her breath, whirled around and dumped the sacks in the dish drainer, the one empty space in her kitchen because she hadn't done the dishes in…she didn't want to think about how long it had been. Alex looked around at the mess and tipped her face toward heaven.

"God, did you have to give Cousin Grace *all* of the domestic genes in the family? I could've used a few, you know, especially since I'm never going to be rich and famous."

As if to tell her that God didn't appreciate her grumbling, the satchel slipped out from under her arm, spilling the essays across the grungy floor she could never find the time to scrub. Alex stared at them in dismay and felt a fierce, sudden urge just to sit down on the floor and cry until she ran out of tears. But what would that solve? She shook her head, but the urge to weep grew even stronger.

She closed her eyes tightly, inhaled a deep breath, then held it a moment before slowly releasing it. There, that was better. She repeated the process until she finally felt in control of her emotions. Then she went back to work, gathering up the papers and putting the kitchen as close to rights as she ever managed to get it.

By seven o'clock, she served a quick but nutritious dinner of chicken breasts, microwaved potatoes and broccoli. The dishes were done by eight. She put on a pot of coffee and sat at the kitchen table, slogging through the first stack of essays, correcting spelling, punctuation and grammar, commenting on the content.

Long after Tasha retired to her room for the night, however, Alex worried about the incident when she'd dropped her satchel. She occasionally wept during sad movies or at poignant moments on TV, but rarely indulged herself in tears of frustration or self-pity; she simply couldn't afford to. In fact, she rarely had such urges in the first place.

But ever since the decision to shoot *Against the Wind* at the Flying M had been announced, she'd been more distracted, more restless and a lot more emotional than was normal for her. She knew the cause, of course. Talking about her old, unfulfilled dreams—first with Nolan, and today with her seniors—had resurrected them. And it was only going to get worse.

Her love of acting was so well known in Sunshine Gap, it was inevitable that she would have similar conversations with other well-meaning people while the cast and crew were in town. Which, unfortunately, would probably make her feel even more distracted, restless and emotional than she already did. Sighing, she laid her red pen on top of the stack of ungraded papers and propped her elbows on the kitchen table.

Well, she couldn't change the situation. Her best course of action was simply to try and keep things in perspective. There was no sense in wishing for what she couldn't have, and an acting career was still number one on that particular list. She had a wonderful daughter who was doing well in school, productive work with decent benefits and plenty of family and friends around her. It wasn't a particularly glamorous life, but it was a good one. Good enough, anyway.

And how many times would she have to repeat that entire litany to herself before she really believed it? Especially the last part about her life being good enough as it was?

"However many times it takes," she said, in a loud, determined voice that grated on her own nerves. She rubbed her tired eyes, then grudgingly picked up her red pen again, muttering, "Yeah, my life's terrific, but actresses don't have to grade dorky English papers."

Nolan rapped his knuckles on Alex's back door and waited until he heard her call, "It's open," before he stepped inside and closed the door behind himself.

"You really should lock your doors," he said, turning back to face her.

Alex sat at the kitchen table, a coffee mug at one elbow and a stack of papers in front of her. She looked tired and perhaps a little pale, but she smiled at his opening salvo. They had carried on this particular argument ever since he'd discovered that few people in Sunshine Gap, including Alex, ever bothered to lock anything. While there was very little crime in the area, he would never be able to go off and leave his car or his house completely unprotected.

"No self-respecting serial killer would come to Sunshine Gap," she said. "There's not enough bait."

"But he might be more interested in quality of victims, not quantity. And even if a serial killer wouldn't come here, we might well attract a rapist or a lowly burglar."

While Alex chuckled, he crossed the room. Holding a copy of the Cody newspaper behind his back, he stopped beside her chair and studied her face. Yes, she definitely was pale, and there was a pinched look around her eyes that suggested a headache either now or in the recent past. She held up her coffee mug in a silent offer to get him some. Shaking his head, he sat in the chair adjacent to hers.

"No thanks, it's a little late for me," he said. "Is something wrong, Alexandra?"

"Wrong? Oh, heavens no." She flicked all ten fingers toward the fat stack of papers. "Nothing the end of the school year won't fix, anyway."

Nolan tipped his head to one side and studied her even more closely. His profession required an ability to read people and accurately judge when they were or were not telling the truth. At the moment his instincts told him that while Alex wasn't exactly lying, she wasn't telling him the whole story, either. Something was upsetting her.

"Just the old paperwork blues?" he said.

Shrugging, she gave him a bland smile that might as well have been a Keep Out sign. "So, what are you hiding behind your back there, Larson?"

Unsure of her mood, he hesitated about showing her the article he'd brought. This might not be the right time to talk her into anything. On the other hand, it would distract her from her despised paper grading, and therefore it might cheer her up. Acting nonchalant, he set the little newspaper on top of her tests, or whatever those papers were.

"I thought you might be interested in this," he said, pointing to the appropriate spot on the front page.

She picked up the paper and read aloud. "'Cattle Call

in Cody.' Oh, there's a catchy headline, isn't it?'' Alex shot him a wicked grin before reading on. '''When a Hollywood casting director issues a cattle call, she's not referring to one of Eddy Arnold's hit songs or critters with four hooves. She's looking for movie extras, the folks who populate the backgrounds of movie scenes. That's what Ms. Nancy Kryszka will be doing in Cody and in Sunshine Gap in just two weeks. If you want a chance to appear on the silver screen, bring a photo of yourself to the Elks Lodge in Cody on May 5 or 6, from 1:00 to 3:00 or to the high school gym in Sunshine Gap on May 7, from 1:00 to 3:00. Men will be required to grow facial hair due to the movie's historical nature.''''

She tossed the newspaper into the center of the table. ''Whatever that guy paid for journalism school, he got robbed.''

''Forget the writing,'' Nolan said. ''What about the cattle call?''

''What about it?'' Her eyes shifted to the left of his face. She picked up her pen and twirled it around and through her long, slender fingers in an intricate pattern.

''It's in two weeks. You're going to go, aren't you?''

''Oh, Nolan. I really don't think it's such a good—''

He cut her off before she could finish her refusal. Once she'd stated a position, Alex was lousy at backing down. ''I'll help you figure out a way to keep Tasha entertained. Or maybe she'd like to be an extra, too.''

''Maybe.'' Alex's eyebrows arched in the middle, as if the possibility of Tasha's wanting to participate in the movie had never occurred to her. ''But it'll be hot by the time they start shooting, and we'd have to wear period costumes with long, heavy skirts. She probably wouldn't like that much.''

''She'd get to see Keith Stanton, wouldn't she?'' Nolan

said, naming the handsome young actor who would play the male lead in the movie.

Chuckling, Alex shook her head. "Nice try, but I don't think so. If I remember the script correctly, his character isn't in any of the town scenes."

Nolan frowned at her. "Enough excuses. It doesn't matter whether Tasha's involved or not. Will you stop being so negative and just do this for yourself?"

"Did it ever occur to you that I really might not want to?"

Resting one forearm on the table, he leaned closer until his nose nearly bumped hers. "It's not that you don't want to, Alexandra. You want to do it so bad your bones ache. But you're afraid to reach out and take this opportunity, and—"

Color flooded into her pale cheeks, and temper glinted in her eyes. "I'm not afraid of anything, so mind your own damn business, Larson."

"You are my best friend, and that makes this my damn business. Are you going to go to that cattle call or do I have to start clucking every time I see you, Ms. Chicken?"

"You wouldn't."

"You don't think so?"

He shoved his chair out of the way, tucked his hands into his armpits and gave his "wings" a couple of trial flaps. Making jerky pecking motions with his head, he let out a string of squawks and clucks that sounded more like cartoon chickens than real ones, but he thought they served their purpose well enough.

Alex gaped at him for at least ten full seconds after he sat down again. Then she leaned back and howled with laughter until he felt a bit...well...insulted.

"It wasn't that bad," he said, when she paused to gasp

for breath. "I thought it was actually quite a good chicken."

She wiped her streaming eyes with her knuckles, inhaled a shaky breath, looked at him...and promptly lost her composure all over again. This time, however, she flopped forward, slapping her palm on the tabletop with each new gust of laughter. Though she clearly was releasing some sort of tension that included territory far beyond the bounds of this conversation, he began to feel seriously annoyed.

"Shut up, Alexandra," he said. "It wasn't that funny."

Nodding, she grabbed a tissue and wiped her nose and eyes. "You're right, Nolan. Of course, you're right. It wasn't that funny, and I'm sorry. I don't know why that hit me so hard."

"If nothing else, it allowed you to avoid giving me an answer. You will go to that cattle call, won't you?"

She met and held his gaze, but he couldn't readily identify any of the emotions in her expression. Interesting reaction, he thought. Then she straightened her spine, squared her shoulders and smiled at him. A knowing, taunting smile, that immediately put his guard up.

"You want me to go to the cattle call?" she said. "Fine. I will if you will."

"Me? No, Alexandra. I'm not an actor."

"You don't have to be. Extras are like pieces of furniture. You just show up and do whatever they tell you."

"But I'm not the one who's interested in making movies."

"Tough. I'm not doing this all by myself. If you want me to try it so bad, you and the kids have to come with me."

"But I'll be working."

She waved his words aside. "You always take a lot of time off in the summer to be with Rick. If the casting office calls on a day you have to be in court, you just tell them you're not available. It's not like they're going to fire you. And, if they did, so what?''

"But I'd have to grow a beard."

"Will you stop making these pathetic excuses? It's not open for negotiation. Either all four of us do this together, or I don't do it at all."

"Come on, Alexandra, play fair. My beard is like steel wool, only not that soft." Even thinking about it made his chin, jaw and neck itch.

Her smile widened. "Gee, that's a shame, Nolan. Guess we can't do it after all."

It was the false note of sympathy in her voice that made the decision for him. The whole thing was ridiculous, but he couldn't let her win this one. There was something going on with her that he still didn't understand, but whatever was driving her away from something she obviously loved so much, needed to be dealt with. The sooner the better.

"You're not getting off that easily," he said, scratching at his jaw. "Mark those dates on your calendar and watch these babies grow."

Chapter Four

The schools provided an important focal point and gathering place for the far-flung residents of Sunshine Gap, which made almost any school-sponsored event a big deal. There were folks living out on isolated ranches nobody ever saw unless there was a ball game or a band concert. People whose children were already grown or who had never had any children of their own still attended to show their community spirit, see their friends and encourage their friends' youngsters.

A senior class play was a long-standing tradition in the Gap; as such it was considered a very big deal, indeed. Alex knew that nearly everyone in the county would attend. She also knew that however the performance went, it would be discussed and dissected for months afterward.

While she wanted to give the audience an evening of fine entertainment, more than anything else, Alex wanted this performance to give her drama students an opportunity to shine in front of their families and their community. Given the lack of budget and dilapidated equipment at her disposal, it wouldn't be easy to put on a quality production.

She badgered local merchants into donating food for the rehearsals and building supplies for the sets. She raided trunks and attics all over town, searching out just the right costumes and props. She relentlessly rehearsed the kids until they could say their lines from any page in the play book without prompting.

The day of the performance, she raced around, making sure the programs were ready, the metal folding chairs properly set up in front of the curtained stage at one end of the gym, the ancient lighting and sound systems working.

As curtain time approached, the kids were understandably nervous. Acting out a role in front of a small group of one's peers was hard enough; acting out that same role in front of the whole town was a quantum leap in intimidation. Even Mike Sullivan, who was only handling the lights, looked terrified.

In the midst of the chaos and jitters, Alex felt energized. There was nothing she enjoyed more than the excitement that came with seeing a cast and crew's hard work come together in a solid performance. Teaching and mothering kept her so busy she could only participate in one or two plays a year. During the long, dry spells between productions, she sometimes felt as if she were starving for this delicious mixture of smells and noises, of adrenaline and the edgy sense of anticipation brought on by raw, stretched-to-the-limit nerves.

Peeking through a gap in the stage curtains, Casie gave a soft moan. "Ms. Talbot, the gym is packed. I think I'm going to hurl."

Alex hauled the girl away from the curtains and shooed

her toward the wings. "No, you're not, Casie. Trust me, a little stage fright is a good thing. It'll keep you sharp and focused."

"But you don't know how this feels," Casie said. "You're never scared to do this stuff."

"Oh, huh," Alex said with a chuckle. "Every time I walk onto a stage, I feel exactly the way you're feeling right now. Take a deep breath, honey. You'll be fine once you get started."

"You promise?" Dallas Teague asked, his voice tinged with an edge of desperation. Even with his stage makeup on, his face looked sickly pale.

God, but she loved teenagers, Alex thought, straightening his tie. They looked like adults and tried so hard to act like adults, but in moments of stress, their masks often slipped, revealing the frightened, insecure children hiding inside those grown-up bodies.

"Yes, Dallas, I promise." She gave his shoulder a reassuring squeeze. "You've all worked hard, and you're ready for this. Just do your best, and your best will be good enough."

"Now, Ms. Talbot?" Chuck Finster asked in a tense whisper, his hands gripped around the curtain rope.

Alex glanced at her watch, then gave her fretful cast a smile and a thumbs-up sign. "Break a leg." She signaled Mike to get the lights, and, knowing any further delay would only make them more nervous, she nodded at Chuck. "Now, Mr. Finster."

The audience hushed when the lights dimmed. The curtain creaked open, Dallas walked onto the stage and began Tom Wingfield's opening monologue. His strong, deep voice commanded attention, and the magic of the theater filled the school's ratty old gymnasium.

Once the play started the kids *were* fine; Alex was a

wreck. Aching to be out on stage with them, she haunted the wings, lip-synching every line, watching every gesture with all the breath-holding anxiety of a mother witnessing her baby's first wobbly steps. She had performed her own first leading role on this small, utilitarian stage, felt the giddy kick of power when she realized the audience had suspended disbelief and followed her into the world of the play. That one experience had forever changed the way she saw herself and expanded her horizons far beyond the confines of life in the Gap.

Suddenly she didn't have to be "just another one of those McBride kids." She could be anyone or do anything she wanted. Furthermore, she could make other people believe in the illusions she created. God, but she hoped her students were getting at least some of those feelings out of this experience.

They wouldn't all become actors; probably none of them would. That didn't matter. She simply wanted them to see new possibilities that they had never before dared to dream for themselves. Dallas was so much more than a "a big, dumb jock." Casie was more than an "airhead cheerleader." Tina was more than a "quiet little bookworm."

Those were the small-town labels each of those kids carried, however, and Alex knew from firsthand experience how incredibly durable such labels could be. Sometimes a label took on enough power to become a self-fulfilling prophecy that directed the entire course of a person's life. She wanted something better than that for these students, but first *they* had to believe they had other options.

Oh, they were doing such a great job she could hardly stand it. They were hitting their cues and marks like pros, and showing an impressive amount of emotion for high school kids. And they were having a ball out there. The audience barely moved during the brief intermission.

By the time the final curtain closed, she felt as exhausted and exhilarated as if she'd just finished a ten-mile run. The community responded to the young actors with a generous blast of applause, whistling and foot stomping. The kids took their bows the way she had shown them, then dragged her on stage with them, ignoring her protests that this was their moment.

Impossible as it seemed, the applause grew louder. Alex smiled and nodded her appreciation toward the crowd, picking out various friends and relatives. A sweet, almost painful sensation filled her chest, momentarily making it difficult to breathe. If only she could bottle this feeling, she would be rich.

When she saw Nolan, Rick and Tasha clapping with everyone else, she realized she already was rich. Extremely rich. She had three special people she could always count on to be there for her. What more did anyone really need?

The lights came back up. People began collecting their belongings and shuffling out of the building. Alex congratulated her students and left to make sure the cleanup crew had started to work. She did *not* want to listen to another one of Horace's ghastly lectures.

Nolan, Rick and Tasha pitched in to help put the school back in order, and when the work was all done, Alex initiated a group hug. "Thanks, troops. Anyone want to go to Cal's for pie à la mode? Or a milk shake? Or a banana split?"

"Works for me," Rick said.

Chuckling, Nolan clapped his son on the back. "Any kind of food works for a bottomless pit."

Rick shrugged. "Well, now that you mention it, I could do with a burger and fries, too."

Cal's Place was still busy with the after-the-play crowd when they arrived. Alex's brother, Cal McBride, led the group to a table at the back of the restaurant that still had a stack of dirty dishes on it from its last occupants. He whisked the mess away and swiped a wet cloth over the table.

"Sit down before you fall down, sis," he said. "When was the last time you ate anything?"

Alex always lost her appetite before a performance. Until that moment she hadn't been aware of feeling particularly hungry, but now that Cal had mentioned it, she realized she was ravenous. "Don't fuss, Cal," she said. "Just feed us."

"All right." Cal grinned and winked at Tasha. "I'll send Sylvia over to take your order."

"Oh, Cal…" Alex started to protest, but her brother had already made a quick exit. He would pay for that someday, the wretch.

Sylvia Benson was a hefty, fiftyish, loudmouthed waitress Cal had inherited when he bought the restaurant. She was basically a good soul and a skilled waitress, but she'd taken it into her head that it was her mission in life to be a one-woman news service and stand-up comedienne. She always thought she was highly entertaining, and she often was. Tonight, however, Alex would have preferred quieter, more peaceful service than Sylvia was likely to provide.

"Howdy, howdy, howdy," Sylvia said, topping off coffee cups left and right on her way to their table. "Well, if it ain't Alexandra Talbot, the director. You got great reviews from everyone tonight, hon. Everybody says the play was terrific. What can I bring you folks?"

As soon as they'd finished telling her, Sylvia swooped over to the kitchen and bellowed their orders to the cook. In what seemed like only seconds to Alex, she swooped back to them, arms and hands loaded with plates and drinks, talking nonstop while she plunked everything down.

"Yup, everybody says the kids did an outstanding job

tonight, especially that Teague boy. Word is, they were almost as good as your class, Alex.'' Sylvia nudged Nolan with her elbow. "Hey, Counselor, that's a fine crop of whiskers you're growin'. Makes you look dashing. You gonna go over to Pinedale this summer and play mountain man at the Green River Rendezvous?''

Scratching his chin, Nolan grinned and told her about their agreement to attend the cattle call. Sylvia shot Alex a surprised look.

"Now that's funny," she said. "I wouldn't think you'd need that much coaxin'. Shoot, I can remember a time when you would've cut school and hitchhiked or even walked all the way to Cody to get to somethin' like that.''

Alex gave her a polite smile. At least, she hoped it looked polite. "I'm a teacher now, Sylvia. And it's a busy time of year for teachers.''

"Aw, fiddlesticks," Sylvia said with a laugh. "If anybody in this town oughtta be in that movie, it's you. You've always been real talented at that sort of thing.''

Sylvia braced one hand on the edge of their table as if she meant to stay awhile and turned her attention to Tasha. "You shoulda seen your mama in her senior play, honey. Lord, but she was the best.'' She glanced over at the next table, straightened up and whacked an elderly rancher on the arm.

"Hey, Harry, you remember seein' Alex McBride in the senior play, don'tcha? They did *Arsenic and Old Lace* that year.''

Harry smiled at her, then nodded at Alex, Nolan and the kids. "Why, sure, Sylvie. Funniest dang thing I ever saw. She was great.''

"See what I mean?" Sylvia said. "We all thought she'd probably run off to Hollywood and be a movie star someday.''

''Well, I'm glad she didn't,'' Tasha said.

''Oh, yeah?'' Sylvia said. ''You don't want to be one of them spoiled rich kids?''

Tasha laughed. ''No, I just think it'd be really gross to see your own mom kissing guys and doing all that racy stuff at the movies.''

''Tasha,'' Alex said with a groan, but of course it was too late to call back the words.

Sylvia leaned back and brayed out a laugh loud enough to turn every head in the restaurant and bring a few curious faces to the doorway that connected the restaurant with the bar next door. Then she had to repeat Tasha's remark so everyone else could enjoy a good laugh. And then, thank God, the cook yelled at her to pick up her orders before they grew mold.

Alex's stomach felt as if she'd swallowed a large hot rock. She looked at her turkey sandwich and knew she wouldn't be able to choke down a crumb of it. To her relief, Nolan, Tasha and Rick ate their own food without noticing her sudden lack of appetite. She spread her napkin over the top, shoved her plate to one side and sipped her coffee.

Still chuckling when she came back, Sylvia started loading their empty plates into her arms. ''I swear, Alex, that little gal's your kid, all right. She's gonna be just like you—''

''No, she's not.'' Slamming one hand flat on the table, Alex came halfway out of her chair and glared into Sylvia's startled eyes. ''Tasha's not anything like me now, or the me I was twenty years ago. She's a normal, happy, *nice* kid, so let's just leave it at that, shall we?''

Sylvia backed up a step. ''Well, uh, sure, Alex. I didn't mean nothin' bad by that.''

''I'm sure you didn't. You probably even meant it as a compliment, but there are people around here who wouldn't take it that way, Sylvia. People who don't remember me very fondly."

"Aw, you weren't such a bad kid. You were just sort of a wild one," Sylvia said.

"Thanks, but I wouldn't want anyone to treat Tasha poorly because of something stupid I did years ago."

"Yeah, I hear ya," Sylvia said. She dumped the dirty dishes into a plastic tub, then scribbled out a check and dropped it in the center of the table. "Have a nice evening, folks." She started to leave, then turned back and added, "Oh, and Alex? You really oughtta go to that cattle call, hon. Everybody'll be real disappointed if you're not in that movie."

"I suppose," Alex muttered as Sylvia walked away.

"Jeez, Mom, did you have to yell at her like that?" Tasha said. "I'm so embarrassed, I wish I could die."

Knowing she needed to get out of there in a hurry or lose her temper all over again, Alex stood up so fast her chair screeched halfway across the aisle between the tables. The only civil reply she could manage was a curt nod. After delivering it, she rushed out of the restaurant, ignoring the startled looks and shouted congratulations directed her way.

Well, great. Now she'd created another public scene, and they could all enjoy themselves, discussing her behavior, digging up her past sins, speculating about her relationship with Nolan and whether or not they were sleeping together and yakety, yakety, yak. And so what? It was her job to keep the old hometown livened up, wasn't it? The biddies in Sunshine Gap must have missed her terribly while she was gone. Who else gave them so much juicy material to talk about?

The cool night air was a blessed relief for her hot face. Leaning back against the log exterior of the building to wait for Nolan and the kids, she closed her eyes and breathed in the scent of steaks frying on the grill inside and pine trees from the little park across the street. The familiar, homey smells made her ache in a way that made no sense. Sunshine Gap was her home, but she had never, in her whole life, felt more like a stranger.

Later that night, unable to sleep, Nolan stood at his bedroom window, gazing across the hedge at Alex's house. There were lights burning on both floors, and he wondered what she was doing. After stomping out of Cal's Place, she'd been silent all the way home, then refused to talk with him in private. Damn, she'd worked so hard on that play, this should have been a triumphant evening for her. He regretted the way it had ended, though he still wasn't sure what exactly had happened to spoil everything.

He was also worried about her.

Alex was a complicated woman with an unpredictable temperament to match. She felt every emotion passionately, and if you added in her flair for dramatizing the most mundane situation, one of her bad moods could be an unpleasant experience at best. However, her anger tonight had come from someplace deeper than a mere bad mood.

He didn't understand why she had allowed Sylvia Benson, of all people, to upset her. Everybody in town knew Sylvia loved to hear the sound of her own voice, and he doubted that anyone took much of anything she said seriously. Besides, Sylvia had hardly launched an attack. In his opinion she'd actually been complimenting Tasha and, in an indirect way, Alex herself. What was so terrible about that? He suspected the most crucial element in the conversation had been the topics under discussion, Alex's past and acting.

Alex rarely talked about her past with him, or to his knowledge, with anyone else, and acting had been a touchy subject with her since a couple of weeks ago. Now that he thought back over the times he'd teased her about his growing whiskers and her debut as an extra, he realized she'd become more tense and withdrawn on every occasion. He sighed and scratched the underside of his chin. Damn whiskers were driving him crazy.

Obviously there were still pieces of Alex's past he hadn't yet discovered, but that didn't matter. A friend was supposed to know when enough was enough. Alex was suffering some real stress, and whatever her problem was, he wouldn't add to it with more teasing about the movie. As long as they were both still up, he might as well end his share of her misery right now.

Sliding his bare feet into a pair of loafers, he hurried downstairs and over to Alex's house. She didn't answer his knock on the back door, but he could hear music playing, something with a driving rock beat that was too melodic to belong in Tasha's CD collection. He knocked harder; if Tasha could sleep through that music, nothing short of a stampede was likely to disturb her.

The porch light came on, nearly blinding him. Then the door jerked inward and Alex appeared. Hair tousled, clothes rumpled and wet in places, a streak of dirt decorating one cheek, she glared at him. "What do you want, Larson?"

Uh-oh. Her mood hadn't changed. In fact, she'd gone past angry and straight on to livid. "May I come in?" he said. "There's something we should talk about."

"I'm busy."

She started to shut the door in his face. He stuck his foot into the opening and prayed she wouldn't smash it.

"Doing what?" he asked.

"If you must know, I'm cleaning out my refrigerator."

"Now? Alexandra, it's after midnight."

''So? Refrigerators are just as dirty at night as they are in the daytime. Not that it's any of your business when I choose to clean the darn thing.''

''Fine. You clean, I'll talk. It won't take long.''

She continued to glare at him for a moment, then turned away with a shrug. ''Suit yourself.''

He followed her inside, nearly stumbling when he saw the state of her kitchen. It was the heart of her house, and he'd always thought its warm, perpetual messiness somehow reflected Alex's heart, as well. He'd probably go nuts if he had to live with her unfinished projects and piles of ''stuff'' everywhere, but the cheerful chaos seemed to suit her.

But this...well, it looked as if a platoon of Stepford wives had raided the place. The dish drainer was empty. All traces of clutter had vanished. Every visible surface, including the top of the refrigerator, sparkled. Even the floor shone.

When she was upset, Alex invariably tackled some job that would keep her hands busy; the bigger the job the better she liked it. But this...she must have been cleaning like a demon ever since she got home. It was not a good sign.

She fished a dishrag out of a sinkful of soapy water and wadded it up in one hand. ''One crack about looking for pods, and I swear I'll throw this at you.''

Raising his hands beside his head, he approached her. ''No jokes, honest. And no more teasing about the movie.''

''What do you mean?''

He leaned one hip against the cupboards and crossed his arms over his chest. ''Forget the cattle call. I'll shave in the morning, and we'll both be happier.''

Had he thought she would appreciate his offer? Perhaps

even thank him for letting her off the hook so easily? How wrong could one man be?

Her eyes narrowed. Her cheeks reddened. Her jaw jutted forward. Then she pitched the dishrag back into the sink, splashing them both.

"No way." She aimed her wet index finger at his chest and shook it in time with her words. "We made a deal, and you're sticking to it. We're all going to that cattle call, and we're all going to get hired."

"I thought you didn't want to do it."

"I've changed my mind."

"Why?"

"I just did. All right?"

"No, it's not all right. I'm not the enemy here, Alexandra. Stop treating me as if I am."

Her eyes widened at his words, then quickly closed, but not before he glimpsed a stricken expression in their depths. Her nostrils flared as she inhaled a deep breath. She cleared her throat, opened her eyes and said softly, "I know. And I'm sorry I took my foul temper out on you. You didn't deserve it."

"If I knew what really was going on, perhaps I could help."

"You got a magic wand you can use to change the past?" Her sad smile wrenched his heart worse than tears would have.

"No, but the past is gone. You don't have to live in it."

"Don't I?" Uttering a bitter laugh, she turned back to the sink and yanked out the plug. "That's how much *you* know about living in the Gap."

"What's that supposed to mean?"

"The past never dies here. People remember every stupid thing you ever did, and once you're classified in a certain way, you're never allowed to change. And God help you if your family doesn't fit 'the norm.'" She gave the dishrag a vicious twist and slammed it back into the sink.

"Calm down, Al—"

"I don't *want* to calm down!" she shouted. "I finally figured out tonight that no matter what I do, in the eyes of this stupid, podunk little town, I'm always going to be a flaky screwup. It's been fifteen years since I graduated from high school, I've been a full-time teacher here for ten years, and they still see me as nothing but a wild, irresponsible kid."

"That's not true."

She glanced around as if looking for something else to clean. Not finding anything, she pulled open the junk drawer and started banging the odd bits and pieces of life that never seemed to fit anywhere else onto the counter. Matchbooks, thumbtacks, batteries, penny wrappers, washers and drapery hooks bounced in turn as they hit the smooth surface.

"It *is* true," she insisted. "You heard that woman tonight. Now they're going to assume that Tasha will be just as wild as I was, and they'll treat her that way, too."

"After you ripped into Sylvia that way?" Nolan said, unable to repress a chuckle. "I doubt it."

"Oh, thanks, Nolan. Thanks a hell of a lot for your support. If you think this is so damn funny, go home."

"No." He reached out and grabbed Alex's hands, forcing her to hold them still. "I'm not saying she didn't have it coming. In fact, I think it was a good thing you spoke up. But she's not the whole town."

"Same as." Alex struggled, but couldn't break his grip. "You big jerk, let go of my hands."

"It's the only way I know to help you calm down," he said. "You get hyper when you're this angry, and then your anger and your hyperactivity feed off each other until you don't think rationally. Now, breathe, Alexandra.''

Scowling at him, she obeyed, inhaling and exhaling until he felt the humming fury in her muscles relax. He cautiously released her hands, ready to duck in case she decided to hit him for manhandling her. She gave him a stiff smile and turned away.

''I'm sorry,'' she said. ''I guess I'm not very good company tonight.''

''You don't have to be. I meant what I said, Alexandra. I'll be happy to forget the cattle call, and I'm sorry if I've made things worse for you by teasing you.''

She looked over her shoulder at him. ''It wasn't just you. Sooner or later everyone would have been on my back to go to one of those cattle calls. I should have realized from the beginning that it would be expected of me.''

''You don't always have to do what's expected.''

Wiping her hands on her jeans, she turned back to face him.

''Well, Larson, it's like this,'' she said. ''You were right about me all along. I do want a part in this movie, however small it might be. I want to hang around the action and watch every single thing they do, and I want it so bad, I can taste it. You were right about that part, too.''

''Then why did you pretend otherwise?'' Nolan asked.

''Because it hurt too much to give up the dream of being in the movies the first time. I was afraid it would hurt even worse to be that close to the real thing. I was trying to be responsible when I brought Tasha back to the Gap, but...''

Her voice trailed off and she mashed her lips together so hard her chin quivered. Blinking rapidly, she turned her face away from him. Nolan finished the sentence for her. ''But it still hurt to give it up.''

She gave a jerky nod, then whispered, ''It nearly broke

my heart. It still does sometimes. I suppose that sounds awfully selfish and immature.''

Instinctively reaching out, Nolan pulled her into his arms and held her, stroking the soft curls on the back of her head. She rested her cheek against his chest. She shed no tears, but held her back and shoulder muscles rigid, as if she feared relaxing completely might make her release a torrent.

''Not at all,'' he said. ''A sign of maturity is when you're able and willing to put your child's best interests before your own desires. You did that, Alexandra.''

She raised her head and met his gaze then, her eyes filled with a misery he didn't understand. ''Oh, please...don't...I wasn't being noble. I've tried to tell myself that I was, but...oh, hell, Nolan, I haven't even told you the whole truth about why I gave up on having an acting career.''

''Do you want to tell me now?'' he asked.

''Not really. I don't want to tell anyone, but I might need your professional services if I go to that cattle call.''

''My professional services? That doesn't make any sense.''

She gave a helpless shrug, then gestured toward the table. ''Why don't we sit down?''

Mystified, he crossed the room and sat on the side of the table closest to the windows. Alex took a bottle of white wine from the fridge before joining him. She opened it, poured them each a glass and handed him one.

''Dutch courage?'' he asked. ''How bad can this be?''

She cleared her throat, then pulled one foot up onto the chair seat and wrapped her arms around her shin. ''Everything I told you before is true. It's just not...everything.''

''What did you leave out?''

''Well, it involves Tasha's father.''

"How?" Nolan said, surprised at her response. "You haven't seen him in what? Ten years?"

"Something like that. But, I guess it really involves his mother as much as it does Brad." Alex sipped from her glass and fiddled with the long, slender stem. "She never forgave me for trapping her beloved son with an unplanned pregnancy. She, uh, wanted me to have an abortion. When I refused, she was absolutely livid."

"Nice lady," Nolan said.

A haunted, faraway expression entered Alex's eyes. "She made my life a living hell for the year Brad and I were married."

"He didn't stand up to her?"

Alex's snort of laughter held a bitter edge to it. "Are you kidding? Mommy paid for everything and always took his side. Besides, in his opinion, I wasn't good for anything but keeping his bed warm, and not even that when I got too fat for his tastes."

"Fat? I thought you were pregnant."

"After five months Brad couldn't tell the difference between fat and pregnant. I didn't think I was terribly big, but the way he carried on, you would have thought I was enormous. God knows I repulsed him."

Remembering how he had enjoyed watching Jennifer's body change and grow when she was carrying Rick, Nolan shook his head in disgust. "Sounds immature."

"Bingo," Alex said. "Marrying Brad Talbot was the biggest mistake I ever made. If I hadn't been pregnant, the marriage wouldn't have lasted two weeks."

"I still don't understand how this relates to your giving up acting."

"His mother's obsessed with keeping the Talbot name 'respectable,'" Alex said, making quotation marks in the air with her fingers. "When I filed for divorce, I decided to keep Brad's name for Tasha's sake. Mrs. T didn't like the idea at all, and she told me that if I ever sullied the family name with a tawdry acting career, she would do everything in her power to take Tasha away from me.''

"She could have tried, but I doubt she would have succeeded," Nolan said.

Alex shrugged. "Maybe not, but you have to remember I'd been a pretty wild kid. I barely graduated from high school. My college grades for the classes I completed before I had to drop out weren't great and I had no job prospects. I wasn't willing to risk that she might succeed."

Nolan frowned. Though the McBrides had occasional spats like any other family, they had a well-known tradition of looking out for each other. He couldn't imagine Alex having to face the problems she was describing by herself.

"Wouldn't your family help you?" he asked.

"They would have tried if I'd told them, but everybody was pretty disgusted with my hell-raising by then. I really wasn't too sure how any of them would react if they knew what was going on. Besides, there was one other issue."

"What was that?"

"The Talbots have been powerful in Wyoming since before statehood."

"So have the McBrides," Nolan said.

"But the divorce proceedings were held down in Laramie, which is Talbot country," Alex said. "They've always been more politically active and connected than my family. I thought there was a good chance they owned the judge."

"There are ways to fight that sort of thing."

"Hey, you know this stuff, Mr. Attorney, but try to remember I was barely twenty years old and scared to death I'd lose my baby. There was plenty of mud that could have been slung from both sides if we'd had a custody battle, but I didn't want that for Tasha's sake or my family's sake, or my own. I just did what I thought I had to do at the time.''

''You didn't sign any agreements?''

''No. It was all done by threats and innuendos, but I knew what Mrs. Talbot was saying. I felt like such a piece of garbage when she got done with me, I took my baby, went back to school and prayed she'd leave me alone if I kept my nose clean. First chance I got, I ran home like a scared little kid, and I stayed here, where my own family could buy a judge if necessary.''

Alex turned her head away, gulped, then inhaled a deep breath. The sight of her struggling to hold back tears angered him. No matter how wild she had been, she hadn't deserved such treatment.

''I didn't mean to sound critical,'' he said.

She gave him a tight-lipped smile. ''It's just…I still have strong feelings about the whole situation. It wasn't a happy time for me.''

''No wonder. The damn woman blackmailed you.''

''Yeah, well, now you know why I didn't jump at the chance to be in Marsh's movie. I still don't want to risk losing custody of Tasha.''

''There's no way anyone could take her away from you without her consent now, Alexandra. If the Talbots wanted to fight you, they wouldn't have any grounds. They've shown no interest in her for years, and you've got a whole town full of witnesses who'll testify to your fitness as a mother.''

At last, she gave him a real smile again. ''You don't know what a relief it is to hear you say that.''

''Oh, I think I can imagine it. And here's a bonus. I'll even help you change your legal name back to McBride if you want. No charge.''

''I might take you up on that offer.''

"You should." He stood and stretched the kinks out of his back. "I'm a hell of a good lawyer."

"And modest, too." She got up and walked with him to the back door. "Thanks, Nolan."

He held out a hand to her. "Come outside and get some fresh air. You'll sleep better."

She slid her hand into his and accompanied him down the steps to her patio. Together they gazed at the stars, enjoying a comfortable silence along with a cool, westerly breeze. After a few moments he heard a quiet sigh, glanced down at her and found her studying him with a warm, inviting look in her eyes he'd never seen there before.

Giving her plenty of time to avoid it in case he'd misread her expression, he turned to face her and put his arms around her. Still moving slowly, he lowered his head and kissed her. She went absolutely still, as if she weren't sure how she wanted to react.

He made it a gentle kiss at first, just a sweet, simple, joining of lips to lips. She exhaled another soft sigh, slipped her arms around his waist and slowly tipped her head to the right, her lips seeking a firmer contact with his. Sliding his fingers into her hair, he cradled her head in his palms and touched the tip of his tongue to her lower lip.

Without a heartbeat's hesitation, she opened her mouth, inviting him to deepen the kiss. He accepted the invitation, and found the answer to a question that had kept him awake during more than a few long, lonely nights. Alexandra tasted like...well, not like any one thing, exactly.

There was a ripe, luscious sweetness, that made him think of fat, juicy strawberries or maybe fresh bing cherries. There was tartness, too, like that of a kiwi fruit. And there was a spicy, tangy sort of taste that was pure Alex. He could have stood there, tasting her, enjoying her, holding her for hours.

But once his hormones realized this wasn't simply a friendly kiss like others he'd occasionally shared with Alex, it abruptly transformed into a hot, passionate, definitely sexual kiss. And the warm, beautiful woman in his arms responded, kissing him back with equal passion, pressing her breasts against his chest. He felt somebody's heart pounding fast, heard ragged breathing and guttural moans, and he was painfully hard and hungry and dangerously close to losing control.

Grasping at his rapidly shredding sanity, he pulled himself back, ending the kiss. Alex stared at him, her lips pouty and still slightly parted and a stunned look in her eyes.

"Wow," she murmured, her voice sounding raw. "Some sparks, huh?"

"Yeah." His own voice sounded equally husky, but he didn't care. He was too busy basking in the ego boost of Alex's awed expression to care about anything but convincing her to kiss him again. It didn't take much, just a slight lowering of his head, and she reached up to meet him halfway.

Any fears that the first kiss might have been a fluke evaporated in the instant, sizzling heat of the second one. He'd never felt anything close to this before, not with Jennifer or anyone else. They were so attuned to each other, so able to give whatever the other wanted, it was as if they could read each other's minds.

If they could do this much to each other with a kiss, what kind of heat would they generate if they made love? He found the notion incredibly erotic. Before he could carry the idea any farther, however, Alex flattened her hands against his chest and none too gently pushed herself out of his embrace.

"Whoa," she said, panting and shaking her head as if to clear it. "That's far enough."

Nolan shook his own head and chuckled. "Sorry. I didn't mean to get so carried away."

"Me, neither. I never dreamed it would be quite that...exciting to kiss you."

"Gee, thanks a lot, Alexandra."

She grinned. "Don't get your ego in an uproar. I just meant that we've been such good pals, I was afraid it might be like kissing one of my brothers or cousins. But it wasn't. It was great."

"Yes, it was." Touching a reddened patch on her chin, he grimaced. "Damn. I told you my beard was rough."

"Well, don't you dare shave a single whisker." Her eyes narrowed as if she were deep in thought, and then her mouth slowly curved into a calculating, decidedly wicked smile. "We're going to go to that cattle call, all right. It won't really be acting, but what the heck? I don't have to make such a big deal out of this. I'll get everyone off my back, and we'll all just have some fun."

Chapter Five

"Hurry up, will you?" Nolan grumbled. "We're going to miss the cattle call if you don't."

Framing his face between the comb in her left hand and the barber scissors in her right, Alex shot him an exasperated glance. "I would if you'd stop wiggling around like you've got ants in your drawers. Just be quiet and hold still, and we'll be done in a second."

"That's what you said five minutes ago."

"And you weren't quiet and you didn't hold still, and look where it's gotten you," Alex said. "I've never seen a beard quite like this before. I can't believe how fast it's grown, and every single whisker has a mind of its own."

"That's why I never grow it out. I look like Brutus in the Popeye cartoons."

Alex chuckled and ran the comb through the renegade hairs on his chin. "Not quite. You're way cuter than Brutus."

"Right."

He shifted around on the chair again, as if something really was making him uncomfortable. Alex snipped an offending whisker, then straightened up and studied him. His cheeks were flushed, his eyes narrowed, and his mouth was turned down in a frown that threatened imminent rebellion.

She had a pretty good idea what his problem was. It had been a week since they'd shared those sizzling kisses, and neither one of them had dared to discuss the inevitable changes in their relationship if they became sexually involved. Both of them had, in effect, retreated to a neutral corner and tried to pretend that their friendship was the same as it always had been.

It wasn't, of course. In fact, nothing had really been the same since the night Nolan had confessed to thinking her breasts were magnificent. Despite their mutual efforts to avoid physical contact, however, the sexual attraction between them seemed to be growing stronger.

Trimming a man's beard required a certain amount of physical intimacy. She'd been working on Nolan's for a good twenty minutes now, and being this close to him had revved her hormones into high gear. The way his eyes kept focusing on her breasts whenever she leaned over to trim another wiry whisker suggested that his hormones were giving him fits, too.

She didn't know whether to be happy about that or not. Her feminine ego liked the idea just fine. In his own, quiet, conservative way, Nolan was an extremely attractive man.

But she and Nolan weren't the only ones affected by their friendship. She had been a surrogate mother for Rick. Nolan had been a surrogate father for Tasha. In doing so, they had formed a family.

It was a family based on a friendship rather than a marriage, but a family nonetheless.

She wasn't ready to make a decision that might harm or even destroy their family unit. Nolan obviously wasn't, either. And they were both doomed to suffer the pangs of sexual frustration until they addressed the issue they were so carefully trying to postpone. Smiling ruefully at that thought, she combed through his beard one last time.

"What?" he said.

"What do you mean, 'what?'"

"What are you smiling at?"

"You sure are cranky."

He whipped one arm out from under the towel tied around his neck and grabbed her comb hand. "Don't tease me today, Alexandra. I'm not in the mood."

Startled by his quick strike and the low, harsh note in his voice, Alex looked into his face and felt a surprising flash of uneasiness. She wasn't afraid of him, exactly; she'd heard Nolan yell when he'd been provoked, but she'd never seen him actually lose control of his temper. But only a fool would fail to respect the fierce glitter in his eyes.

He looked...dangerous. A week ago she would have laughed at the thought of using that word to describe Nolan. Not anymore.

There was something unsettling about seeing those scruffy whiskers on a face and jaw that had always been clean shaven before. Perhaps they were an unspoken reminder that even the most polished and sophisticated man could have a hidden, less civilized aspect to his personality. Did Nolan? He'd always been such a gentleman around her, it was hard to imagine him behaving any other way.

On a purely sexual level, it was also very...intriguing.

Oh, brother, she had now officially lost her mind. She wasn't sure she should even kiss him again. Furthermore, she was a modern, professional woman. She didn't want a caveman, for heaven's sake. Or a cowboy, either, for that matter. Some of the best-looking cowboys she'd grown up with were such appalling chauvinists she'd never found them the least bit sexy.

Then why did those darn, scraggly whiskers make Nolan look so attractive to her? They weren't actually all that scraggly since she'd trimmed them. His beard was thick and coarse, and it made him seem exceptionally...virile. Not that heavy beard growth had anything to do with virility, of course, but it did look awfully...sexy on him.

"Al-ex. Don't look at me that way, Alexandra."

She heard and understood the warning in his voice. She just couldn't find the presence of mind to heed it. Spreading his knees apart, he slowly pulled her toward him. When she offered no resistance, he wrapped his other arm around her waist, pulling her closer and closer still, until she wrapped her arms around him, cradling his head against her breasts.

Groaning softly, he nuzzled her cleavage, his warm, moist breath penetrating through layers of blouse and bra to her skin. Arousal spread through her body, softening her joints, making her feel pliant and hot and itchy, all at the same time. She transferred the scissors to her left hand, then grasped a handful of his hair and let it slide across her fingers, admiring the way the light played off the golden strands and made the brown ones brighter.

Oh, she *did* want to kiss him again, "should" or "shouldn't" be damned. She was tired of always playing it safe. Tired of pretending she had no physical needs. Tired of going to bed alone every night, and then aching to have a man hold her, really hold her, as if she mattered.

Tucking her index fingers under his chin, she lifted, coaxing him to meet her gaze. His eyes were a pure, dark green, with only a hint of brown around the irises. He searched her face, slowly, carefully, as if he were seeing her for the first time and needed to record every detail in his memory in case he never saw her again. Shaken, but oddly thrilled by his intensity, she cupped the sides of his face with her palms, then leaned down and gently kissed his eyes closed, gliding over his cheekbones and down his nose.

"Alexandra," he murmured. "Alex, I—"

Whatever he would have said next evaporated with the opening of her back door. Tasha and Rick followed, arguing their way into the kitchen, as usual.

"Did not," Tasha said.

"Did too," Rick said.

The kids cleared the doorway too quickly for Alex and Nolan to separate with any kind of dignity. Tasha came first, spotted them and stopped walking so fast, Rick bumped into her.

"Dipstick," Rick said. "What the hell did you do tha—"

He broke off as comprehension dawned, and actually took a step backward. The silence stretched out as both teenagers continued to gape. If she hadn't felt so confused and embarrassed herself, Alex thought she probably would have found their dumbfounded expressions hilarious. Nolan nudged Alex out of his way and stood.

"Are you two ready to go?" he asked, pulling the towel away from his neck.

Rick and Tasha turned to each other, their eyes huge, tentative grins lurking at the corners of their mouths. Then Rick looked over at Nolan, let out a whoop of laughter and crossed the room. Hands in his front pockets, he stood with his feet spread wide apart and grinned up at his father.

"Hey, Dad, what have you guys been doing?"

"Yeah, Mom," Tasha said, coming to stand beside Rick. "What have you guys been doing?"

Alex wanted to vanish. A cloud of smoke would be nice, or a convenient hole opening up directly beneath her feet. She didn't need anything fancy, just as long as she could get out of facing the two young wiseacres she and Nolan had raised. Nolan cleared his throat, then scratched at his chin, while sending Alex frantic help-me-out-here messages with his eyes.

Alex held up the comb and scissors. "I was, um, just trimming Nolan's beard."

Rick let out another whoop of laughter. "That's not what it looked like to me."

"Rick."

The lash in Nolan's voice might have made Alex pause. She suspected it might have made a big, hairy biker wearing black leather and chains pause. Rick knew his father too well to fall for the tactic. His grin widened into a smirk.

"Well, jeez, Dad, you were all over each other. How long has this been going on?"

Tasha stepped closer, an eager, wistful look in her eyes that wrenched Alex's heart. Despite all of the affection her uncles lavished on her, Tasha still wanted a father. At one time she had hounded Alex to marry Nolan. Nolan hadn't asked her to marry him, of course, but that didn't matter to Tasha. It had taken months to convince her that would never happen; it had taken all of five seconds to rekindle her hopes.

"Are you like, in…love or something?" Tasha said.

"No," Alex said quickly. "It just, uh…happened, Tash. Believe me, it's nothing for you to get excited about."

"That's right," Nolan said. "There's no big romance here."

Tasha looked at Rick, who looked back at Tasha. The knowing smiles they exchanged made it clear that neither one believed a word the adults had said. Nolan opened his mouth as if he would try again to convince them, but Alex tapped his arm and shook her head. The more they protested, the guiltier they would appear. Only time would help them now.

"Well, then," she said, giving them both a cursory inspection. "You look great. Let's go, shall we?"

Rick's smirk faltered. "Aw, do we really have to do this? It'll be so dorky."

"Yes, we have to do this," Nolan said. "It'll be your first real job if you get hired. You might even earn enough to buy that bike you want."

While Nolan herded the kids out to the car, Alex ran a comb through her hair, dabbed on some lipstick and grabbed the portfolio of photographs and résumés she'd prepared for each of them. The kids whispered and snickered all the way to the high school. Alex exchanged a rueful smile with Nolan, then settled back, willing herself to relax.

It wasn't easy. Her mind either kept going back over those heated moments in her kitchen with Nolan, which was hardly relaxing, or it launched into fantasies in which the casting director took one look at her résumé and begged her to take over an important role because the actress who had been hired for it had broken a leg, contracted the measles or developed some other nonlife-threatening problem. The butterflies in her stomach stubbornly refused to listen to her silent, but stern reminders that this cattle call was simply something to do for fun, not even close to a "real" acting job.

Battered ranch pickups competed with shiny four-wheel-drive wagons and cars for space along the street in front of the high school. Alex wondered how many people were serious about working and how many had come today simply because they hoped to catch a glimpse of a movie star. Summer was such a busy time for ranchers, she doubted that many of these folks would be able to spare the time from their own work to take on a part-time job, even a temporary one.

Eager to get inside once Nolan finally found a parking spot, she practically jumped out onto the street, then had to wait in an agony of impatience for the others, who seemed intent on moving as slowly as possible, to haul their lazy carcasses from the car and catch up with her. Wasn't that the story of her life? she thought with a wry smile. She'd always been out of step with her siblings and cousins, either moving too fast or too slow, or wanting to go off in a different direction from the rest.

She managed to restrain her natural tendency to try to hurry everyone else up, however, and was glad she did when Blair DuMaine stepped outside just as they were getting ready to enter the building. A troubled expression flitted across Blair's face when she first saw them, but then she flashed a big smile and came forward to greet them, and Alex dismissed that quick, worried scowl as unimportant.

"I heard the play earned great reviews," Blair said. "I wish I could have seen it."

"I wish you could have, too," Alex said, "but now that it's over, I've got more free time. Give me a call when you want me to come out and help you work on your lines again."

Blair hesitated, appearing to be at a loss for words. After a moment, however, she said, "I appreciate the offer, Alex, but Dillon's been helping me lately."

"Dillon?" Alex demanded with a surprised laugh. "My cousin *Dillon's* been running lines with you?"

"Yes, he has."

Amazed and amused at the soft, rosy blush coloring

Blair's cheeks, Alex lowered her voice to a murmur. "That's not all he's been doing with you, is it?"

Blush deepening, Blair gave Alex a naughty yet girlish smile and shook her head.

"Well, I'll be darned," Alex said. "How did you coax that wounded old badger out of his den?"

"He's not that bad," Blair said.

"We're talking about the same guy, aren't we? Scarred face? Missing thumb? Cantankerous? Bossy? Stubborn?"

"Yes, of course. But I think he's actually rather sweet."

"Sweet? Dillon?" Alex touched the backs of her fingers to Blair's forehead as if she were checking for a fever. "Honey, we've got to have a drink and talk about this."

"First I think we need to catch up with the kids," Nolan said. "They sneaked inside without us."

Blair smiled and offered him her hand. "Hello, Nolan. Oh, what a...lovely beard. You must be here for the cattle call."

"Yes, Alexandra made me come with her."

Alex snorted at his blatant lie. He ignored her and scratched at his whiskers.

"She's been excited about it since the story came out in the Cody newspaper," he said. "Actually, I think she'd be wasted as an extra. She's quite a talented actress."

Blair shifted her weight to the opposite foot and glanced longingly toward the street. "Yes, I've, um, noticed that."

Alex decided she might have to kill Nolan for putting Blair on the spot. Grabbing his hand, she gave it a hard squeeze to shut him up, plastered a cheery smile onto her face and yanked him toward the school's big front door.

"We'd better get going," she said. "Good to see you again, Blair. Don't be a stranger."

The smile Blair gave her in return looked as strained as

Alex's own smile felt. "I won't. But you know, the closer we get to June, the busier I'll be."

"I understand perfectly. Bye now."

Blair left then, although *fled* might have been a more accurate description of the way she rushed out to her car. Alex waited until she was out of earshot before turning on Nolan.

"I can't believe you said that to her," Alex said, forcing the words out between clenched teeth.

"You wouldn't do it for yourself," Nolan said, his tone infuriatingly calm and logical. "She could do your acting career a lot of good if you'd only ask."

"She's a *friend* and you don't impose on your friends that way."

"Everyone in Hollywood imposes on their friends."

"But I'm not in Hollywood, am I? I'm a teacher, remember? I don't have an acting career."

"And with that attitude, you never will."

"If I can't make it on the basis of my own talent—"

"There are thousands of starving but talented actors out there. You need contacts with insiders like Blair to get noticed enough even to get auditions."

She hated it that he was probably right in everything he'd said. "How do you know so much about it?"

"I knew a few entertainment lawyers from L.A. You need an agent, too."

"Well, I didn't hire you to be one for me," Alex said.

"Maybe you should have," Nolan said. "I'd be good at it, don't you think?"

His smug grin made her laugh in spite of her irritation. Nolan was simply being Nolan, after all.

"You're such a cowboy," she said, rolling her eyes in mock disgust at him.

Nolan scowled. "Very funny. I'm no cowboy, and I've never tried to pretend otherwise."

"Oh, yes you are. You're an urban cowboy, but you're still a cowboy."

"And how did you reach that brilliant conclusion?"

"My brothers and my cousins do the same thing you just did. When you see something you think needs to be done, you don't wait around for permission. You go right ahead and do it."

"That makes me a cowboy?"

"Sure it does. What you did with Blair fits right under the heading of 'taking care of the womenfolk,' whether the woman in question wants your help or not."

Nolan had the grace to look chagrined. "I see. It seems I've seriously overstepped myself. I'm sorry, Alexandra."

"I'll forgive you this time, Larson, but see that you don't let it happen again."

Nolan saw the glint of amusement in Alex's eyes, heard the wryness in her voice and knew that he really had been forgiven. While he was glad of that, he also felt irritated to realize that once again in Alex's eyes, he had become a source of entertainment. How she did enjoy laughing at his alleged stodginess. The brat.

He opened the door and made a sweeping gesture with his right hand. "We should find the children. It's nearly one."

Alex glanced at her watch, squawked in surprise and hurried into the building. A section of bleachers had been pulled out for the occasion. Rick and Tasha waved from a row near the top, indicating that they'd saved two extra seats.

Nolan followed Alex up the stairway, admiring the sway of her long denim skirt and the glimpses of her trim calves and dainty ankles he caught with every step. Smiling to himself, he decided she wouldn't think he was stodgy if she could read his mind right now. She might slap his face, but she wouldn't call him stodgy.

A plump, middle-aged redhead came forward to address the crowd. Dressed in a wrinkled gray pantsuit, a yellow blouse and scuffed gray pumps, she looked harried, but friendly. Introducing herself as Nancy Kryszka, the casting director, she gave a quick synopsis of the movie's plot and went on to describe a typical day of work for a typical extra.

Nolan was impressed. With a clever, fifteen-minute presentation, she established an easy rapport with her audience. While she was funny, she was also informative and highly professional. She obviously loved her work, and she radiated an infectious energy and enthusiasm guaranteed to attract eager candidates for the jobs she needed to fill.

She answered questions at the end of her spiel and had everyone who was still interested in working fill out an information card. While her assistants collected the cards and attached the applicants' photographs, Ms. Kryszka asked anyone who had previous acting experience to stay behind and dismissed the rest of the crowd, telling them they would be called closer to the shoot. Nolan turned to tell Alex he would meet her at the car and promptly forgot what he'd planned to say.

Alex's skin looked awfully pale, but her eyes glowed with an intense emotion he couldn't readily identify. Although excitement was likely a major component, what he saw in Alex's eyes went deeper than that. Her expression actually reminded him of someone experiencing a religious conversion. The thought made him uneasy. Surely she wasn't getting too hyped up over being an extra.

Rick and Tasha stood up, jarring the bench. Alex

blinked, shook her head as if to clear it of confusion, then uttered a soft laugh and jumped to her feet.

"Come on, Nolan, let's go." She leaned down, grabbed his elbow and tugged. "I want to talk to that casting director."

Nolan obediently led the way back down the steps. The four of them gathered for a moment at the bottom.

"Is this gonna take all day, Mom?" Tasha said.

"I doubt it," Alex said. "Why? Did you and Rick have something in mind?"

"We want to go to Cody," Rick said. "We can see a movie and get a pizza."

"Or go bowling," Tasha said.

"Fine. You three decide," Alex said. "I'll meet you at the car as soon as I'm done."

Nolan experienced another flash of uneasiness while he watched her approach Ms. Kryszka, then told himself not to be ridiculous. Alex was a sensible woman. She knew this was only going to be a summer job, and a short-term one at that. No need to worry about anything other than getting Rick and Tasha to agree on what they wanted to do in Cody.

Alex joined them at the car twenty minutes later, bubbling over with enthusiasm. They saw a movie, shared a pizza and drove back to Sunshine Gap. Alex and Tasha retired to their house. Nolan and Rick retired to theirs.

Rick went straight to his room. Assuming his son would spend the rest of the evening playing computer games, surfing the Internet or reading, Nolan went into his den and decided to pay his bills. He'd barely gotten started, however, when Rick interrupted him.

"Dad? Have you got a minute?"

Nolan looked up and felt his heart sink. Rick stood in the doorway, his shoulders tense, his eyes worried. Damn.

There hadn't been that much anxiety in Rick's face since they'd moved to Sunshine Gap. Nolan had hoped never to see it again.

"Of course, Rick," he said, forcing his voice to remain calm. "Come in. Have a seat."

Rick hesitated a moment, then stuck his hands into his front jeans pockets and crossed the room. He sprawled in the overstuffed chair on the other side of the desk and studied Nolan with unnerving intensity.

"What is it?" Nolan asked.

"Are you in love with Alex?"

"I don't know," Nolan said slowly. "I'm attracted to her."

"Duh, Dad," Rick said. "We saw you two playing kissy-face, remember?"

Nolan frowned. "Love and physical attraction aren't necessarily the same thing."

"Are you sleeping with her?"

Rick's gaze was direct, and his voice carried an accusing note.

"That's none of you business," Nolan said.

"Why not? Wouldn't you want to know if I was sleeping with somebody?"

"Of course. But I'm an adult, Rick. I don't discuss my sex life with you or anyone else."

Rick slung one leg over the chair's arm and tapped his foot in the air in time with a frantic rhythm only he could hear. "I think you should discuss it with me. I don't want you to screw things up with Alex."

Nolan rubbed his tired eyes. "What makes you think I'll do that?"

"She's…cool, Dad. Really cool."

"Too cool for a stodgy old geezer like me? Is that what you're trying to say?"

"No. But I don't get why you're encouraging her to do this movie thing. Don't you think that's a little dangerous?"

"No, the stunt people do all the dangerous work. The extras just walk down the street or stand around in the background."

"Not *that* kind of dangerous." Rick rolled his eyes. "I mean, didn't you see how excited she was today? What if those movie people see how good she really is and offer her a shot at something bigger than being an extra?"

"She'll do it and have a great time," Nolan said. "What's wrong with that?"

"She could get the acting bug really bad, that's what. She could get other job offers. And then she just might pack up and move to L.A."

"She wouldn't do that," Nolan said, hoping he sounded more certain of his answer than he actually felt. In fact, the uneasiness he'd experienced at the cattle call returned, only now it was ten times stronger.

"Why wouldn't she?" Rick asked.

"Her whole family's here. Tasha's doing well. And Alex already has a job."

Rick huffed, then rolled his eyes again. "Dad, get a clue. Would you teach high school if you could be in the movies?"

Nolan's gut clenched. He knew Alex enjoyed teaching in general, and she enjoyed working with her students. But there were things about her job she despised, such as dealing with Horace the Moron, for instance. She always had a stack of papers to grade or lesson plans to figure out, and there were frequent, idiotic meetings that never accomplished anything and useless classes she had to take to keep her teaching certificate renewed.

The hours were long, the pay was low and the public

rarely appreciated how hard teachers worked. Would he do what she did if he knew he could practice law instead? The obvious answer made him sweat. He didn't want Rick to see that, however.

"She's always wanted to be in the movies," Nolan said in his most reasonable tone of voice. "Once she sees the process up close and finds out it's not as glamorous as she thought it would be, she'll get it out of her system and everything will be fine."

"You don't know that'll happen." Rick put both feet on the floor and leaned forward, elbows on his knees, hands outstretched toward Nolan. "What if she really likes it? What if she wants to leave?"

"I can't give you any guarantees about what Alexandra will or won't do. I don't think she'll want to leave Sunshine Gap, but if she does, we'll have to be her good friends and wish her well. Won't we?"

"But, Dad—"

"She's a grown woman, Rick. She can go anywhere and do anything she pleases. What is it you expect me to do?"

"You could marry her. She wouldn't go anywhere if you were married."

"You don't marry someone just to stop her from leaving."

"Alex has more going for her than that," Rick said. "She's pretty, she's funny, and you like each other. Tasha likes you, so you won't have any problems with stepkids hating your guts. Alex is even young enough to have more kids if you want. You'll never find anybody better, Dad."

"I can see you've thought a lot about this, and you're right in everything you say," Nolan said. "But this isn't just about you and me and what we might want. What about Alexandra and what she wants? Even if I asked her, she might not want to marry me."

Rick grinned and his eyes took on a wicked gleam. "She wasn't beating you off with a bat when Tasha and I walked in on you two."

"No, she wasn't." Nolan chuckled at his son's lecherous expression. "But we've never even dated officially. We're a long, long way from being ready to discuss marriage."

Rick snorted, rudely expressing doubts about Nolan's intelligence and/or his sanity. "You've been best friends for almost five years, so I'd say you know each other pretty well. And you love Alex, Dad, I know you do."

"Yes, I love Alexandra. But it's not the same thing as being *in* love with someone."

"I don't get it." Rick shoved himself to his feet and glared across the desk at Nolan. "We'd be happy with Alex and Tasha, and they'd be happy with us. You can't just let them go off to L.A. by themselves. It's too dangerous for women there."

"Calm down, son. You're getting way ahead of yourself. You're worrying about things that may never happen."

"I never worried about Mom dying, either, but she did," Rick said quietly. "I don't want to lose another one."

Chapter Six

"Oh, Nolan, that's awful," Alex said later that night when he finished telling her about his encounter with Rick. "Tasha's got the same idea, and she refuses to listen to reason. What are we going to do?"

Raking one hand through his hair, Nolan paced to the other side of her living room. "I don't know. I never dreamed one kiss could create such huge expectations."

"It wasn't just one kiss." Alex pulled her bare feet onto the sofa cushion and tucked them under her. Propping her elbow on the sofa's back, she supported her head with a loose fist and watched him make another lap. "We weren't even really kissing when they caught us. It was the... tenderness of the moment."

"That's hardly the point, Alexandra."

Alex turned her head away and hid a smile at his aggrieved tone. Oh, he *was* in a snit. While she hated to see him upset, she had to admit she enjoyed being "the calm one'' for a change. Not that she blamed him a bit for flipping out over his son's remarks.

Rick had not recovered from his mother's death quickly or easily. With the unconscious cruelty of the young, he had, in fact, blamed his father for not being able to ''make everything be okay again.'' Although Rick was older and more mature now than when his mother had been diagnosed with ovarian cancer, Alex certainly understood why Nolan felt so besieged at the moment. The situations were much too similar for comfort.

When Nolan paced closer again, she thumped the cushion beside her. ''Sit down and relax before you wear out my carpet. We've handled our little varmints before, and we can do it again. We just have to outsmart them.''

''I don't know if we can do that anymore.'' Nolan sat, but he didn't relax. He leaned forward, elbows braced on his thighs, his hands tightly clasped between his knees. ''They're both so blasted quick. What one doesn't dream up, the other one does.''

''Come on, Nolan, get some perspective. They're just teenagers, and young ones at that.''

Nolan gave her a baleful stare. ''They know where the guilt buttons are, and they don't hesitate to use them. And they're going to be watching everything we do. One small slip of the tongue, one exchanged glance that lasts too long, one impulsive hug that's not quite platonic enough, and they'll have us engaged to be married in a week.''

Alex chuckled, but knew he wasn't exaggerating the situation by much, at least in the minds of their children. When he would have scolded her, she held up her palms to stop him.

''I know what you mean, and I'm taking it seriously, Nolan. I really am. But other than refusing to have anything to do with each other, I don't see what can we do about it.''

"We can't do that." Nolan raked his other hand through his hair. "Then Rick *will* have lost you."

"I didn't mean we wouldn't have anything to do with each other's children. I could still do things with Rick and Tasha by myself. So could you."

"We could," Nolan said. "It wouldn't have that same 'family' sort of feeling, though. I doubt that would satisfy either of them."

Nothing short of a wedding would satisfy them, Alex thought, but she refrained from saying so. Nolan's eyes already looked haunted and his fingers drummed nervously against his pant legs. He didn't need any more anxiety.

"We could date other people," Alex said. "That would throw them off."

"Too obvious," Nolan said. "Especially right now. They'd see through that in a second."

"They might think so at first, but if we were consistent, I think eventually they'd realize we weren't really...serious about each other."

Nolan shook his head, but didn't say anything. Alex threw up her hands in exasperation. "I'm getting a little tired of coming up with ideas for you to shoot down, Larson. It's your turn to come up with one."

"I'm sorry. I didn't mean to do that." He surged to his feet and paced across the room again. "I'm just extremely frustrated."

"Me too. I thought we might be ready to explore a new relationship, but..." She pulled her feet out from under her and looped her arms around her knees. "We can't risk raising their hopes if we're not sure where the relationship is going, and there's no way to make sure we know where it's going, without raising their hopes. It doesn't seem quite fair, but that's the way it is."

"You're right." Nolan rested one elbow on her fireplace mantel, rubbed his other hand over his face and heaved a disgruntled sigh. "Of course, you're right. We have to think of what's best for the kids. But where does that leave us?"

"Where we've always been," Alex said. "Best friends."

"We go on as if nothing has changed?"

"Nothing *has* changed, Nolan. We've only shared a few kisses." Granted, they were the best kisses she'd ever had, but she could live without them. Not happily, perhaps, but she would survive.

"All right, friends it is," he said, though he didn't sound any happier about the idea than she felt. "I suppose there's really nothing else we can do."

She thought Nolan would leave then, but he turned his back to the fireplace, shoved both hands into his front pockets and studied her with a thoughtful frown. She studied him in return, and found herself wishing they could have come up with another solution. His continued, silent regard began to grate on her nerves.

"What is it?" she finally asked.

"You wouldn't leave Sunshine Gap, would you?"

"Leave the Gap?" The question was so unexpected, she laughed. "You mean escape, don't you? Jeez, I've been trying to get out of this town my whole life. The farthest I ever got, besides on a vacation, was Laramie."

He pulled his hands out of his pockets and folded his arms across his chest. "Are you saying that, given the right opportunity, you *would* leave?"

"This is about Rick, right? Do you want me to talk to him?"

"No, I'm asking you a question, and I'd like an answer.

Would you leave Sunshine Gap for, say, a career in Hollywood?''

"Hollywood? Are you nuts? It's never going to happen.''

"But if it did—''

"Nolan!'' She laughed again, shook her head and got up off the sofa. "Trust me, that's not going to come up. Nobody ever got to be a movie star by signing up as an extra.''

"Just answer the question, will you?''

"No.'' She crossed the room, slid her hand through the crook of his elbow and walked him to the back door. "It's too ridiculous to deserve an answer. Now, I want you to go home, get some sleep and don't worry your handsome little head about it, okay?''

He stepped outside, then turned to face her, planting one large foot in the middle of the threshold. "Why won't you answer the question, Alexandra?''

"Because there isn't one, simple answer.'' When he still didn't move his foot, she huffed in exasperation, then tried again. "Listen, as of right now, this minute, I have no intention of going anywhere. But, given the right opportunity, I suppose I *might* leave the Gap.''

"But it's your home.''

"So? L.A. was your home, and you left it. You didn't move up here on a whim, though, and I wouldn't move to California or anywhere else on a whim. The decision would depend on what the actual opportunity was and how it would affect Tasha and a long list of other things.''

"But—''

"But nothing. I answered your question as honestly as I could. Now, go home and at least let me get some sleep.''

With obvious reluctance, he removed his foot from the doorway, then turned and went down the steps. "All right. I'm sorry to have bothered you.''

"Hey, we're friends, remember? And you still have to take me to the prom next weekend."

"Sure. No problem, Alex. See you around."

"Yeah. 'Night, Nolan."

He vanished through the hole in the hedge without his usual cheery wave. The wretched man knew that would bug her, she thought, scowling after him. And whenever Nolan said, "No problem," it usually meant there was one. Well, maybe she *had* been a tad short with him, but honestly, what had he expected?

Assuring herself she had nothing to feel guilty about, she shut her door, turned out the lights and wearily climbed the stairs. Pausing at the doorway to her bedroom, she surveyed the water stain on the far corner of the ceiling where the roof had leaked last winter, the usual mess of clothes she'd tried on and discarded but hadn't taken the time to hang back up, the big, rumpled, lonely bed.

Pulling her T-shirt off over the top of her head, she flung it at the overflowing laundry hamper and raised both arms wide above her head. "Jeez, I don't know," she muttered to an imaginary audience. "If somebody offered me a whole new career in Hollywood, how could I ever stand to leave all of this?"

Alex saw very little of Nolan during the next week. They still jogged every morning, but neither had much to say. She told herself he was probably just too busy to socialize right now. She told herself she didn't care, when he didn't come over to help the way he always did while she did the spring cleanup bit in her backyard. She even told herself he could be so annoying at times that it was actually rather nice to have a break from his company.

Lies. They were all lies, and she darn well knew it. The truth was she missed having him show up at her door with a bottle of beer and an invitation to chat about work, the kids, her day, whatever. She missed hearing his laugh and his opinions. She missed...him.

They'd had spats before, but nothing serious. Nolan usually got over being mad at her within an hour. They'd never, ever stayed mad at each other for longer than a day.

But this time was different.

She sensed it, even if she couldn't put her finger on exactly what had changed. He didn't seem angry, but he didn't act like a best friend, or even a regular friend, for that matter. He had withdrawn to a place where she couldn't begin to guess what he was thinking or feeling. She couldn't talk to him about her own feelings, either. It was pretty darn hard to fix a problem when neither of them would admit one existed.

By the time Saturday rolled around she considered calling off their date. She really didn't need an escort in order to be a chaperone. She'd probably have more fun going to the dance by herself than if Nolan tagged along like a silent but dutiful Saint Bernard.

On the other hand, the music was usually so loud, very little conversation was possible. Why should he get out of suffering through it with her, when she'd already suffered through a bar association dinner and a chamber of commerce party with him this year? And, since she was in a mood to make him suffer, maybe she'd have to do a little digging in the back of her closet and find something really...interesting to wear.

For once she allowed herself plenty of time for a leisurely soak in the tub, a facial, a manicure and a pedicure. She used the rich, scented body lotion and matching perfume her brother Jake had bought her for Christmas, and styled her hair with less curl for a sleeker, more elegant look. She paid particular attention to her eyes when she put on her makeup, and when she slipped into the deceptively simple royal blue cocktail dress, she was well satisfied with her efforts.

Nolan might not talk to her anymore, but he wasn't going to ignore her.

"Hey, Mom," Tasha hollered up the stairway, "Cousin Grace is here."

"Be right there." Alex grabbed her evening purse and a lacy shawl, then took one last look at herself in the mirror. She looked good, if she did say so herself, but was it too much? Too blatant? Too outrageous? She didn't know, couldn't trust her own judgment with such things.

"Holy smokes, Alexandra," Grace said quietly from the doorway, "you look…fantastic."

Grace McBride Kramer was two years younger than Alex. They were close in height and build and had similar features, but the similarities ended there. Grace wore her hair in a long, single braid, little makeup and seldom bothered to put on a dress. She was a natural born homemaker who had been widowed while she was still in her twenties. She was raising her two boys at the Flying M Ranch where she cooked and kept house for whichever family members were in residence.

Though their personalities were very different, Alex and Grace had become good friends as adults, and often traded baby-sitting chores. Grace had come into town to pick up Tasha, who would be spending the night at the ranch with her cousins. Alex looked at Grace and tried to smile past a sudden wave of anxiety.

"Thanks, Gracie. I got this dress years ago and never found the right time to wear it. Do you think it's all right?"

"All right?" Raising her eyebrows, Grace ambled farther into the room and walked around behind Alex, studying her from every angle. "Honey, any man with a pulse is gonna think that little number's fine and dandy. Who's the guy?"

"The guy?"

"The guy you're plannin' to seduce with that...frock."

"I'm not planning to seduce anyone. I'm going with Nolan."

"Nolan?" Grace sputtered with laughter. "You're wearing *that* to go out with poor Nolan?"

"What do you mean 'poor Nolan'?" Alex asked. "He's not some loser. He's handsome, intelligent and successful."

"I know that," Grace said. "I've always liked him a lot. I just didn't think you were smart enough to notice what a great guy he is. You always treat him like a pal."

"Well, that's what we are. Pals."

Grace grinned. "Uh-huh. You wear that around him, you won't be pals for long."

"Oh, jeez," Alex said, caught in a panic of indecision. "I'd better take it off, then." She tossed her purse and shawl at the bed, turned and headed for her closet. "I don't know what else I'll wear, but—"

Grace caught her arm and stopped her in mid-fret. "Don't you dare change that dress. It's perfect on you."

"But Nolan will think—"

"So? Let him think. You could do worse. A lot worse."

"It's not like that. You don't understand, and I don't have time to explain—"

As if on cue, Tasha hollered up the stairs again. "Mom, Nolan's here."

Alex froze. "I can't do this. It's a mistake. I have to change."

Frowning, Grace stepped in front of her and gently grasped her shoulders. "Hey, Alex, calm down. The dress is beautiful, but it won't cause a scandal or a riot or anything. What's going on here?"

"I'm not sure," Alex whispered, struggling to catch her breath. "I was just so...angry, and—"

"At Nolan? What did he do?"

"Nothing, really."

"It doesn't look like nothing," Grace said. "If I need to call in some McBride muscle—"

"No," Alex said, emphatically shaking her head at the thought of one of her overly protective brothers or cousins going after Nolan. "It's not like that, Gracie, honest. Don't you dare say a word to any of those guys."

"Mom," Tasha yelled, making two long syllables out of the word. "Didn't you hear me? Nolan's here."

"She heard you, Tash," Grace called down the stairs. "She'll be right there."

Alex took a deep breath, then another and another until the sensation of panic eased. "Okay, I'm fine now," she said. Giving Grace a grateful smile, she picked up her purse and shawl. "Thanks."

"You *will* tell me what this is all about tomorrow when you come to pick up Tasha," Grace said.

"It's a long story," Alex said, heading carefully down the stairs.

Grace followed behind her. "That's the best kind. I wouldn't miss it for the world."

Nolan stood near the windows in Alex's living room, battling a fierce urge to fidget with his bow tie or the corsage box. It was silly to feel nervous about taking Alexandra to a high school dance, but he did. Of course, Rick's smart-aleck lecture about condom use just before he left to spend the night at his friend Jeff's house hadn't helped. Having Tasha poised on the sofa, ready to note every facial expression, every tone of voice, every...everything that passed between himself and Alexandra, didn't help his nerves much, either.

Rotten kids. As if Alexandra wasn't driving him crazy enough. Or was he simply driving himself crazy? How many times had he picked up the phone to call her this week and tell her he didn't want to be "just friends" with her? Twenty-five? Fifty? A hundred? At least that many.

And every single time, he'd changed his mind at the last second. He wouldn't call it chickening out. Well, all right, now that he thought about it, maybe he *should* call it that. If the sweating palms, the pounding heart and the sick feeling in the pit of his stomach hadn't been symptoms of fear, he didn't want to know what was wrong with him.

He cleared his throat. Tasha smiled at him. He smiled back, wishing she would go away. He wished Alex would hurry up. Tasha had already called her twice, for God's sake. What was she doing up there?

The sound of voices drew his attention to the stairway. A pair of dainty, high-heeled sandals came into view first, followed by a trim pair of ankles and long, slender legs. He would know those legs anywhere, but the sheer nylon stockings certainly were an improvement over running tights.

Then he glimpsed a bright flash of blue, lifted his gaze to take in the whole woman and wondered if it was possible for a man his age to die from a stroke, brought on by having all of the blood in his brain suddenly rush down to a certain…unruly part of his body he'd been trying not to think about. If so, he could be in big trouble. He could only pray his tuxedo jacket would cover it.

What Alexandra was wearing wasn't a dress; it was a declaration of war. War on what? Celibacy in general? It would be an effective weapon. His dignity? Nobody looked dignified while drooling. Any platonic feelings he might ever have had toward the woman wearing it? Already dead and buried.

Oddly enough, the dress had a full skirt and a sweetheart neckline that adequately covered everything that was supposed to be covered. It wasn't tight, and it really wasn't too short. Viewing it objectively, he couldn't have said what made that particular dress so damn sexy. It simply was.

Or was it Alexandra?

She reached the bottom step and strolled into the living room, approaching him with a welcoming smile. "Hi, Nolan. Sorry to keep you waiting."

His own smile felt stiff. He wasn't at all sure his voice would sound any better than a croak, but he couldn't just stand here and gape at her. "You look beautiful, Alexandra."

"Thanks. You look great, Nolan." She glanced over at the sofa. "Tasha, would you mind getting Nolan's boutonniere out of the fridge for me?"

While Tasha walked past him with a definite smirk on her face, Nolan shoved the corsage box at Alex with a lack of finesse that surprised even him. He'd been smoother than this as a high school kid, but he'd never felt more flummoxed in his life. Thank God the corsage had a wrist band so he didn't have to fumble around trying to pin the thing on her dress.

Still smirking, Tasha returned carrying a cellophane-wrapped rosebud and a camera. She knew how much he hated having his picture taken at the best of times. He might have to pay her back for this someday, say when she went to her first big dance.

Alex took the boutonniere and expertly pinned it on his lapel. *She* wasn't nervous. And really, why should she be? As far as she was concerned, he was just an accessory to go with that dynamite dress. All week long she'd seemed perfectly happy to go back to their old friendship.

If she hadn't acted so content, he might have found the nerve to complete one of those phone calls he'd wanted to make. But she had, and he hadn't found the nerve, and so here he was, doomed to spend the evening with this incredibly alluring woman, who thought of him only as a…buddy. He didn't know how he was going to keep his hands to himself and maintain his sanity at the same time. It served him right for being such a coward.

"I want pictures," Tasha said. "Stand close together now."

Alex turned around and snuggled into Nolan's left side. He automatically slid his arm around her back, letting his hand rest on the upper curve of her hip. She fit perfectly against him, and glanced up and smiled at him as if she felt the rightness of it, too.

"Okay, turn to your left," Tasha ordered. "Nolan, put your hands around Mom's waist. That's right."

Tasha probably would have posed them again and again if Alex's cousin Grace hadn't announced she needed to get back to the ranch. Tasha reluctantly put her camera away, then collected her backpack and hugged her mother. She hugged Nolan, as well, and his heart melted at the misty, wistful smile Tasha gave him on her way out the door.

He couldn't blame her for wanting a father, and he felt terribly flattered that she wanted him to fill such an important role in her life. If he were honest, he'd admit to loving her as much as if she were his own daughter, anyway. Sighing inwardly at the tangle of emotions the Talbot women created inside him, he escorted Alex out to his car.

The Sunshine Gap version of a prom had a sweet, old-fashioned atmosphere. The school cafeteria had been decorated with crepe paper streamers and balloons, and small

tables were placed around the perimeter of the room. A
disc jockey had been imported all the way from Casper to
provide the music. A group of parents made snacks in the
kitchen. The girls all wore formals; the boys wore dark
suits.

Alex's main job as chaperone was to prevent the kids
from spiking the punch bowl. Nolan's job was to provide
backup for Alex, but she didn't need much help. An experienced booze smuggler in her own teenage years, she
could spot a suspicious bulge in a coat pocket or a guilty
grin from fifty yards.

Her real skill came, however, in relieving the kids of
their contraband with such good humor, they rarely even
bothered to argue with her. Nor did they hold any apparent
grudges. The girls all complimented her dress, and when
the football coach and his wife took a turn guarding the
punch, several of the boys she had busted even asked her
to dance.

As the evening wore on, Nolan found it more and more
difficult to invent small talk. He'd never minded sharing
silences with Alex before, but tonight they made him uneasy. Her perfume teased him with a constant reminder of
her nearness. His fingers tingled with the memory of how
soft and cool and smooth the material of her dress had felt
when they were having their pictures taken. Her smiles
made him ache to taste her mouth again.

Dancing with her during the occasional slow numbers
only increased the torture. They had danced together often
enough to anticipate each other's moves, which freed them
up to talk and laugh and enjoy themselves. Tonight he was
so painfully aware of her breasts and hips brushing lightly
against him, he could hardly feel the beat of the music,
much less dance to it.

By the time the last song played, Alex's smiles appeared

less and less frequently, she avoided meeting his gaze, and her own seemingly endless supply of chitchat had completely run out. He hated the new awkwardness between them. He desperately wanted to fix it, but he didn't know how.

The silent drive home took only ten minutes, but the tension made it feel like forever. When he pulled into Alex's driveway, she unbuckled her seat belt and opened her door before he could put the transmission into Park. God, she couldn't wait to get away from him, and he couldn't blame her.

"Thanks for coming with me," she said. "I know chaperoning a high school dance isn't much fun, but I really apprecia—"

He shut down the engine, ripped off his own seat belt and, turning to her, reached for her hands. "Alexandra, stop. It was a lousy evening. It's my fault and I'm really sorry."

She shot him a surprised glance, then looked down at their joined hands. "Don't blame yourself, Nolan."

"There's no else to blame," he said. "I started this whole stupid thing, and then I kissed you and the kids caught us and I thought we could go back to being friends, but it's not working for me."

"It's not?"

"No, dammit, it's not." He released her hands, then wrapped his fingers around the steering wheel as if he didn't know what else to do with them. "Have I ruined everything, Alex? Even our friendship?"

Chapter Seven

In the glare of the dome light, Nolan's face looked flushed and his eyes were filled with misery. Alex pulled her door shut, wrapped the shawl closer around her and turned toward him.

"Wait a minute," she said. "Back up, Nolan. What's not working?"

"Everything. I mean, nothing's working. Every time I'm around you now, I don't have platonic feelings. They simply aren't there anymore. I stayed away from you all week because we agreed that we would just be friends, and I didn't think I could hold up my end of the bargain."

"*That's* why you've ignored me all week?"

"*Ignored* you? I haven't ignored you."

Alex folded her arms across her breasts. "That's what it felt like."

"Well, that's not what I intended. I didn't enjoy staying away from you, Alexandra. I missed you."

"Good."

"Good? You like knowing that I suffered?"

"When you deserve it," she said. "You deserved it for making me suffer right along with you. I missed you, too."

"You didn't act like it."

"Neither did you," she said.

"A man's got to have a little pride, you know."

"You think a woman doesn't?"

"I didn't say that."

"You didn't have to." She sniffed and turned her head away. "You 'oinked' it just fine."

"I did not."

"Did, too."

Nolan snorted. Then he chuckled. Then he let out a deep, rumbling laugh that bounced off the car's roof and the windows until Alex had no choice but to join him.

"Can you believe how much we just sounded like the kids?" he said later, wiping at his eyes.

"No," Alex said, still chuckling as she dabbed at her own eyes with her fingertips. "I think we were so busy acting immature we missed the most important thing either of us said."

"Which was?"

"That we missed each other."

"Yes." He leaned closer and took her left hand in his right. "Talking with you has become an important part of my day. I felt...lost without it."

"Same here. We've shared a lot over the years."

He traced playful, random patterns on her palm with the fingers of his left hand, his touch light, affectionate and terribly arousing. She wondered if he knew what he was doing to her. Casting a sidelong glance at him, she caught a flash of white teeth in the darkness and decided in the affirmative. The stinker.

She pulled her hand away and popped open her door again. "We need to talk and I need coffee." She led the way to her house, pausing at the top step before opening her back door. Looking over her shoulder at him, she added, "But I'm not inviting you in for sex tonight."

"Well, that's direct enough, even for an oinker like me," Nolan said with a wry grin. Then his grin turned wicked and his voice dropped to a husky murmur. "Does that mean you might invite me in for sex some other night?"

Alex's pulse skittered. Whew, she hadn't been the target of Nolan's charm quite like this before. The man was a champion flirt. "We'll see," she said, opening the door. "I suppose it's in the realm of possibility."

She kicked off her shoes under the kitchen table and went to fill the coffeemaker. When she returned, Nolan had taken off his bow tie and his jacket, and his white, pleated shirt was open at the neck. With another week's growth, his beard had developed a more defined shape, but it still gave him a rough edge that provided an interesting contrast to his elegant clothes.

He glanced up from removing a gold cuff link as if he'd felt her regard. He returned the favor, his gaze leisurely roaming from her hair to her toes, carrying an intensity that gave her gooseflesh on her arms and thighs. When he looked up again, she saw a stark hunger in his eyes that would have frightened her had he been someone she didn't know and trust implicitly.

"That is one damn sexy dress," he said, his voice low and raw. He removed the other cuff link and rolled up his sleeves with calm, deliberate movements. "You wore it just to torture me, didn't you?"

She nodded. "I was…angry that you could just drop out of my life so easily. I wanted to get your attention."

"It worked."

"Do you want me to change?" she asked.

He slowly shook his head. "It's a little late for that. I won't forget how you look in it."

Feeling like a tease, Alex clasped her hands in front of her waist. "I'm sorry, Nolan."

"I'm not." His lips curving upward, he looked her over again, raising more goose bumps in the process. She shivered, and his smile widened, but he only said, "Come on, Alexandra. Let's sit down and talk."

The coffeemaker gurgled and hissed behind her. She grabbed the excuse to turn away and collect herself. Her hand trembled when she reached for the coffeepot. She made a fist, lowered it to the counter and took a deep breath.

It was ridiculous to feel so shaken. Nolan was her friend, her very best friend. Yes, she was seeing a different side of him, a side he'd concealed from her. The atmosphere between them now felt strange, but he hadn't become a stranger. He was still Nolan. It shouldn't be so hard to remember that.

Grabbing two mugs, she filled them and carried them back to the table. Nolan took one from her, then pulled out a chair for her before settling himself on the side of the table adjacent to hers. They sipped in silence, surreptitiously glancing at each other. Tension grew between them again, swelling with each quiet breath either of them took until Alex feared it would smother her. She carefully set her mug down and wrapped both hands around it.

"So," she said. "Where do we go from here?"

"Forward," Nolan said. "We've already agreed we can't go backward, haven't we? Or was that just me?"

"No, it didn't work for me, either," she said. "But define *forward*. What does that mean, exactly?"

"You know, for someone who's supposed to be so impulsive, you can be awfully cautious and analytical."

"I'm never impulsive when I'm not the only one who will have to pay the consequences." She smiled. "Answer the question. What do you mean when you say *forward?*"

"Immediately or ultimately?"

"Both. But start with immediately."

"Immediately, I see a few casual dates." He paused, tilted his head slightly to one side and raised both eyebrows. "How honest do you want me to be here?"

"As honest as you want me to be with you," she said.

"Okay. At first, I see casual dates, followed by some serious necking in the car, and, if I get lucky, some heavy petting."

The bluntness of his answer didn't surprise her. Nor did the content. Still, she had to groan, if only to reward him for telling the truth.

"Jeez, Larson," she said, shaking her head in mock disgust. "I thought you were more...evolved than that."

"I'm evolved. We've already spent five years building the relationship. The only thing that's ever been missing is sex."

He looked so pleased with himself she had to laugh. "Spoken like a real man. Is that all you guys ever think about?"

His smile faded. "Of course it isn't. Come on, Alexandra, this is *me* you're talking to. I'll always care about you and Tasha, whether or not you and I ever make love. You know that."

"Okay, I'm sorry, Nolan. It's not fair to treat you like you're just some guy I met in a bar. But I still don't know what you want to happen. If we make love, the whole relationship will change."

"It already has. Haven't you noticed it's not nearly as

easy to talk to each other as it used to be?'' He raised his eyebrows at her again, and when she nodded in response, he continued. ''I want to be at ease with you again. I liked being able to say anything, without having to worry you'd take it the wrong way.''

''I miss that, too, but I'm not sure adding sex to the relationship will bring that back. And what about the kids?'' She sipped her coffee. ''We've got two bright, impressionable, pubescent kids watching everything we do. We have to set a good example for them.''

''Of course we do,'' Nolan said. ''That's why I don't see us hopping into bed together right away. I want to do what you said before—explore a whole new relationship. We could pretend we're just meeting each other now.''

''And if it doesn't work out?'' she said. ''You saw how hopeful Tasha was tonight. If we start really dating each other, her expectations are going to go through the roof. Rick's will, too. I'd hate to disappoint them.''

''Has it ever occurred to you that perhaps we're not doing our children a favor by trying to make everything all neat and tidy for them? Life seldom is, you know.''

Alex sat up straighter. ''What do you mean?''

''Life is full of uncertainty. We've worked hard to minimize it for Rick and Tasha because they both were cheated out of a parent and we feel guilty about it. We were probably right to do that for them when they were younger, but now that they're older, don't they need to learn how to handle a little uncertainty in their lives? Maybe even an occasional disappointment?''

''That sounds reasonable in theory,'' Alex said slowly.

With a soft laugh Nolan tossed his hands up beside his head. ''I don't know if it's reasonable or selfish as hell. Maybe I'm just trying to rationalize doing what I really want to do for a change, whether or not it's the best thing for the kids.''

''I don't believe that.'' Alex leaned forward and patted his forearm. ''You've always taken Rick's needs into account before you did anything important. I've always admired that about you.''

''Same here. But dammit, we can't just keep going around and around in circles. We have to make a decision. What do you want to do?''

''I probably want exactly what you want, but what if we end up hating each other?''

''Come on, Alexandra. You don't really think that would happen, do you?''

Reflecting back over the course of her relationship with Bradley Talbot, Alex shrugged. ''It's possible. We could lose our respect for each other, our friendship, everything.'' Even saying those words made her throat ache.

''Or we could fall in love with each other.'' He leaned closer, reached out and smoothed an unruly lock of hair back from her face. ''And live happily ever after.''

''I don't think I believe in happily ever after anymore.''

''I'm not asking you to,'' he said. ''Not just yet.''

Her stomach knotted up so tightly it hurt. ''What do you mean?''

''You know exactly what I mean. Someday we're probably going to have to talk about the *M* word.''

Pushing her chair away from the table, Alex got up and vehemently shook her head while she walked to the coffeemaker. ''Oh, no. Please, don't go there, Nolan. I used to think about getting married again someday, but I really wasn't very good at it the first time.''

''That was a long time ago.''

''No.'' She shook her head even more vehemently. ''This subject is not open for discussion.''

His eyebrows drew together in a puzzled frown. "Too soon?"

"Probably never." She poured them each another cup of coffee, then returned the pot to the counter. "I know you're never supposed to say 'never,' but..." She let a shudder finish the sentence for her.

"The situation is completely different. You're not twenty years old and pregnant, and I'm not your ex-husband."

"I know that." But he was like Brad in certain ways. They were both lawyers, logical to a fault and neat in their personal habits. "But there are certain...expectations that go along with being a wife that I'm not capable of fulfilling."

"What are you talking about?"

"I'm just not good marriage material." She came back to the table and opened her arms wide. "Look around you. This is how I live. I'm a lousy housekeeper and a mediocre cook. I'm not proper and dignified. Give me a drink or two at a party, and I'm way too outspoken and outrageous for your kind of crowd."

"I've never complained about any of that."

"That's because we've been friends. The rules change when you put on a wedding ring."

"I never realized you were still so bitter."

"That's not bitter," Alex said. "That's just realistic. Look, I don't think this is such a good idea, Nolan. I know things have been strained between us this week, but don't you think it might get better over time?"

"No, I don't." He touched a finger to her lips when she would have argued. "There's no need to panic. Let's just be ourselves and see what happens."

"But—"

"We'll go very slowly. Start with a few simple dates. Be honest with each other."

How like him to make ground rules, Alex thought, smiling in spite of her doubts. "Either of us can back out at any time?"

"Absolutely. With no hard feelings."

"I don't think you can guarantee that one, Counselor."

"Probably not, but it's a good thought." He stood and held out his hand to her. "It's late. Walk me to the door?"

She took his hand, let him help her up and felt her heart flutter when he laced his fingers through hers. Eyes crinkling at the corners, he turned to face her at the back door, slid one finger under her chin, tipped it up and planted a warm, sweet kiss on her lips. "It'll be okay, Alexandra. You'll see."

He left then, and she watched him get into his car, start the engine and back out of her driveway. When she could no longer see him, she stepped inside, closed the door and murmured, "It'll be okay? Why don't I believe that?"

Frustrated and more uneasy than he wanted to admit, Nolan locked up his house for the night, poured himself three fingers of Scotch, tossed in a couple of ice cubes and carried the glass upstairs to his room. He set it on his nightstand, stripped off his tuxedo and went into the bathroom to wash his face. When he was done, he reclaimed his drink and stood at the window while he drank it.

He looked up at the distant sparkle he'd come to think of as Jennifer's star, but didn't feel the usual warmth at the thought of his wife. It wasn't any wonder her spirit wouldn't come to him now, he supposed, not when he finally was seriously considering a replacement. Guilt pinched at his heart, and he swore softly.

Jennifer wouldn't have minded his finding another wife. In the days immediately before the end, she had reminded him several times that the wedding vows would no longer be in force after death had parted them. He'd always known, however, that her concern had been more for Rick to have a mother than for him to have another wife, and she never would have expected him to choose a woman so unlike herself. Most of his guilt came from knowing full well that she would not approve of a woman like Alexandra taking over either of her roles.

He had loved his wife and grieved deeply at her loss. With the distance of five years, however, he could view their relationship more objectively than had ever been possible before. If he were honest with himself, he would have to admit that he'd always known something was missing in their marriage.

Now he knew what that something was—the sizzle that comes with an attraction of opposites. Jennifer had been conventional, conservative, logical, neat, organized, or in other words, too much like him. It had made for a serene relationship, but not a very exciting one.

He wouldn't be disloyal to Jennifer or disrespectful of her memory, but he knew he needed more of what Alexandra had to offer. The stimulation of different ideas, the challenge of keeping up with her zest for new experiences, the sheer sense of fun she stirred up wherever she went; all these things had loosened him up, made him a more tolerant, understanding father and a better human being. He doubted Jennifer would have understood that, nor would she have liked Alex.

Hell, if he hadn't needed her help quite so desperately when he'd first moved to Sunshine Gap, he probably would have brushed Alex off as being too kooky for anything more than a nodding acquaintance. And what a loss that would have been, both for himself and for Rick. When it came to the things that really mattered, Alex wasn't kooky at all. He'd never known anyone with a stronger sense of responsibility or a more stringent set of personal ethics. She didn't get enough credit for that.

Most of the talk in Sunshine Gap about her outrageous behavior referred back to her adolescent days. She had the creative flair and confidence of a trendsetter. Given her love of brightly colored, eye-catching clothes, she stood out like an exotic bird in Sunshine Gap. Other people checked out what she wore and commented on what she did, but in L.A. or any other city, she wouldn't have registered a two on the kooky scale.

He understood all of those things about her, probably better than she understood them herself, but he didn't understand why she was so afraid to let their relationship grow. She trusted him, she knew him, knew he wouldn't hurt her or Tasha. He looked across the hedge at her house, noting that the light in her bedroom was still glowing around the edges of her blinds. Damn. He wanted to be there with her right now.

Both kids were gone for the night. It seemed like a sin to waste such a great opportunity to grab some privacy. But the lady wasn't quite ready, so he would have to be patient.

"Soon, Alexandra." He held up his glass in a toast, then tossed back the rest of his Scotch and went to bed, confident that in the end his patience would pay off and Alexandra would be his. Thank God he had plenty of time to convince her they belonged together.

Chapter Eight

During the next couple of weeks Alex immersed herself in wrapping up class projects, grading term papers and other end-of-the-school-year details that always seemed to pop up unexpectedly, no matter how carefully she planned. She saw Nolan more often than during the week before the prom, and felt pleased that their friendship had once again become "normal." True to his word, he seemed perfectly content to let her set the pace in developing a more romantic relationship.

So far she hadn't had the nerve to instigate more than a few kisses. She enjoyed kissing him so much, she knew it wouldn't be long before she was ready to move on to, how had he put it? Oh, yes, "some serious necking and heavy petting." She grinned every time she remembered him saying that.

The actual necking and the petting didn't sound half-bad. If only she didn't have so many doubts about the wisdom of doing what felt natural and right when she was kissing him. In Nolan's embrace everything felt natural and right, and therein lay her problem. With him there was no inner alarm signaling the need to quit; she just wanted to go right on kissing him, holding him, loving him until they were both...satisfied.

But she did have doubts. She had huge, hairy, horrible doubts about her ability to satisfy him, about her ability to keep her heart intact if he satisfied her as devastatingly well as she suspected he might, about her ability to recover if she fell in love with him and it didn't work out. Most nights she lay in bed, worrying, wondering, wishing she had half the sexual experience most people in Sunshine Gap probably assumed she did. Ha! What a joke.

She debated with herself endlessly, leaning one way one day, the other way the next. By the time the last Friday of May rolled around, she was frustrated and disgusted with herself, but still unable to make a decision.

As if sensing her mother's potential for crankiness rising, Tasha begged to spend the night with a girlfriend. Nolan and Rick were elbows deep in an old car they were restoring together.

When Grace called and said the family was getting together at Cal's Place for dinner and socializing with the movie's cast and crew members, Alex jumped at the chance to go out and think about something other than her relationship with Nolan. She dropped Tasha off, then drove to her brother's bar and restaurant. Main Street was so crowded with unfamiliar cars and trucks she had to park around the corner.

Cal's restaurant was equally crowded, and Alex paused in the doorway, looking for Grace. A pair of hands waved from the back. Alex squinted, saw Grace's oldest son, Riley, then threaded her way through the swarm of customers.

She'd expected to meet a lot of strangers, and there were plenty of them present.

She hadn't expected to see so many locals, however, and it wasn't until she spotted Blair DuMaine sitting beside her cousin Dillon that it began to make sense. Blair had spent very little time in town since she'd arrived at the Flying M, and the residents of the Gap had all come out to get a look at a famous actress. The phone lines were probably still smoking. Chuckling to herself, Alex spotted Sylvia Benson balancing a heavily loaded tray on one shoulder, heading right for her.

Alex dodged out of Sylvia's way and quickly slid into an empty chair between Riley and his little brother, Steven. "Hi, guys," she said. "What's shakin'?"

His dark eyes practically dancing with excitement, ten-year-old Steven leaned over and whispered in her ear. "I think Mom's got a boyfriend."

"Really?" Alex stole one of Steven's french fries and sneaked a peek at the other occupants of the long table. Grace sat between two good-looking men, both of them strangers to Alex. "Which one?"

"The blond guy," Steven said. "He's the wrangler for the movie company. She's been showin' him all over the ranch and stuff. I think he even kissed her."

"Really?" Alex said again, shamelessly pumping the kid for information. Not that the little blabbermouth ever needed much encouragement to tell everything he knew. Alex thought Steven would probably make a great reporter someday. Before he could tell her more, however, his mother noticed Alex.

"Hi, Alex," Grace said with a startled laugh. "I didn't see you come in."

"Just got here," Alex said. She inclined her head toward

the blond man sitting on Grace's left and winked. "And you were otherwise occupied."

Grace blushed, much to Alex's surprise. Grace hadn't paid any attention to men since her husband had died several years earlier. If the big blond wrangler could get that much of a reaction out of her, more power to him. Grace introduced him as Wade Kirby and the other man as Randy Lorenzo, the location manager for the production company.

The evening progressed in a blur of new faces and names, talk and laughter, and a general move into the adjacent bar for dancing. Grace wasn't the only one showing signs of changing. Dillon, who had acted surly and reclusive ever since he'd been disfigured in the same accident that had killed Grace's husband, tonight was dancing every dance and showing every sign of having one heck of a good time.

Alex shook her head in amazement, ordered a drink and made her duty rounds, greeting old friends and introducing herself to the newcomers. She enjoyed hearing all the movie talk, until she found herself cornered at the family table by one of Cal's more-eccentric employees, Sunshine Gap's favorite retired teacher.

If Miz Hannah had a last name, nobody remembered it or used it; she was simply Miz Hannah. She had lovingly taught second grade for two generations and had started on a third one before failing eyesight had forced her to retire. When Cal had accidentally discovered that her pension wasn't large enough to support her, he'd hired her to act as a hostess at his restaurant. She despised charity and wouldn't have accepted help from him or anyone else under any other circumstances.

Well into her eighties, Miz Hannah moved too slowly now to be a great restaurant hostess, but she did love to visit. Most of Cal's customers had been in her class at one time or another, and many of them enjoyed spending time with her when the need arose. She was small and plump, and she had a refined manner that went well with the string of pearls she always wore.

Alex nearly groaned out loud when Miz Hannah sat down at her table. She was whipped. She'd almost decided to ask her brother Zack to drive her home, as he'd volunteered to be the family's designated driver for the evening. But she couldn't possibly be rude to Miz Hannah; it simply wasn't done. When Miz Hannah wanted to visit about something, one was expected to cooperate.

"Well, Alexandra," Miz Hannah said, "I heard wonderful reports about the senior class play this year. Everyone who saw it enjoyed it very much."

"Thank you, Miz Hannah," Alex said.

"I noticed the other day that your neighbor, Mr. Larson, has grown quite a lovely beard."

"Yes, he has," Alex said.

"He came into the restaurant for coffee, and we had a nice visit. He's such a sweet man, isn't he?"

"Yes, he certainly is," Alex said, wondering if Miz Hannah would think he was so sweet if she'd heard him talking about necking and petting.

"Well, Alexandra, he said something that started me thinking about you."

"What was that, Miz Hannah?"

"He told me that he and his son had signed up with you and your little Natasha to become extras in Marshall's movie."

Wondering where on earth this conversation might be going, Alex nodded cautiously. "That's right."

"But, Alexandra, that simply won't do."

"Excuse me? We're only doing it for fun. It won't hurt the children in any way."

"Oh, I know that." Miz Hannah patted her fluffy white curls, then pushed her glasses farther up on the bridge of her nose. "But being an extra is not nearly a big enough role for you. Surely, Marshall knows you're much more talented than that."

"That's not Marsh's decision to make," Alex said.

Miz Hannah gave an imperious sniff. "I beg your pardon. He wrote the script, didn't he?"

"Yes, he did. But when he sold it, it became the property of the production company that bought it. He really doesn't have anything to do with the casting decisions."

"But, Alexandra," Miz Hannah protested, her high, wavery voice cutting through the other sounds in the room like the whine of a buzz saw, "you *must* be in this movie. It's about your very own ancestors, after all, and—"

Alex reached across the table and patted Miz Hannah's hand. "I didn't expect to have a part, Miz Hannah. It's all right."

Miz Hannah pursed her lips, then firmly shook her head. "No, it most certainly is not all right. I'm very concerned about this. You mustn't fight your destiny."

Had anyone else made that statement, Alex doubted she would have been able to stop herself from laughing out loud. Goodness, had the old darling gone on a New Age kick? "My destiny? I'm afraid I don't understand what you mean."

Miz Hannah gazed directly into Alex's eyes. "Yes, you do. You were born to be an actress. I've known that about you since you were in the second grade, and I believe you've known it even longer. Just as your cousin Marshall was meant to be a writer, you were meant to be an actress. And not just in those little amateur productions they put on around here."

Keenly aware that people at several nearby tables were

listening to every word coming from Miz Hannah's mouth, Alex felt her face grow warm. At the same time her stomach clenched so hard it ached. It took everything she had to reply in a soft tone, but somehow she managed it.

"There's nothing wrong with amateur productions," she said.

"Of course not," Miz Hannah agreed. "Without them, most of us would never see any live theater. But you are no amateur, and you will never reach your full potential as an artist if you don't push yourself to accept an occasional challenge. Don't waste the talent God gave you, Alexandra. You've been stagnating here for too long."

Though Miz Hannah's criticism had been mildly stated, a shocking number of angry, defensive, frustrated words roared up inside Alex at the injustice of it all. She had to take a long, deep breath to prevent them from spewing out. She took a second one, just to be safe, but her voice still shook when she replied.

"I know you mean well, Miz Hannah, and I appreciate your concern, but I'm really not an actress. I've been a teacher for ten years now, and if I do say so myself, I'm a pretty darn good one."

"Of course you are," Miz Hannah said. "I hear wonderful things about your teaching all the time. But there is a lot of acting that goes into being a teacher, and that's the part you love the best, isn't it?"

"Perhaps," Alex said, "but I don't have any intention of changing careers. I've built a good life for Tasha and myself, and I'm content with what I have."

Miz Hannah gave her an affectionate smile. "I understand, dear. You go on now and dance and have some fun, but do think about what I've said, won't you?"

Grateful for the dismissal, Alex got up and headed straight for the bar. Cursing under her breath, she slid onto one of the padded stools and ordered another drink. When it arrived, she took a sip, then sighed as the icy rum and cola soothed her jangling nerves. Honestly, it was silly to let Miz Hannah rattle her cage. She was just a sweet, little old lady who thought she knew what was best for everyone.

After a second sip, Alex glanced to her right and recognized Nancy Kryszka sitting beside her. The casting director had the bleary-eyed look of someone who's made a serious dent in a bottle of alcohol. She picked up her drink and saluted Alex with it.

"Hi, there," Alex said, returning the gesture.

"You're one of the McBrides, aren't you?" Ms. Kryszka held up a hand like a cop stopping traffic. "No, don't tell me which one. I'll get it in a sec. I have a great memory for faces."

Alex wondered how great anyone's memory could be when it had been pickled in vodka. "Okay."

"Aha! I've got it. You're...Alexandra McBride... something or other. Don't know your last name, but you're the one with all the acting experience."

"That's right," Alex said. "You must have met so many people here, I'm impressed you remembered that much."

Ms. Kryszka made a slapping motion and let out a cackle of laughter. "Oh, honey, I wouldn't forget you. I got special orders about you."

"You did?" Alex asked.

"Sure did. It's a shame, too. A damn shame." Ms. Kryszka lit a cigarette and blew a smoke ring at the ceiling.

Mystified, Alex frowned. "What kind orders did you get?"

"I'm not s'posed to cast you for anything. You don't even get to be an extra."

"Are you sure?"

"Yep." Ms. Kryszka nodded, then giggled and blew another smoke ring. "That sounded real Western, didn't it?"

"Uh, certainly," Alex said. "Who gave you the orders?"

"Ms. Blair DuMaine herself."

Unable to believe what she was hearing, Alex swiveled around on her stool and searched the crowd for Blair. Whatever the problem was, surely she could fix it. "Do you have any idea why she gave you that order?"

"Said she promised...s-s-somebody she wouldn't encourage you to go prof-f-feshn'l."

The instant she spotted Blair shuffling around the dance floor to a romantic ballad with her arms wrapped around Dillon's neck, Alex understood Ms. Kryszka's slurred message. "By any chance, was that somebody my dear cousin Dillon?"

"Yep, tha's the name." Ms. Kryszka giggled again. "Damn, I'm getting this Western lingo down good."

"You sure are." Literally seeing red, Alex downed the rest of her drink, slid off the bar stool and headed for the door. She'd almost made it outside when her big brother Zack, the town's sole law enforcement officer, intercepted her.

"Hey there, sis," he said. "Where do you think you're goin' in such a hurry?"

"Home. Get out of my way, Zack."

"I can smell the booze on your breath, Alex. You're not drivin'. I'll take you."

"No need. I'll walk." She planted one hand in the center of his chest and gave him a hard shove.

Zack staggered but quickly caught his balance and followed her through the doorway. "Alex, what's the matter with you?"

"Not a damn thing." She turned in the direction of her

house, but he grabbed her arm before she could take a step and swung her back around to face him. She didn't dare look at him. Zack was her favorite brother, and if she saw any sympathy in his face right now, she'd probably bawl her eyes out. After taking a moment to compose herself, she said, "I'm fine, Zack, honest. Go back inside and watch for drunks. I promise I won't drive."

"I'm not so sure it's a good idea for you to be out walkin' around after dark. Got a lot of strangers in town these days."

"Oh, pu-lease," she said. "Everybody walks around Sunshine Gap after dark. You can watch me until I turn off Main Street if you want, and I'll be home two minutes later."

"Sure I can't help you with anything?" he said.

"Yeah." She yanked her arm out of his grasp and set off at a brisk pace, fearing he might still try to stop her. He didn't, but she felt his troubled gaze following her until she turned the corner two blocks later. She'd have to remember to call Zack's home answering machine and let him know she'd arrived home safely. Otherwise the big lug was bound to worry about her.

Nolan hung up the phone, grabbed a sweatshirt and pulled it on, then went out his front door and sat on the steps to watch for Alexandra. He couldn't imagine what would have upset her so much, but Zack McBride wasn't known to exaggerate. If she didn't show up in the next ten minutes, Nolan intended to go looking for her.

Two minutes later he heard her coming. From the low, furious sound of her muttering, he concluded the walk hadn't calmed her down. When she marched into view with her head down, arms swinging like a power walker's, he suspected she could have stomped all the way to Cody and it wouldn't have helped much.

He waited to speak until she'd just passed his front walkway.

"Hi, Alex. Nice night for a walk."

She halted, turned her head toward him, then said something he couldn't hear, did an abrupt about-face and stomped back toward town. Nolan jumped off the steps and ran after her. He reached for her and she turned on him, hitting and cursing like a demented thing.

"Alex." He shielded his face with a forearm and wrapped his other arm around her waist. "Alexandra, stop."

"Don't touch me. Let me go. I have to go kill that son of a bitch right now."

"Kill who? Zack?"

"Yes, dammit. Zack and Dillon and Blair and Miz Hannah."

"Will you stop hitting me?" Nolan grabbed her flailing hands and trapped them between their bodies. "Zack and Dillon, I can probably understand, but why would you want to kill Blair and sweet old Miz Hannah?"

"They're all a part of it," she said, panting as she struggled to free her hands again. "It's a big fat conspiracy."

"How much did you have to drink?" he asked.

"That's right, you buzzard." She twisted her whole torso, but he managed to hang on to her. "Go ahead and laugh at me, too. Just like the rest of them."

Her voice broke then, and so did her heart. It sounded that way, anyway, when the fury in her eyes dimmed and her face crumpled in on itself and a ragged cry rose from her throat. He raised one hand to the back of her head and pressed her face into the crook of his shoulder.

Her whole body shook with the force of her sobs and

her tears dampened the front of his sweatshirt. She wept on and on, as if she had an endless supply of heartache and gallons of tears to shed. He rocked her back and forth, stroking her hair and crooning wordless, comforting sounds to her that he had once crooned to his son.

"Shhh. Alexandra, sweetheart, don't," he said, hugging her closer. "You'll make yourself sick."

She raised her head from his shoulder and glared at him from red, swollen eyes. "You're damn right, I'm sick. I'm sick and tired of being treated like a slow child. I'm sick of this damn, stupid little town and everybody in it."

"I believe you," he said. "Why don't you come inside and tell me what happened tonight?"

"Oh, Nolan." A fresh wave of tears gushed down her cheeks. "You wouldn't understand. You're always so... regular."

"Regular?" He gently turned her around and slowly led her back to his house.

"You know, regular," she said. "Normal."

"And you're not?"

"Well, I think I am, but obviously nobody else does. I'm thirty-three years old, and my own brother doesn't even think I can find my way home."

"That's not what he said. He was only worried about you because you were upset."

She paused on his front steps and swiped at her eyes with the backs of her hands. "I don't want Rick to see me like this."

"It's all right. He's already gone to his room for the night," Nolan said. "He won't come out of hibernation again for at least twelve hours."

Alex uttered a weak laugh. "He's not a bear."

"You've never seen him when he first gets up in the morning." He ushered her through the living room and into the hallway, pausing at the powder room to let her splash water on her face. When she'd finished, he continued on to the kitchen, filling the teakettle while she slid into the breakfast nook and curled up in the corner. "Tea or hot chocolate, Alexandra?"

Her only answer was a shrug. He made them each a mug of hot chocolate and slid into the booth beside her. He gave her a few moments to compose herself.

"What happened?" he asked.

She related the events of her evening in a soft, dreary monotone that didn't even sound like the Alex he knew. An air of depression settled over her like a dark, polluted cloud, worrying him more than either her temper or her tears had. In fact, he far preferred the temper to this...hopelessness.

"No wonder you were furious," he said. "I didn't know Dillon was such a jerk."

"He's not a jerk," she said with a sad smile. "He's a cowboy. Tasha and I are his womenfolk, and he's just trying to take care of us. Since all of our parents are jaunting around the world, I'm sure he feels especially responsible for us now."

"But you're an adult."

"Oh, huh." Her laugh had a bitter edge. "It's exactly what I tried to tell you before. Nobody's ever allowed to change in Sunshine Gap. Certainly not the town flake."

"You're not a flake."

"Then why does everyone feel a need to run my life for me? Of course, it might help if they'd get together and make up their minds. I mean, Miz Hannah's saying, 'Act,' Dillon's saying, 'Don't act.' What's a poor, stupid child like me supposed to do with that?"

"Ignore them," Nolan said. "Ignore all of them."

"I've tried that for years and years, but I can't do it

anymore," she said, pounding her fist on the table with a conviction he found alarming. "I just can't."

"What do you mean?"

"I have to get out of this town."

"No, Alexandra, that's not necessary."

She raised her chin and gazed at him with a steady regard that made him squirm. "I see. You know what's best for me, too? Well, let's hear it, oh, wise one."

He held up his hands, palms out. "I'm sorry. That was uncalled for. It just seems a bit...extreme to me."

"I don't know why. People move all the time."

She was right, of course, but the thought of her leaving made his chest hurt. "Where would you go?"

"It doesn't really matter, as long as it's someplace where no one knows me. If I call the placement office at the university on Monday, I may even be able to find another teaching job for next fall."

"What about Tasha? Won't it be hard on her to move, when she's so close to starting high school?"

"Not as hard as it will be on her if we stay here," Alex said. "It's not in her best interests to grow up as the daughter of the flake. And don't tell me I'm not a flake. It doesn't matter what you think or what I think about it. I'm talking about what the whole community thinks."

"Tasha's the one who really matters here, and she doesn't think you're a flake," Nolan said.

"Yes, she does." Alex told him about the day Tasha had come home and found her dancing. "She says things like how much she wishes she had a 'normal' mother all the time. To her, I'm this...wacky wild woman who does things nobody else's mom would even think about doing."

"That's just adolescence talking. All kids think their own parents are weird. Believe me, you're well within the boundaries of normal."

"You really think so?"

"Of course I do."

"Yeah, but you're from California," she said. "What do you know about normal?"

Nolan grinned. "I'm the stodgy one, remember? If I say you're normal, you're normal. Besides, most of those other people who are always giving you grief can't even run their own lives. What do they know about running yours?"

"Not much."

Encouraged by her grumbled reply, he continued. "I think you've been trying too hard to win everyone's approval, when that's clearly an impossible task. As you pointed out, they can't even agree on what it is you should be doing."

She frowned, propped her chin up on one hand and gazed off into some distant place only she could see. Nolan imagined he could hear angry thoughts buzzing around in her head like a swarm of wasps. Gradually, however, the frown lines across her forehead eased and she nodded.

"You may have a point," she said thoughtfully. "I never used to care much about what anyone else in Sunshine Gap thought of me, because no matter what I did, somebody always disapproved. It seems funny, but even after all these years, that still hasn't changed, has it?"

"No, it hasn't," Nolan said. "And you're hardly the only one who gets discussed over coffee at Cal's Place. Gossip is a form of entertainment in Sunshine Gap, Alex. Everybody seems to have an opinion about everybody else, but that doesn't mean any of those opinions are right."

"I know that," she said. "I used to know that, anyway. Do you suppose I've been so worried about losing Tasha for so long, I've become a little…paranoid about my image in the community?"

"Possibly. It's hard to let go of a fear like that, and at

one time your fears may have been realistic. But you're not in danger of losing Tasha now. You've certainly proved you can hold a responsible job and provide her with a nurturing, stable home. Beyond that, what you choose to do with your life is no one else's business.''

Lowering her hand from her chin, she drummed her fingertips on the table and slowly started to smile. A moment later she smacked her palm on the table, laughed, then scrambled onto her knees, threw her arms around his neck and hugged him so hard he could barely breathe.

''You're a genius, Larson,'' she said, ''an absolute genius.''

When he tried to loosen her stranglehold, she pulled back, cupped her hands on either side of his face and gazed into his eyes as if she were searching for something. Whatever it was, she must have found it. The next thing he knew, she brought her mouth to his and kissed him with a sweet, wild passion that momentarily stunned him.

She had been so cautious before, so hesitant to start any sort of love play and so quick to end it, he'd begun to wonder if he'd dreamed those very first kisses they had shared. But this kiss was like a gift...a gift with her whole heart and soul inside. It reminded him of hiking for hours under a blistering sun and then jumping into the sheer bliss of an alpine lake.

Only this time, he wasn't jumping by himself. He was jumping with Alexandra in his arms, and her lips were pulling him down and down and down into the depths of pleasure so fast his head reeled. Her fingers tangled in his hair as if she feared he might try to get away, when in fact, he would have swallowed her whole if only he'd known how.

His senses were hyperalert, greedy to experience and savor every aspect of her kisses. He tasted the salt of tears on her lips and the bite of rum on her tongue. Her hair felt silky against his hands and his cheek, and it carried the tang of tobacco smoke on top of the familiar strawberry scent of her shampoo. Her breasts rubbed against his chest, tantalizing him with mental pictures of his palms and fingers shaping her, caressing her, drawing erotic whimpers from her luscious lips.

Leaning back, she silently studied him, her eyes huge and wary, but oh, so hot and hungry. She whispered his name, traced his eyebrows and his cheekbones with trembling fingertips, slid onto his lap at the urging of his hands on her hips. For long, quiet moments, he simply held her there, giving both of them time to absorb the newness of these feelings.

She trailed her thumb across his lower lip. He teased it with the tip of his tongue, then gently nipped it with his teeth. Her laugh filled the room, soft and low and vibrant, stroking his nerve endings like a favorite song.

He supported the back of her head with his shoulder and brought his other arm across her hip to protect her from banging it against the table. This wasn't the most comfortable place he'd ever tried to make out, but he wasn't about to risk losing the moment by trying to move anywhere else. Besides, he couldn't take this too far because Rick was upstairs. While he didn't expect to see his son again before morning, he couldn't absolutely guarantee it.

Raising his free hand, he slid it into her curls behind her ear and stroked the soft skin at her nape. "This is nice."

"Mmm-hmm." She looped her arms around his neck and rubbed the tip of her nose against his. "Better than nice. I wish I'd found the nerve to do this before. You're always so sweet, and I'm really grateful for everything you've done."

"This isn't just gratitude, is it?" he said, instantly despising the idea.

She gave him a chiding look. "Don't be silly. It's not *just* gratitude, but I am grateful to you, Nolan. You've taken away a huge burden I've carried around for years."

"I haven't done anything."

She tipped back her head and laughed like a delighted child. "Oh, yes, you have. All of a sudden I feel so...free. You can't imagine how wonderful that feels."

"You mean the community approval thing?"

"Exactly," she said. "You're absolutely right. Whatever I do with my life, other people are going to think whatever they want to about me. So, I might as well stop trying to prove how much I've changed and how responsible I've become and do whatever I darn well please."

In the depths of her beautiful dark eyes burned an angry, reckless defiance he'd never seen there before. He suspected, however, that her family and the residents of Sunshine Gap had seen it many times when Alex had been growing up. To say it made him feel nervous was an incredible understatement, but he managed to keep his voice reasonably calm.

"And what might that be?"

"I haven't figured it all out yet." She raised one hand to the back of his head and leaned closer until their mouths were aligned and he could feel the puffs of her breath hitting his lips. "But you'll be the first to know when I do. With a wild woman like me, anything's possible."

She closed the tiny space between them, kissing him back into the depths of pleasure. Once again he felt the bliss, but the chill came from deep inside himself, not some imaginary mountain lake. He was not by nature a worrier, but he couldn't escape a nagging sense of anxiety.

If Alex truly felt free, she might leave Sunshine Gap, and then he would lose her. He didn't know why he was so certain that would happen; he simply was. His chest hurt in the same spot that had pained him earlier, but he didn't need a doctor. Alex was the only one who could fix this kind of chest pain.

It was a hell of a way to figure out he was falling in love with her.

Chapter Nine

The last day of school fell on Friday, the third of June. At the end of that long-awaited day, Alex locked up her classroom, handed in her paperwork and went home, where she collapsed on the sofa, insisting that she needed a minimum of one week's personal vacation before tackling any other summer activities. Her personal vacation schedule included sleeping in until she awoke—on her own—around noon, afternoons spent lying in a hammock in the backyard reading novels in between naps and, in the evening, mindlessly watching one taped movie after another until bedtime.

This year, as in every other year, she thoroughly enjoyed her life as a lazy, shiftless blob for the first two days. By the third day she began to notice that her house could use a good cleaning, but she bravely forced herself to ignore the mess and rented another movie. By the fourth day, she realized her car was dirty, the grass was "belly high on a tall horse" and the weeds were taking over her flower beds, but she gritted her teeth and stuck to her regimen of rest, rest and more rest.

On the fifth day she was wide awake by eight o'clock, showered and dressed by nine and on the rode to Cody with Tasha and Rick by ten. Visiting the Buffalo Bill Historical Center before all the summer tourists descended and having a late lunch at the Irma Hotel with Nolan could hardly be counted as work. They stopped at a grocery store on the way home and bought steaks for the barbecue, fresh vegetables for a salad and all the makings for banana splits.

The kids teased her about caving in and doing something productive before her week was up. She smiled and turned up the tape player, blasting them with vintage rock and roll until they begged for mercy. Back at her house, she shoved the perishables into the fridge, changed back into her "resting" clothes, an ancient pair of khaki shorts and a faded purple tank top, and headed back out to the hammock.

Tasha and Rick asked for permission to wash her car. Alex gave it with an indolent wave, knowing the project undoubtedly would lead to a full-fledged water fight that might conceivably end up involving every kid in the neighborhood. She could only hope. Much more of this peace and quiet, and she would go loony for sure.

Putting one foot on the ground to start the hammock swinging, she heard the first ear-splitting shriek. She sighed happily and opened her book, an erotic thriller that would probably keep her up half the night. The story grabbed her interest right away, and with the cheerful sounds of garden-hose warfare playing in the background, she turned page after page, completely losing track of time.

A car door slammed out front somewhere. Uh-oh. Tasha knew better than to try to wash the inside of the car, didn't she? Maybe it was time to check on the kids. Alex set her book on the grass under the hammock and carefully swung her feet over the side before climbing to her feet. She'd learned the hard way that getting in and out of this thing was an art form. Before she could do more than brush off the seat of her shorts and tug down the hem of her tank top, she heard voices coming around the side of the house.

An instant later Blair DuMaine stepped onto the patio, followed by Alex's cousin Dillon. The good feelings Alex had been storing up all week evaporated in a heartbeat. Every drunken word Nancy Kryszka had said to her at Cal's Place came back to taunt her, and the anger she'd struggled to bury since that humiliating evening roared back to life. Squaring her shoulders, she turned to face them.

"Hello, Blair. Dillon. This is a surprise," Alex said, letting her tone tell them she didn't find it a particularly pleasant one.

"Hello, Alex." Blair's smile faltered, but she radiated an air of suppressed excitement.

"Alex," Dillon said. "Mind if we sit down?"

"I guess that depends on what you want," Alex said.

Dillon tipped the brim of his Stetson back and frowned at her. "You lose your manners somewhere?"

"Dillon, please." Blair shot him a warning glance, then turned back to Alex. "We'd like to talk with you, if you've got a few minutes. It's important."

Raising her chin, Alex propped her hands on her hips. "I can't think of a thing either one of you could say that would be worth my time to listen to it."

"Alex!" Ignoring Blair's restraining hand on his arm, Dillon stepped forward until Alex had to tip her head back to look into his eyes. It was an old intimidation tactic the male McBrides all used, but it had never worked worth a damn on Alex. "What the hell is the matter with you?"

"Nothing's wrong with me, you big jerk." She jabbed her index finger into his chest. "What the hell's the matter with you?"

"Me?" Dillon said. "What'd I ever do to you?"

"You're a meddling, interfering, busybody, that's what. Why don't you go off somewhere, like to China maybe, and mind your own damn business for a change?"

"Stop, both of you, please. Whatever the problem is, surely, we can fix it." Blair took a deep breath, but when she spoke again, her voice wavered as if she might be fighting tears. "Alex, I really, um...well, I really need your help."

It wasn't easy to harden her heart against the distress in Blair's eyes, but Alex tried. "My help? What for?"

Dillon muttered something unintelligible, but subsided when Blair touched his arm again. "Look, Alex," he said, "if I've done something to upset you, I'm sorry. I'll be happy to talk it over with you, but couldn't we please just sit down for a minute here, so Blair can tell you what she wants?"

Curious in spite of her anger, Alex waved toward the patio. "All right."

They all grabbed a lawn chair and gathered around her battered umbrella table. Blair cleared her throat, then folded her hands together on the table's stained surface and gazed into Alex's eyes. "I need you to be in the movie, Alex."

"What?" Alex said, jerking back in surprise. That was certainly the last thing she'd expected to hear.

"I need you to play Belle Flannigan. You'll need to do a screen test, but I've seen home videos of you and I know you'll be marvelous."

"Wait a minute." Alex gave her head a violent shake. "I know I didn't hear that right. Have you two been in Cal's bar all afternoon?"

"Cut it out," Dillon said. "She's dead serious."

Alex turned on him with a glare. "Oh, yeah? Way I heard it, you didn't want her or anybody else encouraging me to go professional."

Dillon had the grace to flush. "You heard that?"

"You betcha. You know how it is in small towns, Dillon. People talk. Word gets around."

"Aw, jeez, Alex, I'm sorry." Dillon shrugged. "I just thought you and Tasha were doing so well lately, I didn't want to see you get all…sidetracked."

"What did you think I might do?"

"Well, hell, I don't know." He shot Blair a desperate glance, but she only raised her eyebrows at him and shook her head. "Take off for Hollywood, I guess."

"You didn't think I could make it there, did you?"

"I don't guess I thought it out all that well, hon. It was just sort of an instinctive thing to protect you, same as I would Grace." He gave her a lopsided, apologetic smile. "The folks are gone, and I know they never wanted you to go there, so I played the big brother. I sure never meant to hurt you."

The honest regret in his eyes took the heat from her anger. Even when they'd been kids, she'd never been able to stay mad at Dillon for long. Still, it wouldn't do to let him off the hook too easily. If he didn't suffer from this experience, he wouldn't learn anything from it.

"All right," she said. "I'll forgive you this time, but I want you to take some time and think back to how long I've been teaching school here and how long it's been since I did anything really outrageous. I've grown up, Dillon. Get used to the idea, will you?"

"I'll do my best." Then, to Alex's surprise, he stood, crossed to her chair, pulled her to her feet and gave her a rib-crunching hug. It was something he might have done before the accident, and she couldn't help hugging him back.

Blair jumped to her feet, came over to stand beside Alex and grabbed her hands the second Dillon released her. "Alex, please, tell me you'll do this," Blair said. "It's not a big part, but it's a good one, and you're perfect for it."

"What happened to Whitney Morgan?" Alex asked, mentioning the actress who had already been signed to play the role.

"Nothing. We have to change the shooting schedule, and she's not going to be available when we need her. We'll have to buy out her contract as it is, and if we have to start looking for a replacement from scratch, we'll have a huge delay and go way over budget. You're my only hope to stay on schedule."

"Come on, Alex, you can do it," Dillon said.

"You really think so?" Alex said.

"Hell, yes. Piece of cake. I double-dog dare you."

"Oooh, you're really pulling out all the stops," Alex said with a grin. She turned to Blair. "Do you really think I can do it? You haven't seen me do that much."

Blair's eyes glittered with something that looked to Alex like hope. "I knew you could do it that night you ran lines with me. Reading through it the first time, you gave Belle a wonderful personality. If you can just give me that much on camera, I'll be absolutely thrilled. Will you?"

Alex glanced down at her arms and laughed at the goose flesh covering them. "Well, I'd really love to give it a shot," she said. "But what'll I do with Tasha? And I always keep an eye on Rick for Nolan, you know. They don't really need a baby-sitter, but I can't just leave those two to their own devices."

Dillon grinned. "I'll take 'em off your hands for a few days, maybe a whole week. Those kids can both ride pretty well, and Grace just happens to need some help drivin' our herd up to summer pasture. We'll take 'em back to the ranch with us tonight, and they can help her get ready to leave.''

"Lord, Dillon, they'd love that," Alex said.

"And by the time they're done with that," Blair said, "we'll be ready to start shooting the town scenes in Cody, and they can be extras. Will that help?"

"I think so," Alex said. "Let me check with Nolan."

"I'll do that," Dillon said. "I can answer any questions he has about where they'll be goin' and such."

He headed for the back door, and Alex watched him for a second, feeling slightly confused. "Wow," she said, "what's the big rush?"

Blair laughed. "Welcome to the world of feature films, where everything is always hurry-up and then wait forever. I'm afraid we have a lot to do to get ready before we start shooting next week. We'll do your screen test tomorrow, and you can meet with the wardrobe mistress. You don't have a SAG card, do you?"

"A SAG card?" Alex said, feeling more confused by the moment. She should know what that was, but her mind had so many things whirling through it, she couldn't seem to focus on any one of them very well.

"Screen Actors Guild."

"Oh, of course," Alex said. "Uh, no, I don't have a card."

"It's all right," Blair said with a smile. "We'll take care of it. We'll take care of everything for you, Alex. All you have to do is show up and act. Do you still have your script?"

Dillon poked his head out of the back door. "Nolan agreed. I'll help the kids pack their gear."

"All right, Dillon. Thanks," Blair said. She turned back to Alex. "Now, where were we? Oh, yes, the script."

Alex nodded. "I still have it, I'm sure. I mean, I wouldn't throw something like that away, and I haven't lost it. I don't think I have, anyway."

"Alex, are you all right?"

"Oh, yeah, I'm fine," she said, although she really wasn't all that certain about the matter. "This is just such a surprise, you know?"

"I hope it's a nice one," Blair said.

Alex laughed. "Are you kidding? Of course it's a nice surprise. What should I do for the screen test?"

"We'll run through our scene together. Try to memorize your lines, but don't get uptight about it. We just want to see how you come across on film."

"You really thought I was okay? When we did that scene before, I mean?"

Blair took her hand, led her back to her chair and gently pushed on her shoulders until she sat down. Then she pulled her own chair close and sat facing her. "Alex, I wouldn't ask this of you if I didn't believe you could do it. What's really worrying you?"

"I'm sorry," Alex said. "I don't mean to be such an insecure pain in the rear, but I don't want to make a fool of myself or let you down. I, uh, really expected you'd want to work with me again, and when you didn't...well...I guess I got the idea you must have thought I wasn't very good."

"That wasn't it at all," Blair said, firmly shaking her head. "I enjoyed both of the times we acted together, but Dillon was so adamant about my leaving you alone, I didn't know what else to do. I'm sorry you were hurt."

"You really care about him, don't you?"

The expression in Blair's eyes softened, and her cheeks

flushed a lovely shade of pink. "Oh, yes," she said softly. "He's a wonderful man. A bit...old-fashioned sometimes, but he's got a good heart. He loves all of you so much."

Wondering if Blair knew she was falling in love or had, perhaps, already fallen, Alex grinned. "You've been good for him, Blair. He's changed since he started working with you, and believe me, it's an improvement."

Blair's blush deepened. Before she could say anything, however, Dillon came out of the house with both teenagers in tow. His eyes warmed as he approached Blair, and Alex felt a tug at her heartstrings on his behalf. Shoot, she was feeling the same protective impulses toward Dillon that he had for her; he'd already been hurt too many times by women. Was there a way he and Blair could get together on a permanent basis? Or was he headed for another heartbreak?

There was a flurry of activity then, getting everything loaded into Blair's rental car. Alex gave Tasha a goodbye kiss and hugged Rick, ignoring his adolescent horror of such affectionate gestures. Blair promised to call later with details and drove away before Alex could get fully into her mother mode and check everything the kids had packed.

When the sporty little red car disappeared from sight, Alex strolled around the side of the house, whistling under her breath as if nothing important had happened. She lived at the end of a quiet street that ran out of pavement fifty yards past her property line and turned into a country road. Nolan was her only close neighbor, but a person never knew when some rancher's wife would come into town the "back" way and drive past Alex's house. She didn't want anyone to see her doing something unusual, such as jumping around and screaming like a maniacal game-show contestant, and stop to find out what was going on.

The news would get out soon enough. More than anything else, Alex wanted a few moments of absolute privacy to get used to the idea that Blair DuMaine had asked her—well, more like begged, really—to be in her movie. Confident that no one would see her, she pinched herself. The pain assured her she hadn't dreamed the entire episode, which meant that Alexandra McBride Talbot was actually going to have a screen test tomorrow.

No wait, why use the name that had given her nothing but grief and trouble for the past fourteen years? For acting purposes, why not use Alexandra McBride? Or just Alex McBride? No, that sounded too masculine. Alexandra McBride it would be.

Now that she thought about it, she decided it was time to take Nolan up on his offer to help her change her legal name back to McBride. Oh, she wished he would hurry up and come home. She had the most wonderful news in the world, and no one to celebrate it with her.

"He doesn't beat ya. He doesn't rape ya. He gives ya food to eat, clothes to wear and a roof over your head. Honey, what more do ya want in a man?"

Putting both hands behind his back, Nolan ducked through the gap in the hedge and stopped on Alex's side. His heart contracted at the sight of her standing in the middle of her patio wearing wrinkled khaki shorts and a disreputable purple tank top. Her bare feet were grass stained, her hair wildly tousled, her eyes focused on some smoky, old-time saloon in her imagination. God, she was gorgeous.

As soon as he'd hung up the phone after talking with Dillon, he'd closed his office, made one stop for flowers, another for champagne and broken every speed limit on the way home from Cody. His single thought had been to get to Alex in time to be the first to congratulate her, but maybe he was making too much of this...business. He glanced down at his suit and shook his head, feeling foolishly over-dressed.

"Ha! Love ain't all it's cracked up to be, Lizzie, and don't you forget it." Alex's voice took on a cynical, soul-weary note that made Nolan ache with pity for the disillusioned woman who spoke those words. "You marry that Swanson fella, or you're gonna end up in some stinkin' saloon just like me. Believe you me, you don't want that."

Hell. He should go home and change into something more casual. He stepped back toward the hedge. His movement must have caught her attention. She paused, then pivoted toward the hedge, and for a moment he had the impression she saw someone other than himself. A second later her gaze focused more clearly on him and her whole face brightened at the instant of recognition.

She let out a joyous whoop, ran across the yard and launched herself at him, obviously expecting him to catch her. Unfortunately the bouquet of flowers he held in his left hand and the champagne bottle he held in his right slowed his reaction time considerably. He managed to get his hands out from behind his back, but before he could brace for the impact, her arms wrapped around his neck, her breasts smashed into his chest and her momentum tipped him right over into the hedge. She landed on top of him, driving the air from his lungs.

Struggling to inhale, he propped himself up on his right elbow and set the bottle in the adjacent bush. Alex started giggling and thrashing around in search of a way to disentangle herself. It might have been an erotic situation if he hadn't been worried about the placement of her knees in relation to his groin. She finally managed to gain her feet without emasculating him and reached down to help him sit up.

"Oh, jeez," she said, giving him a delightful eyeful of

cleavage while she brushed at his suit coat and picked leaves and twigs out of his hair. "I'm so sorry. I didn't realize…oh, flowers? And I squished them? God, I'm mortified. Absolutely mortified. Are you hurt anywhere?"

"I'm fine." With Alex fussing over him like a sweet, voluptuous nurse, he was in no particular hurry to extract himself from the bushes. He gave her a weak smile and drew a shaky breath into his lungs. She leaned closer, gently touching his ribs and tsking over a scratch on the side of his neck.

He thought he felt a swoon coming on, whether it was from the view or the snootful of pheromones he received from her closeness, he couldn't have said. He only knew she smelled like sunshine and fresh air and soft, warm…woman. Hey, it wasn't *his* fault his nose was practically buried in the neckline of her tank top.

"Nolan," she said, her forehead wrinkled with worry. "Nolan, are you sure you're all right? You look a little funny. Maybe I'd better call Zack and ask him to bring the ambulance."

The thought of her burly brother wrestling him onto a stretcher shattered the last of Nolan's lusty daydreams. He gave his head a shake, then scrambled to his feet over Alex's objections. He brushed off his seat, tucked in his shirttail and retrieved the champagne bottle.

"Congratulations," he said, offering it to her. "You're going to be a star."

"Oh, Nolan." She sniffled as she took the bottle from him and carefully set it at her feet next to the crumpled flowers. Then she looked up at him again and lifted her arms in preparation to give him a hug. "Is this okay now?"

"More than okay."

He hugged her to him, savoring every second of contact with her curves. She pulled out of his embrace long before he was ready to release her, her smile tinged with uncertainty, as if she wasn't quite sure what should come next. He wasn't sure, either, and they just stood there looking at each other with an awkward silence leaching the fun from their celebration before it could even properly get started.

"Thanks, Nolan," she said softly.

"You can hug me anytime, Ms. Movie Star Talbot."

"No, not Talbot." She scooped up her gifts and led the way to the patio, chattering as they walked. "We're going to change my last name back to McBride. My credit will read—" she stopped and swept one hand across an imaginary movie screen "—Alexandra McBride." She grinned at him over her shoulder. "You think?"

"Definitely. It's a fine stage name."

"I think so, too. God, I love this, Nolan!"

Waving her fists above her head, she performed the manic victory jig that always cracked him up. He'd never seen her look so excited or so happy, and he was fiercely glad he'd thought to make an occasion of this day for her. When she finished dancing, he sent her into the house for glasses, draped his suit coat over the back of a lawn chair, rolled up his shirtsleeves and began opening the champagne.

After being tossed about in the hedge, the wine undoubtedly would spew everywhere, but Alex wouldn't mind. In fact, knowing Alex, she'd love watching it go off like a geyser, and he gave the bottle an extra shake just for her. She returned with two slender flutes as he removed the wire cage covering the cork.

"Ready to catch?" Aiming the bottle's mouth out into the yard, he put his thumbs under the cork's rim and slowly pried it loose. Alex stood beside him, grinning eagerly, bouncing from one foot to the other, glasses at the ready. He grinned back at her, applied the last smidgeon of pressure and sent the cork flying with the distinctive popping sound they'd been waiting for.

The champagne sprayed from the bottle like a fountain. Alex filled both glasses, and when the wine continued to gush, she gulped one glassful and shoved it back under the bottle, filling it again.

"Careful," he said with a chuckle. "If Tasha and Rick catch you guzzling like that, you'll never hear the end of it."

Grinning wickedly, Alex took another healthy gulp. "Tasha and Rick aren't here."

"Where are they?"

"They're at the ranch." She flicked drops of wine from her fingertips, then licked them clean, one by one. "I thought Dillon told you they're going to drive the herd up the mountain with Grace and the boys."

"He did." Nolan froze, his glass a tantalizing inch from his mouth as the implications of what she'd just told him sank in. "But I didn't realize they'd be gone this...soon."

Alex's gaze jerked up to meet his. Her eyes widened as if she suddenly could read his lecherous thoughts, or maybe the catch in his voice had given him away. She smiled, a sweet yet naughty little smile that made his heart lurch and then pick up a hard, driving rhythm as it pumped blood straight to his groin.

"Well, well, well," she said, using Belle Flannigan's smoky, seductive voice. She set her champagne glass on the table, turned back to face him and placed her hands on his chest. "Here we are, alone at last. What do you think we should do about it?"

Chapter Ten

Nolan gripped her wrists, pinning her hands against his white shirt. "Are you serious?"

Taken aback by the unusual fierceness in his voice, Alex studied his face, noting the flush on his cheekbones, the flaring of his nostrils, the intensity burning in his eyes. She went very still, hardly daring to breathe until she figured out the answer to his questions, the one he had spoken as well as the others she could see so clearly in his eyes.

Was she serious? Was she ready to take the final step that would forever change him from a friend into a lover? Was she prepared to live with all of the possible consequences?

He raised one hand to the back of her head, tangled his fingers in her hair and tugged, forcing her to meet his gaze. His voice was low and gritty and his cheekbones looked even more prominent. "This is your last chance to say no."

She wished he would just go ahead and kiss her, sweep

her off her feet and make the decision. And yet, there was something so dear and so, well...Nolan about asking for her consent at a time like this. It seemed as if she'd wanted him forever, and during the past two weeks the frustration had grown unbearably, with no hope for relief because one or the other of their wretched, nosy children was always underfoot. If he was half as sexually frustrated as she was...

"If you say yes, you can't take it back." He wrapped his other arm around her waist and pulled her hips flush against his. Oh, goodness, he most definitely was as frustrated as she was. And maybe that heavy beard growth *did* have some relation to virility after all. "For God's sake, Alexandra, don't play with me. What do you want?"

She had no words for what she wanted, but she could show him. She slid her hands up his chest and across his shoulders, linking her fingers together at the back of his neck. Stroking her thumbs over his earlobes, she reached up and pressed her mouth to his tight, dry lips, pouring all the pent-up desire she felt for him into the kiss.

His groan sounded as if it came all the way up from the toes of his wingtips. While his lips softened and his tongue flirted with hers, luring her deeper and deeper into his mouth, his arm tightened around her with a strength that thrilled her. He moved his feet closer and closer to hers, forcing her to move backward in an awkward, shuffling sort of dance that made no sense until he spoke to her between breath-stealing kisses.

"That's it, sweetheart, keep moving," he said.

"Where?"

"Inside."

"Why?" That was a dumb question. She knew it was a dumb question even before she asked it. Her first clue should have been the impressive bulge behind the zipper of his suit pants insistently rubbing between her thighs at every step. Still, she loved the way he spelled out his intentions.

"Because, I'm going to do things to you that should only be done behind closed doors." As if he'd become impatient with their shuffling dance, he wrapped both arms around her, lowered them under the curve of her buttocks and lifted her completely off the ground. Nuzzling at the curve where her neck met her shoulder, he carried her to the steps and set her down.

"What kind of things?" she asked when he finished kissing her as if those few seconds of separation from her lips had left him starving for the taste of them.

"Wild things." He nudged her up the first step and kissed her again. "Wicked things." She negotiated the second step with her mouth locked to his. "Wonderful things." They conquered the final step and shuffled to the screen door. He pressed her back against it; his hands sneaked under the hem of her tank top and slid up her sides, stopping at the band of her bra.

She might die if he didn't touch her breasts in the next thirty seconds. Gripping his tie with one hand, she fumbled behind her with the other, found the latch and managed to maneuver him back far enough to get the door open. They stumbled inside, still kissing madly, already tearing at each other's clothes before the door banged shut. Their hands were shaking and kept getting in the other's way, until he muttered a curse she'd never heard him use before, put his hands around her waist and boosted her up onto the work peninsula.

"I'm going to strip you naked." He pulled her top off and tossed it over his shoulder, and the lusty fire in his eyes as he studied her satin bra and the exposed curves of her breasts nearly melted her into a puddle then and there. He parted her thighs with his hands and stepped between them, then used his teeth to drag her bra straps off her shoulders. "And then I'm going to kiss you, and touch you, and taste you all over."

She slid her hands into his hair and tipped her head back, offering herself to him. Starting at her jaw, he planted hot, wet kisses down the side of her neck, across her collarbones and back across her chest, gradually moving lower and lower. Her bra fell away, and he filled his hands with her breasts, lifting them, gently squeezing them, his thumbs rubbing her nipples. Marvelous sensations streaked along her nerve endings, pooling in a delicious ache between her legs.

"You're beautiful." His voice sounded raw and guttural, and the lusty admiration in his eyes made her feel like the most desirable woman in the universe. "So damn beautiful."

He took one pouting nipple into his mouth, bathed it with his tongue, then sucked on it while she moaned with delight and clasped his head to her. When he moved to the other breast, she wrapped her legs around his hips, pulled him closer and locked her ankles together behind him, seeking relief from the intensified ache by rubbing herself against him. She could feel him trembling with restraint, knew he would torture them both with some misguided attempt to be considerate and go slow for her sake.

But she didn't want slow, dammit. It had already been far too long since she'd experienced this excitement, this freedom, this powerful rush of life in her veins. She wanted down-and-dirty, hot-and-sweaty, no-holds-barred sex.

She barely managed to strip off his tie without strangling him. After fumbling forever just to get three stupid buttons on his shirt undone, she simply yanked at the bottom until it came out of his pants, then ran her hands up under the tails and over his chest. He raised his mouth from her breasts and frowned as if in confusion. She lightly raked her nails through the wiry patch of hair between his nipples, smiling when he inhaled a harsh breath.

While she had the advantage of surprise, she pushed his shirt up to his armpits. He automatically raised his arms, allowing her to pull it off over the top of his head. After so many years of denying her sexual desires, she was greedy beyond belief, not simply wanting, but *needing* to touch and taste and kiss all of him, to take him inside herself and ride this passion wherever it might take them.

"Yes," he said with a groan as she treated his chest to the same loving attention he had given hers.

She went for his belt buckle next, loosening her grip with her legs to create more space to work. He stroked her back, her hair, her shoulders and breasts while she dealt with the fastenings of his trousers and lowered the zipper. The instant she let go of the waistband, his pants dropped to his ankles with a thud from his wallet and a jingle of coins in his pocket.

"Shazaam," she said with a grin. "That was quick. No wonder you lawyers wear suits instead of jeans."

His eyes glinting with mock threat, he placed his hands on either side of her hips and leaned down until their eyes and mouths were aligned. "I don't think I want to know what you meant by that."

"No, you probably don't." Chuckling, she rubbed her nose against his and slid her hands down his sides. "Nice boxers. I've always loved plaid."

He grabbed her by the waist, lifted her off the counter and set her on her feet. With one quick tug, he had her shorts down around her ankles, and while she stepped out of them, he stripped off his shoes, socks and trousers. His gaze holding hers, he took a foil packet from his wallet and set it on the counter.

"Oh, God," she whispered, "I didn't even think about that."

"You didn't need to," he said, pulling her back into his arms. "I would never put you at any kind of risk."

It was true, of course, which was why she finally felt safe enough to be here with him like this. He was not a careless, selfish boy; he was a mature man. He would treat her with the same respect and concern for what happened to her after they made love that he had always shown her before. That was simply who he was, and she loved him for it. And for so many other reasons.

He kissed her then, pushed her panties down over her hips and lowered his boxers, giving her no more time to think or to speak. All she could do was feel—the wonderful pressure of his broad, hairy chest against her aching breasts, his warm, clever hands moving over her waist and hips and buttocks, his hard, hot shaft pressing into her lower belly, making her knees soften and her thighs want to open. He slid one hand between them, stroking, probing, readying her for his entrance.

The sensations were so strong, so sharp, so...exquisite, she could barely breathe. Had anything ever felt this good before? It had been so long since she'd made love, she couldn't remember exactly what it had been like, but surely, she wouldn't have forgotten something this wonderful.

She clung to his shoulders, fearing she would collapse otherwise, and soon they were shuffling again. She yelped when her back and bottom came in contact with the cold, hard surface of the refrigerator's door. Laughing against her mouth, he slid his arms around her, one at her waist, the other across her bottom, lifting her off her feet. She wrapped her legs around his waist and reached down to guide him.

Her body tightened involuntarily at first, as if protesting the invasion, but he moved slowly, carefully, pausing at the slightest hint of resistance, kissing her and murmuring softly in her ear. Gradually, her muscles relaxed, and he pushed deeper and deeper, stretching and filling her completely.

The sensations she had thought so wonderful only moments before, now seemed insignificant. His kisses reached into her heart and soul, and he was all around her and inside of her, and everywhere he was there was pleasure. She reveled in the strength of his arms holding her, the power of his body surging into her again and again, driving her wild with earthy words of encouragement and the blatant expressions of ecstasy crossing his face.

The knowledge that she could affect him so profoundly was as erotic as anything he could have done to her or for her. She felt the sweet tension building in her womb with each thrust of his hips, heard herself whimpering as she strained with him, taking him deeper still, while she clung to his shoulders with sweat-slicked hands. The climax roared through her, radiating outward from the place where their bodies were joined, with enough power to reach the farthest outposts of the galaxy, no doubt.

She sagged against him, gasping for breath, incoherently murmuring his name. Still cradling her in his arms, he knelt, lowered her to the floor and came down on top of her. Her hands were free now, and she used them to caress him, learning what he liked by his moans and sighs.

And it all began again—the pleasure, the building tension, the closeness she had never felt with another human being. He held nothing back. His breathing grew tortured. His thrusts came faster and harder. Finally, he let out a lusty shout, his whole body convulsed, and he collapsed into her arms.

She welcomed his weight, though it pressed her into the unforgiving kitchen floor. Stroking her hand from the nape of his neck to the small of his back, feeling the thunderous pounding of his heart against her breasts, she felt... complete. She didn't realize she was weeping until he raised up on one elbow and gently brushed away her tears with his other hand.

"Sweetheart, did I hurt you?" he said.

She shook her head, sniffled and laughed self-consciously. "No, these are...happy tears...I think." She gulped, then sniffled again. "I didn't know it could be so...spectacular. You're...well, you're just pretty darn... spectacular."

His worried frown eased, his chest expanded, and his shaft twitched deep inside her. "Spectacular? Honey, you haven't seen anything yet," he drawled with a wicked grin. "Wait until you see what I can do in a bed."

"Yeah, I might like to try that sometime." She reached up and tugged on his chin whiskers. "If I don't get squashed like a bug on this hard floor."

Laughing, he sat back on his heels and held out his hands to her. "Would you like to get up?"

"Oh, heavens no." She let him pull her to a sitting position, wrinkled her nose and looked back over her left shoulder. "The kids made orange juice this afternoon."

"How can you tell?" he asked.

"I think my left shoulder blade's been lying in a puddle. It feels...sticky, and it has that unmistakable citrus fragrance, you know?"

"Let me see." He moved around behind her, sniffed at said shoulder blade, then licked it clean, ignoring her giggling protests about how dirty her kitchen floor was. "Yes, that's definitely orange juice."

"Ewww, how could you?" she said.

"As I said, honey," he said, licking his way up the back of her neck and on around to her earlobe, "you haven't seen anything yet."

"Yeah, yeah, yeah," she said, raising her shoulder to her ear in defense against his prickly whiskers. "Talk's cheap, cowboy."

"Cowboy? Oh, now you've done it, woman. Now you're going to have to pay."

He stepped around in front of her, grabbed her hands and pulled her to her feet. Then, before she could guess what he was up to, he bent down, put his shoulder against her belly and lifted her in a fireman's carry. She shrieked with surprise, then with laughter as he calmly opened his wallet, withdrew another condom packet and carried it and her up the stairs to her bedroom.

He dumped her unceremoniously into the middle of her queen-size bed, followed her down and proceeded to prove that she really hadn't seen anything yet. When it came to the bedroom, the man didn't have a stodgy cell in his body.

The birds woke Nolan just before dawn the next morning. He lay on his right side, watching the gray light brighten into rosy sunshine and slowly climb the wall. Alexandra lay curled up beside him, facing the same direction. She was as naked as he was beneath the sheet, and he considered waking her with a kiss and seeing if anything spectacular developed. He reluctantly rejected the idea on the grounds that he'd kept her up most of the night, and she needed rest for the big day ahead of her.

Besides, he enjoyed watching her sleep. And it was pleasant simply to lie there in her bed, identifying objects that had only been shapes at the periphery of his vision the night before. It had been a long time since he'd spent the night in a woman's room, and he liked the carefree, rumpled atmosphere of Alexandra's.

For one thing it smelled good; she had scented candles and dishes of potpourri all over the place. For another, it was colorful and filled with knickknacks, pillows and textures his own, more Spartan room didn't have. Best of all, it had Alexandra herself; nothing had ever felt more right than waking up beside her.

And last night... He wasn't certain he would survive another one like it, but he would gladly give anything he owned for the chance to try. He'd always known making love with Alexandra would be different from anything he'd ever experienced. But he hadn't known it would be so much...fun.

Smiling at a particularly fond memory, he glanced down at her and felt a surge of tenderness fill his chest. Once the decision to make love with each other had been made, there had been no awkwardness, no hesitation, no holding back for either of them. He had felt young, strong and sexy as hell, and it was all thanks to Alexandra, or rather, to the way she had looked at him and responded so freely to him. Lord, what an incredible woman.

She stirred, stretched her top shoulder, then settled back into slumber with a quiet sigh and a contented little smile. She looked adorable, soft, sweet and...and sexy as hell. He wanted to smooth her hair away from her face, but firmly resisted the urge to touch her. It was only a feeble excuse to "accidentally" wake her, and she would wake up when she was ready. He just wished she was ready now.

As if she could hear his thoughts, she frowned, rolled onto her back for a moment, then rolled onto her left side, giving him an enticing glimpse of her breasts as she turned.

Tucking one hand under her cheek, she settled down again, wiggling her rump a little as if she were searching for the most comfortable spot on the mattress. He grinned, linked his fingers together behind his head and prepared himself to wait. In the meantime, he had important thinking to do.

Five minutes later, Alex yawned and slowly opened her eyes. When she caught sight of him, she yelped and scuttled away from him, the top sheet clutched against her breasts. Though her eyes didn't appear to be completely focused, she looked terrified.

"Alex, it's just me," Nolan said. "Are you okay?"

"Nolan?" She blinked, looked at him again, then rubbed one hand over her face. "I'm sorry. I must have forgotten you were here."

"Well, I guess that puts me in my place," he said, ruefully shaking his head. "And here I thought I was spectacular."

"You were. I mean, you are." Laughing softly, she scooted closer to him. "I'm just not used to waking up with a man in my bed."

"I think I already knew that."

She stiffened and pulled the sheet higher. "Is that a complaint?"

"A complaint?"

"About my performance my last night."

"Of course not. What on earth gave you that idea?"

She sank her front teeth into her lower lip, then turned her face away from him. "It wouldn't be the first time."

"From your ex?"

She nodded, but didn't speak. Nolan waited a moment, then swore under his breath, climbed out from under the sheet and crawled over to sit beside her. Taking her left hand in his right, he twined his fingers with hers and held them on his knee.

"The only thing I meant by that remark was that I've been your neighbor for a long time, and I've never known you to have a man stay overnight. I mean, I know you don't...sleep around. I was actually giving you a compliment. Or trying to, anyway."

"Oh." Her cheeks turned a vivid pink. "I seem to be starting this day off all wrong. How about some coffee?"

She moved as if she would pull the bottom of the sheet free of the mattress, but he leaned back on his free hand, trapping it with his weight. "I don't want coffee, and I don't want you to leave this room feeling bad about last night."

"I don't," she said. "Not really."

He didn't believe her. He wished he had some smooth line that would reassure her, but he didn't. That left honesty, which had always worked well for them before.

"Look, Alex, I don't have any particular expectations for my partners. I'll probably get thrown out of the association of guys for confessing this, but I haven't had that many besides Jennifer." She glanced up at him, surprise evident in her eyes. He felt his own face getting warm, but forced himself to continue.

"I never enjoyed having sex with women I didn't know very well, and you know all about what it's like trying to find some privacy when you're raising a child by yourself. You don't need to worry that I'm comparing you to someone else. Last night I thought you were...spectacular."

"Oh, Nolan." She put her arms around his neck and kissed his cheek. "You are the dearest man."

"You really think so?"

She nodded, rubbing her soft, smooth cheek against the base of his neck. "Yes, I do."

"Then marry me."

Alexandra froze. She remained silent for so long, he

might have thought she hadn't heard him if she hadn't stayed completely still. Finally, in a small, cautious voice, she said, "What?"

"Marry me, Alexandra."

She pulled away from him as if he'd just contracted a bad case of fleas, and wrapped the sheet more tightly around herself. "Are you nuts? One night of spectacular sex is not enough for a marriage proposal."

"How many nights do you need? Five? Ten? Fifty?"

Now she gaped at him, her mouth working, but with no sound coming out. Then she exhaled an irritated huff, which only made him smile. Cliché or not, she was damn cute when she was angry.

"Very funny, Larson. Ha, ha, ha. That's not what I meant, and you know it."

"All right, I'll stop teasing you, but the proposal stands. I want to marry you."

With a mighty yank, she hauled the sheet out from under him, tucked in the loose ends and stood up, looking faintly regal as she shot a disapproving glance at his naked lap. Which, of course, only made him smile again. His boxers and pants were downstairs, and she had the sheet. What did she expect him to cover himself with? A fig leaf? A hot pink pillow?

"It's just one of those morning things," he said with a grin and a shrug. "Men have them all the time. Especially when they wake up next to a beautiful, naked woman."

"I've heard that line before, so don't start with me." She sneaked another peek at his lap. "And don't even think about…that."

"Too late," he said, unable to resist a chuckle. "I've been thinking about 'that' since before you woke up."

Her smile looked reluctant, but at this point he'd take any smile he could get. "That's better," he said, holding out a hand to her. Cautiously she came back to the bed and sat down beside him. "Now, tell me what's wrong with my proposal. Did you want more flowers, moonlight and a ring?"

"No, it's…I'm just not ready to think about it yet. It wasn't that long ago you were only my best friend. I can't believe you, of all people, would do something so…impulsive."

"Impulsive? I didn't exactly pick you up in a bar last night. We know each other better than a lot of married couples I see every day."

"Which ones? Your clients, ninety percent of whom are getting divorced?"

"A happy marriage is possible, Alex. I know you didn't have one, but I did, and I'm telling you, we can make this work."

"How can you be so sure?"

"We've been living almost like a married couple for the past three years. We simply haven't been having sex."

"No, there's more we haven't done that married people do. We don't fight over money. We don't fight over household chores or how to raise our children. We don't fight over the remote control or get on each other's nerves, because we're not married and we both can go home alone whenever we want."

"You want to keep your own house? I'd have to think about that. There might be tax advantages."

"Oh, for heaven's sake, Nolan, the whole idea is crazy. We're happy the way we are. Why mess with success?"

"I prefer to think of it as enriching our lives by sharing them even more than we already have. And you know as well as I do that we can't have an affair with our two inquisitive and impressionable teenagers watching us. Unless you want to give Tasha permission to do the same thing.''

Alex shook her head. ''Of course I don't. But people don't get married just to have sex anymore.''

''Excuse me? I thought it was spectacular sex. Now it's 'just' sex? I'm hurt.''

''Will you be serious?''

''Not until you give me a better reason you won't marry me than those pitiful excuses you've been throwing around.''

''They're not pitiful. You know, some of us don't process major life changes as fast as others. I've had to work really hard to conquer my impulsive streak, and I'm not going to make a decision like this without giving it a great deal of careful thought.''

''Will I still have all of my own teeth by the time you finish thinking about it?''

''Probably,'' she said drily. ''But I have too much going on right now even to think clearly. Can it wait until after I'm done with the movie?''

He waggled his eyebrows at her. ''Do we get to have spectacular sex in the meantime?''

She laughed, then put her palm in the middle of his chest, tipped him over backward on the bed and loosened the sheet enough to straddle his waist. ''If we don't get caught by the kids, I could try to…fit you in.''

He groaned at her pun, but she cut him off with a sweet, passionate kiss. Unwrapping her like a birthday present, he kissed her back. In a matter of seconds she was naked in his arms and once again responding to him with an unbridled enthusiasm that made him confident of reaching his ultimate goal. Given the bonds they already shared, he saw no point in putting undue pressure on her for an immediate answer to his proposal.

Her request to postpone further discussion until she was finished filming her part in the movie seemed reasonable to him. He wasn't going to forget it, however, and he wasn't going to let her put him off until they were both in their fifties. He would simply use the time between now and the end of her stint as a movie star to make sure she loved him enough to say yes.

Chapter Eleven

With the kids gone, Alex felt as if they were on a honeymoon. They talked and made love, then made love and talked, and occasionally cooked a meal together. Nolan was warm, he was funny, he was sexy, and he showed such a flattering interest in her new adventures, she found herself eagerly looking forward to seeing him again a minute after they parted each morning. Her life wasn't perfect, but it was so close, it terrified her.

The most terrifying thing of all was Nolan's marriage proposal, lurking in the back of her mind like a guilty secret. Damn, but she wished he hadn't done that. It didn't matter how many times she told herself he wasn't like Brad, or that this situation was completely different, or that she was being silly, paranoid or just plain stupid, the prospect of getting married again made her feel like jumping off a bridge.

Her fear had nothing to do with Nolan personally, but

she doubted she could ever make him believe that. He was a logical, rational man, and there was nothing logical or rational about this...terror she experienced every time she thought about marrying him. His marriage had been a happy one; he couldn't possibly understand the crushing sense of failure that came with a divorce. Or the conviction that being married would somehow rob her of her identity.

She refused to dwell on the negative, however. There were too many good things happening for her to allow irrational fears to spoil this special time. When the fear made itself known in the silent hours of the night, she forced herself to think about her scenes in the movie or how she would spend her acting salary—anything to take her mind in a positive direction.

Once her screen test was declared a success, her days passed in a blur of costume fittings, rehearsals and discussions with Blair and the director, Patrick Quillen. She loved the excitement and the challenge, not to mention the personal acting lessons she received from Blair and Patrick to help her make the transition from stage to film. Even with all of that going on, however, the hours she spent with Nolan were the very best part of her day, and she treasured them.

The casting office called on Sunday night, asking Nolan to come out to Old Trail Town west of Cody for a costume fitting on Monday. He took Monday off, and since Alex finally had a free day, she tagged along with him. Old Trail Town was a tourist attraction consisting of homesteaders' cabins and other historic buildings that had been moved to the site from the surrounding area in order to preserve them.

The set designer had been hard at work, devising ways to make the collection of buildings look like a living, breathing town from the Old West for the cameras. When Alex and Nolan arrived, the actual buildings were practically hidden from sight by rows and rows of trucks and trailers full of equipment, a cluster of huge tents and a whole village of portable toilets. They followed a series of handwritten signs directing the extras to the wardrobe tent.

Crew members crisscrossed the area, stringing fat electrical cables, talking on headphones, tinkering with machinery. Everywhere Alex looked, she saw more preparations underway. The realization that filming was finally going to start in a couple of days began to sink in, and with it came a whole new set of fears to take her mind off her worries about marrying Nolan.

Word of her role in the film had spread through the area like an August grass fire, and it seemed as if every other person in the seemingly endless line of extras waiting for costumes felt compelled to congratulate her and tell her to "break your leg and do us all proud, honey."

After the fortieth or fiftieth time it happened, she gave up trying to explain that the correct phrase was "break *a* leg," and simply accepted the sentiment behind the words as gracefully as she could. Insecurities, old and new, gnawed at her insides like a swarm of termites. A tiny bite here, a little nibble there, and before long her self-confidence was about as substantial as a snowflake.

Her tension built and built, until finally she had to get away or risk saying something she undoubtedly would later regret. She gave Nolan the most casual smile she could manage. "I think I'll go check out the commissary tent and see if I can find some coffee."

Nolan studied her face for a moment, then stepped out of line and left with her.

"You didn't have to lose your place," she said when they'd put enough distance between themselves and the line for privacy.

"I'll go back later," he said. "I take it your adoring public was starting to get to you?"

"Adoring, my foot." Alex kicked at a rock and shook her head in disgust. "They don't really give a damn about me. They just want to be able to say they know somebody in the movies."

"That's a pretty cynical attitude."

"Well, it's true. When I was growing up, most of those 'friendly' folk probably thought I'd be dead or serving time in prison before I turned thirty. And now they come at me with all of these expectations..." She shook her head again. "I'd be surprised if at least half of them aren't secretly hoping I'll fail miserably."

"Too bad they're going to be disappointed then, isn't it?" He cupped the side of her face with one hand and stole a quick kiss. "You're going to be marvelous, Alexandra. Absolutely marvelous."

She smiled and kissed him back. "Have I ever told you how nice it is to have someone around who always believes in me?"

"My pleasure. Now, let's go find that coffee."

The line at the wardrobe tent was much shorter when they returned, and five minutes later Nolan stepped into the men's changing area with an outfit one of the assistants had given him. Alex asked about clothes for Tasha and Rick and found out that Blair had already made arrangements for them. Then Nolan ambled out of the changing tent, and stopped every conversation within ten yards on either side of him.

He had his thumbs hooked into the back pockets of a pair of tight black pants. The rest of his outfit included a sky blue shirt, a beige leather vest and a black string tie. With his thick, bushy beard, the black Stetson he wore tipped low over his eyes and the right accessories, he could have been a gunslinger, a saddle tramp, a rancher or even a sheriff.

Alex took one look at him and felt a familiar heat curling low in her belly. Mercy, but he was one handsome man. The wardrobe assistant, a red-haired beauty in her twenties who spent an indecent amount of time checking the fit of his snug pants and patting all the seams in his shirt, obviously agreed. If he hadn't been giving her distinctly wary glances, Alex might have had to hurt the woman.

Good Lord, I'm jealous.

The thought sounded so loud and clear in her mind, she glanced around, afraid she might have said it out loud. No one appeared to be paying any special attention to her. No one but Nolan, who was grinning at her. He knew. Oh, damn, the wretched man knew, and she hated it. It was the kind of thing he could use against her someday.

No, he wouldn't do that. Brad would have, but not Nolan. The emotion was a warning signal, though. A woman only felt jealous when she cared enough about a man to be hurt by him. When she cared too much.

Not that she didn't love Nolan, Alex told herself. She did. But she didn't want to be *in* love with him. Not to the point that she could feel like a jealous shrew; it was simply too demeaning to feel that…needy. Oh, hell, she didn't know what she wanted. Except to get that witch's hands off him.

"Looks good, Nolan," Alex said with a bright smile plastered on her mouth. "If you're finished, we'd better go."

"Sure thing, honey." He winked at her, then turned and left to change, abandoning her to the interested stares of everyone standing around the wardrobe trailer.

Well, great. That was totally great. Now she had one more thing to worry about—fresh gossip about her relationship with Nolan. There had always been some of that, but it hadn't bothered her because there truly had been nothing going on between them. That wasn't true anymore, and if they weren't terribly discreet, the whole situation could quickly get out of hand. This was just what she needed, more pressure, more stress. Oh, why did she have to fall in love with the big jerk right now?

Wearing his costume, Nolan walked along the main street of the make-believe little cow town on Wednesday afternoon, paying scant attention to the funeral procession passing the other way, as the assistant director had requested. He'd lost track of how many takes they'd already shot of this scene, but he'd already decided that his career as a movie extra wouldn't last more than a day or two.

It wasn't so bad when they were actually filming a bit of action; at least it felt as if something might be happening. That part rarely lasted more than a minute or two, however. Then it was back to standing around in the heat and the dust, waiting for the crew to reset the cameras and the wranglers to bring the horses and wagons back to their original positions and start the process all over again.

Rick and Tasha appeared to be enjoying themselves. As part of the funeral procession, they got to stand around in the middle of the street between takes, listening to Blair DuMaine explain what all of the technical people were doing. Nolan couldn't hear much of what she said, but the production assistants freaked out if an extra strayed too far from his assigned spot, so Nolan stayed put. Blair hadn't been present since the lunch break, however, and everyone missed her cheerful enthusiasm.

When a perky little blond production assistant who looked as if she was barely out of her teens called his name and asked him to follow her, Nolan was more than happy to leave the street scene. Then he realized she was taking him to the back door of the saloon. That was where Alex was supposed to be. Still wearing the threadbare cotton dress she'd worn that morning, Blair DuMaine stepped outside as he approached, shutting the door behind her.

"It's Alex, isn't it?" Nolan said, his heart sinking at the worry in Blair's eyes. "What's wrong?"

"I'm not sure," Blair said quietly. She dismissed the production assistant with a jerk of her head, then grasped Nolan's elbow and led him a few steps away from the saloon. "It looks like an anxiety attack to me. I'm afraid she's trying so hard to be perfect, she's paralyzed herself."

"I know she's had stage fright before, but I don't think it's ever stopped her from performing," Nolan said. "What makes you think I can help her?"

"She asked for you. If you'd rather I called in a doctor, I will, but—"

"No, don't," Nolan said quickly. "Alex would hate that. I'll be glad to see what I can do. Where is she?"

Blair inclined her head toward the saloon. "In there. I think she's really embarrassed over freezing up. If you can, please reassure her that we realize this is completely new to her, and she can have all the takes she needs to do this. She's doing us a huge favor, and as long as she's willing to keep trying, we'll hang in there with her."

"She'll appreciate that. May I see her alone, now?"

"Of course," Blair said. "The crew's gone for their coffee break. I'll keep them out of your way until I hear from you. Just tell one of the production assistants to call me on the radio if you need anything."

"All right. Thanks, Blair."

"Don't thank me. I'm the one who got her into this. I feel terrible that she's having such a hard time."

"She'll be fine," Nolan said with a confident smile that

was only partially false. "Alex is a fighter, and this movie means a lot to her. She won't give up without giving it everything she's got."

Blair smiled. "She's lucky to have you."

"No," Nolan said, shaking his head. "I'm the lucky one. She's a wonderful woman."

Blair nodded and walked away. Nolan went back to the saloon and stepped inside. Though it obviously had been cleaned up for the production, the old building still carried the musty smell of abandonment. The room was dim, the only light coming from the windows facing the street. The long bar and its brass foot rail had been polished to a high gloss, as had the brass spittoons, placed at three-foot intervals.

Alex sat at one of the round wooden tables, gazing at the painting of a voluptuous nude woman hanging behind the bar. Nolan had never seen anyone look more dejected than Alex did at that moment. Her shoulders were slumped. Her eyes were big and sad. Even her bright red dance-hall-girl dress and the matching feather in her hair looked droopy.

He walked slowly across the rough wooden floor, then squatted on his heels beside her chair. "What's going on, Alexandra? Butterflies?"

"More like buzzards," she said. "Big ones."

"Want me to shoot 'em for you?" he said, using his best Western drawl.

"Go away, Nolan." Her voice wavered. She gulped, but kept her eyes trained on the painting. "I changed my mind. I don't want to talk to you."

He dropped the drawl and let one knee rest on the floor. "You know you're going to have to tell me about this sometime, and I'm already here. Why not get it over with?"

"You won't respect me anymore."

"That's not possible, Alexandra."

"But I'm a...I'm a failure."

"Really? What scene were you trying to do?"

"The one just before Elizabeth comes into the saloon. Where I sit on the cowboy's lap and try to get him to come upstairs with me."

"And after one morning of filming, you've decided you're a failure."

"Yes. I thought I could do this, but I...well, I just can't."

"You're sure of that?"

"Of course I'm sure." She shot him an irritated glance. He took it as a healthy sign, but then she subsided back into her pitiful mode, wailing, "I ruined everything. I couldn't find my marks, much less hit them. I blew my lines. I didn't do anything right."

"Sounds bad."

"It was worse than bad. It was awful."

"And there's no hope that any of that will get better when you've had more practice?"

"None. I'm a fraud, I tell you. A fraud and a failure."

That sounded a little melodramatic, even for Alexandra. She thought she wanted him to sympathize with her, but he suspected that everyone else had probably already done that. She desperately wanted to please Blair. If Blair and her crew had been too nice when she made mistakes, they undoubtedly had only fed her fear of making more mistakes until it was so huge, she couldn't see anything else.

What Alexandra needed now was to get past being afraid and go straight on to anger. If he could irritate her enough to stir up her I'll-show-you rebellious streak, she could still pull this off. Heaving a deep, disappointed sigh, he stood up.

"Well, come on, then," he said. "Let's find the kids and go home."

Alex shot him a disbelieving look. "Just like that?"

"You said it was hopeless." Shrugging, he glanced away so she wouldn't see him smile. "What's the point in hanging around?"

"Well, jeez, Larson, don't strain yourself digging for sympathy."

Nolan noted the healthy spots of color on her cheeks with satisfaction and went in for the kill. "You don't need my sympathy."

"I thought you were my friend."

"I am. But you still don't need my sympathy. You're getting more than enough from yourself. Believe me, Alexandra, self-pity is not an attractive trait."

Glaring at him, she sputtered. "You, you, you...jerk. I'm not feeling sorry for myself."

"Of course you are. You're absolutely wallowing in your failure, perhaps even...dare I say, enjoying it?"

"Enjoying it!" Fists clenched at her sides, she came to her feet so fast it looked as if her chair had bucked her off. "I haven't enjoyed one horrible second of this whole, lousy miserable, rotten, stinking day."

"Sure, sweetheart. Whatever you say. Let's go home."

"We're not going anywhere until you believe me."

"I believe you. It's just that...oh, forget it." He turned back toward the door. "Come on."

"No way. What were you going to say?"

He came back to face her. "It's just that I know that you can do this, and I know that *you* know, that you can do this. For God's sake, we've done this scene together fifty times. Unless you're getting something out of all of this attention, I really don't understand what's happening here."

"Is that what you really think?"

"Who cares what I think? It's what *you* think that matters. Do you *really* believe you can't do this?"

Hugging herself tightly, she looked away, inhaled a deep breath and let it out again. Then she slowly shook her head and said softly. "No, I don't really believe that."

"Okay," Nolan said, lowering his voice to match hers. "Then what went wrong? What did you need that you had when you and I did this scene together?"

Her brow wrinkled, and he could almost see the thoughts churning through her mind. "I don't know." She paced two steps to the left, then pivoted and paced two steps back to the right. "I felt too...exposed, I guess. I suppose that sounds really stupid."

"No, it doesn't. Now we're getting somewhere." Nolan eyed the neckline of her dress. It exposed some cleavage, but he wouldn't call it indecent. "Is it your costume?"

She glanced down at herself and grinned at him. The grin looked a tad self-conscious, but Nolan wanted to cheer when he saw it. As soon as they figured out what had thrown her off, she was going to be all right.

"Not that kind of exposed," she said. "It was more like...well, everything was too close. I'm used to the audience being—" she held her hands at arm's length "—out there somewhere. And I usually can't see them very well because of the footlights. But this isn't a big set, so the camera's really close. And with Patrick and Blair and the sound people and the makeup people, and whoever all those other people are, it feels like they're all right on top of me. I'm so conscious of having everyone in my face, I can't concentrate."

"Maybe Patrick and Blair could clear the set."

Alex shot him a horrified glance and shook her head. "It didn't bother anybody else. I can't ask for special treatment. It would be unprofessional."

"Blair wouldn't see it that way," Nolan said. He passed on everything Blair had said to him when he'd arrived at the saloon. "I think she'll be glad to do whatever she can to make it easier for you. She's so used to this system, she just didn't understand what the problem was."

"They'll all think I'm a wimp, Nolan."

"These people don't give a damn about anything but getting the best performance you've got to give them. Ask for whatever you need, Alexandra. Even if they do think you're a wimp, that's better than being a quitter, isn't it?"

Her chin tilted up and her eyes narrowed. "I'm not a wimp. And I most certainly am *not* a quitter."

"So, prove it."

She glared at him. "You think you're so smart, Larson. I know exactly what you're doing."

"It's working, isn't it?"

"Yes, damn you," she said, giving him a grudging laugh.

"Good. I'll call Blair back in here and you can try again."

"All right."

He got as far as the swinging front doors before she called to him again.

"Hey, Nolan?" She waited until he looked back over his shoulder at her. "Will you stay here with me for a little while? Just until I feel more comfortable with these people?"

It touched him deeply that she wanted him to be with her when she felt unsure of herself. "Of course. I'll make some arrangements for the kids, and then I'll be right back."

"Bring them, too, will you? I think I can handle all of those other people in here, if I have some of my own folk to look at. You guys have been my cheering section for so long, maybe I can't act anymore without all of you watching.''

He smiled at her, then stepped out into the afternoon sunshine and went to find Blair.

Alex watched Nolan leave with a lump the size of a fist in her throat. It was scary to realize how well he knew her; he'd known exactly how to handle her, which buttons to push to lift her out of her funk, just as she'd known he would. Scarier still, was realizing how much she had come to depend on him.

And yet, nothing had ever made her feel safer than the sound of his voice and the sight of his face when he'd hunkered down beside her. Of course, now she would have to punish him for some of the awful things he'd said to her. Enjoying her failure, indeed! The stinker. She definitely would have to get him for that one.

How he ever could have believed any of that nonsense was beyond her. She'd never been more miserable in her life than when she'd heard her cue and been completely unable to deliver her lines. Good Lord, she'd longed for this opportunity for a lifetime. It didn't make any sense at all that she conceivably could enjoy blowing it. What a crazy idea!

Or was it? Oh, not that she would *enjoy* blowing it. That was too ridiculous even to contemplate. The human mind, however, was a complicated, even tricky apparatus, and it might be possible that some part of her felt she deserved to fail. Perhaps even wanted to fail. As strange as that sounded, she knew she was on the right track. It simply felt…right.

But why? The chances of failure were great enough. Why would she feel the need to guarantee it?

And if that was, indeed, what she actually had been doing, then why had she felt so paralyzed by fear? The fear *had* been real, dammit; she *knew* what fear felt like. Well, maybe it hadn't been fear of failure. She hadn't lied to Nolan when she'd said she believed she could do this.

So, if she wasn't afraid of failing, then what was she afraid of? Succeeding? Oh, dear, maybe she was crazy after all. What could she possibly have to fear from success?

At one time she'd had good reason to fear a battle with the Talbots over Tasha's custody, but Nolan had assured her that that no longer was the case. Was her fear simply a holdover from an earlier time? Or was it something different? Something deeper?

She had no easy answers, but she knew one thing. Wherever the fear was coming from, she was not going to give in to it. If she was going to do whatever she darn well pleased, this surely was it. Once and for all, she intended to prove, if only to herself, that she could act in this or any other arena she chose.

She would succeed first, by God. If there were problems to face as a result, then she would face them. But she damn well would not spend the rest of her life wondering if she could have made it, if only she'd had the guts to try.

Chapter Twelve

"He doesn't beat ya. He doesn't rape ya. He gives ya food to eat, clothes to wear and a roof over your head. Honey, what more do ya want in a man?"

Nolan held his breath the next day as he watched the scene unfold between Alexandra and Blair, or rather, Belle Flannigan and Elizabeth Clark, a world-weary dance-hall girl and a dead miner's innocent daughter. It didn't matter that there were two movie cameras in the room or twelve other people watching as avidly and silently as he was. Alex and Blair had brought their characters to life, and everyone privileged enough to witness the magic, ached right along with them.

When he'd first heard Alexandra deliver those lines, Nolan had thought they were funny. But now, seeing her deliver them with such sincere puzzlement, it seemed tragic that poor Belle couldn't even conceive of a man who had more to offer a woman than bare survival and a lack of abuse. And what experience had given Alexandra the understanding to play it with so much authentic emotion? Had her marriage truly been that bleak?

"Love. I want love, Belle," Blair said, her eyes brimming with tears. "And I don't love Bear Swanson. I don't reckon I ever will."

"Ha! Love ain't all it's cracked up to be, Lizzie, and don't you forget it," Alex said. "You marry that Swanson fella, or you're gonna end up in some stinkin' saloon just like me. Believe you me, you don't want that."

If Blair's tears had tugged hard at Nolan's heartstrings, the bitterness in Alexandra's voice broke his heart. Damn, what a fine performance. There wasn't another actress in Hollywood, famous or not, who could have played Belle any better than Alexandra McBride. If the rapt expressions on every other face in the room were anything to judge by, he wasn't the only one who held that opinion.

They went all the way through to the end of the scene before Patrick said, "Cut. Fantastic job, Blair, Alex. We'll take a look at it, but I think it's a keeper."

The room filled with chatter as everyone shifted around, released from the demand to be absolutely still while the cameras and sound equipment were rolling. The makeup artists descended on Blair and Alex, getting them ready to shoot the scene again, in case Patrick wanted another take. Nolan turned to Rick and Tasha and, putting an arm around each of them, walked to the one uncrowded corner of the room.

"Well, what do you guys think?" he asked.

Eyes shining, Tasha answered in a voice hushed with awe. "Mom was super. They both were, you know, but I've never seen Mom seem more...real."

"Yeah, she was great." Rick shoved his hands into his front jeans pockets. "She was too good."

"Too good?" Tasha frowned at him. "That's a dorky thing to say. How can she be too good?"

Rick inclined his head toward the group gathered around the monitor to watch the replay. "You might as well start packing your stuff right now."

"Rick," Nolan said, his voice sharp with warning. "That's enough."

"Start packing?" Tasha said. "What are you talking about?"

Rick shot Nolan a scowl, then looked down at his feet. Tasha turned to Nolan.

"What did he mean? Packing for what?"

Nolan tucked a strand of Tasha's dark hair behind her ear, hoping the gesture would calm at least some of the anxiety he saw in her eyes. "Rick thinks that they'll offer your mom other movie roles, and she'll want to move to Hollywood to pursue an acting career."

She gave Rick such a droll look, Nolan had to smile. Tasha continually delighted him, almost as much as Alexandra did.

"Oh, Ricky, she will not," Tasha said. "Mom's way too old to be a movie star now."

"She doesn't have to be a star, stupid," Rick said. "Haven't you ever heard of character actors? You don't have to be real young to do that, and Alex is a natural. I heard that director guy call her that."

Tasha drew back as if he'd slapped her. "Well, I don't want to move to California. All my friends are here, and our whole family and the ranch. And I don't like big cities."

"You've never even been to a big city," Rick said with a derisive snort. "Billings doesn't count."

"Oh, yeah? Well I happen to think Billings is too big,

so I don't need to go see anything bigger to know I wouldn't like it.''

"Hey, stop it, you two," Nolan said. "You're both getting upset over nothing. Alexandra hasn't said one word about moving.''

"Yeah, but, Dad—"

Nolan cut Rick off with a firm shake of his head. "Drop it, son. Just stop worrying about it.''

"I would if you'd marry her.''

Tasha looked at Rick, then up at Nolan. The speculation in her eyes made Nolan feel like a bug pinned to a board in some kid's science project.

"Yeah, why don't you marry her? Is it because of me? I mean, if you don't want to be my stepfather, I guess I could understand, but—"

Nolan felt sweat break out on his forehead. Between Rick's fear of losing another mother and Tasha's fear of being rejected by another father, why didn't these two just rip his heart out with their bare hands? It would take a sterner man than Nolan Larson to ignore the pleas for reassurance in Rick's and Tasha's eyes. Resting his hands on Tasha's shoulders, he leaned down and kissed her cheek.

"I already think of you as my daughter, Tasha, and if your mother would marry me, I would be extremely honored to be your stepfather.''

"Does that mean you're going to marry my mom? For real?''

"Well, I, um, we haven't really made any decisions about that yet.''

Rick's expression brightened as he jumped on Nolan's last word. "Yet? Does that mean you and Alex have talked about getting married?''

Nolan cleared his throat and sent a desperate glance in Alex's direction. Great. The director was kissing both of her cheeks and patting her hands. Some help she was going to be.

"Da-ad," Rick said, his voice insistent. "Does that mean you and Alex have talked about it?"

"Well…yes, we did talk about it." Both kids puffed up like bullfrogs, and Nolan frantically held up his palms before they could cut loose with any loud noises he would have to explain. "Now, both of you be quiet, will you? As I said, we haven't made any decisions. We really need some time to sort everything out. And we'll do that just as soon as this movie's done and out of the way, all right?"

Tasha flung herself against him and hugged his waist with amazing strength for a girl. Then she tipped her head back and gave him the most intense, excited grin he'd ever seen. "All right. I'll be good, I promise. Really. I won't give you any trouble at all. Not ever."

Nolan ruffled her hair. "Don't make promises you can't keep, sweetheart. Nobody expects you to be perfect."

"Can I talk to my mom about it?"

"Oh, uh, sure…eventually," Nolan said. "But why don't we just all stay real cool and quiet about it for now? Your mom's waited a long time to try this. Let's give her a chance to really enjoy it. Doesn't that seem fair?"

"I guess so," Tasha said.

Nolan turned to his son. "Agreed, Rick?"

Rick's nod looked grudging, but he did nod. "All right."

Heaving a silent sigh of relief, he led the kids back to their assigned viewing seats. They were setting up to try the scene again. Alex would kill him if she knew he'd told the kids so much, but the truth was, he was getting worried about her future plans, too. She was so darn good, how could Hollywood not embrace her?

And how would she respond when they did?

* * *

Alex pulled into her driveway at the end of the next week, turned off the engine and just sat there in her car, savoring a moment of quiet and a sense of accomplishment she'd never felt before. This afternoon they had finished filming her part in *Against the Wind,* and she was pleased with her performance. Apparently so was everyone else involved with the production, and she couldn't wait to tell Nolan and the kids about her incredibly wonderful day.

As if her thoughts had conjured them up, Tasha and Rick barreled through the hedge from the Larsons' backyard, spotted her car and ran over to greet her.

"You're home early," Tasha said with a big grin. "Nice you could make it in time for dinner for a change. Nolan said to tell you he'll throw steaks on the grill for us and to come on over as soon as you can."

While Alex collected her purse and the tote bag she used to hold her street clothes, makeup and toiletries at the set and climbed out of the car, Tasha bounced from one foot to the other, arms held out at her sides in anticipation of a hug. Alex happily gave her one, smiling in gratitude at Rick when he relieved her of the tote bag and carried it into the house for her. Nolan had done a superb job of training his son to be a gentleman.

Tasha chattered all the way into the house as if she were starving for attention. Alex tried to listen, but she had so many other things to consider, it was more than a little difficult to focus on Tasha's scattergun rambling. Rick put her tote bag in the hallway, then came back into the kitchen.

Setting her purse on the counter, Alex flipped through the stack of mail, setting aside the bills, and tossed the rest into the trash can. Opening the refrigerator, she scanned the shelves for something cold to drink. Goodness, a trip to the grocery store appeared to be a high priority in the very near future.

"Mom, you're not paying attention," Tasha complained.

Alex shut the fridge and smiled at her. "What, Tash?"

"Aunt Grace called and said Uncle Dillon's going to be tied up with the movie next week. She wants to know if we can come out and go check on the cows with her and the boys. Can we?"

"Probably," Alex said, though even the thought of riding for hours made her buns ache in anticipation. Still, she owned a seventh of the Flying M, and she needed to do her share to keep the place going. "I'll call her in the morning."

"You better do it now or you'll forget," Tasha said.

"I won't forget."

"But, Mom, she said it was really important."

"Tasha, I just got home. Give me a break, will you?"

"Yeah. Sure, Mom."

Tasha turned away, but Alex glimpsed a sheen of tears in her eyes. Guilt-stricken, she squeezed Tasha's shoulder. "I'm sorry, honey. I didn't mean to snap at you. I'm just tired."

Tasha shrugged off her mother's hand. "You're always tired. I'm going to Rick's."

"Okay. I'll grab a quick shower and be right there," Alex said.

The screen door banged shut behind Tasha. Alex sighed, then hurried upstairs to wash off the dust and the traces of makeup she'd missed before she left the set. The spat with Tasha was no big deal, just a reminder that it was time to come back to her real life. After all these days of being treated like a celebrity, it would take time to get used to being a mere, mortal, mom again. But, she told herself with a smile, maybe it wouldn't be forever.

The shower refreshed her considerably. Dressed in clean shorts and a T-shirt, she followed the luscious aroma of barbecuing steaks through the gap in the hedge. Nolan looked up from the grill and waved her over.

"Good timing. The steaks are ready, and so is everything else."

She gave him a quick kiss. "What a guy. You'll never know how much I appreciate everything you've done to help me while my schedule's been so crazy."

He waggled his eyebrows at her. "Let's get rid of the kids, and you can make it up to me."

"We'll definitely have to work on that," she said with a soft laugh.

He led the way into his kitchen, where Tasha and Rick were putting the finishing touches on the table in the breakfast nook. They all piled into the booth, and it struck Alex that they really had become a family. Everyone at this table teased and bickered and cared about everyone else. If that wasn't a family, what was?

"So, how was the magical world of movie making today?" Nolan asked, passing the bowl of salad to Tasha.

"It was pretty amazing," Alex said. "Patrick showed us some of the dailies. It was just a rough cut, of course, but he and Blair both seemed really pleased. And my dear cousin Marsh nearly hugged me to death and told me I was wonderful."

"Well, jeez, Mom, why don't you brag a little more?" Tasha said.

Alex ignored Tasha's sarcasm and simply took her at face value. "All right. Your Uncle Dillon agreed with Marsh, and, if you want to know the truth, I thought I was pretty good, too. I had a really cool day."

"Great," Nolan said. "Any chance we can see the dailies?"

"I imagine that could be arranged." Alex took a baked

potato from the plate Rick passed to her and handed it off to Tasha. "We'll probably have to go out to the ranch."

"Are you all finished with the movie?" Tasha asked.

"For now," Alex said. "I may have to make a trip to L.A. later to do some work in a sound studio if they didn't get all of our dialogue recorded clearly, but we wrapped up my last scene today."

"Well, good." Tasha grinned at Rick. "It's about time."

"Yeah, it took long enough," Rick said. "Now we can do some fun stuff."

Nolan scowled at the kids. "Excuse me? So far this week, you two have nagged me into taking you to the movies, swimming, bowling and riding. None of that was fun?"

"Sure it was, but it's just not the same without Alex." Rick smiled at his dad, then winked at Alex. "We missed you."

Alex reached over and ruffled his hair. "I missed you guys, too, but I don't know how much fun I'm going to be. Something else happened today. I'm not sure if anything will come of it, but things could get...interesting."

"What are you talking about, Mom?" Tasha said.

Flutters of excitement attacked Alex's stomach. She inhaled a deep breath to calm them, but it didn't help much. "Blair has invited her agent to come up for the Fourth of July weekend. She's going to show him the dailies and introduce me to him. If he decides to represent me, I may get more movie work."

"Wow," Rick said. He gave Alex a weak smile before turning to Nolan. "Imagine that. What a surprise."

"All right, Rick. You've made your point," Nolan said. "Don't jump to conclusions."

Suddenly Alex felt as if the conversation had gone somewhere without her. "What conclusions?"

"Rick thinks you're going to become a character actor

and move to Hollywood.'' Tasha wrinkled her nose at Rick. ''I told him you would never do that.''

''Well, I don't anticipate that happening anytime soon,'' Alex said. ''But I wouldn't completely rule it out forever, either. I mean, if the right opportunities came along, it might make sense to move down there.''

Frowning, Tasha sat up straight, set down her fork and folded her arms across her chest. ''Well, if you do, I'm not going with you.''

''Excuse me, young lady.'' Despite her best efforts to control it, Alex's temper was starting to bubble. ''You are thirteen years old. I am your mother. I'm also your sole means of support. That means you live where I live, until you can support yourself.''

''Forget it,'' Tasha said, shaking her head. ''I'm not moving to California with all those gangs and weirdos and perverts.''

Alex sighed. ''Natasha, you don't know what you're talking about. There are lots of nice people in California. Besides, I wouldn't move there if I wasn't making enough money to live in a decent neighborhood.''

''I don't care,'' Tasha said. ''I'm not going, and you can't make me. So don't even think about it.''

Alex had to count to twenty before she could choke out a civil reply. ''You know, that's exactly what your grandparents said to me when I first decided I wanted to be an actress. I had to take it from them, but I don't have to take it from you.''

''Well, jeez, Mom, you don't have to have a cow.''

''That's enough, Natasha.''

''Excuse me,'' Nolan said, ''but this argument is becoming awfully…big for a hypothetical situation. At this point that's all we've really got here.''

"Oh, right, Dad," Rick said. "Like this agent won't love Alex's work? What planet have you been living on?"

"I don't appreciate your tone of voice, son," Nolan said.

"And I don't appreciate being patronized, Dad," Rick said. "You said to wait until Alex was done with the movie. Well, now she's done. Are you two going to get married, or not?"

"I never promised you that, Rick. I only said we'd talked about the possibility."

Alex could barely believe her ears. Surely, Nolan wouldn't discuss something like that with the children behind her back. "You did *what?*"

"It's not what you think, Alexandra," Nolan said, an edge of desperation in his voice. "It wasn't intentional. It just sort of…slipped out."

"What difference does it make if we know?" Tasha said. "Whatever you decide to do, it will affect us pretty directly. And I think you should get married."

Alex covered her eyes with one hand and muttered, "God, I don't believe this."

Nolan slid out of the booth and came around to Alex's side. Taking her hand, he pulled her to her feet, then spoke to Rick and Tasha. "You two are in charge of the dishes. We're going for a walk."

With the kids grumbling in the background, Alex followed Nolan through his house and out the front door. They turned right at the curb and set off along their usual jogging route. Neither spoke. Alex felt pummeled by so many different emotions, she thought she could probably walk all the way to Boston and still be unable to form a coherent thought.

At last Nolan pointed out their turn-around point, a fallen cottonwood tree lying off to the side of the road. Alex approached it slowly, checking for resident critters before she took a seat. Pulling one heel up close to her bottom, she wrapped her arms around her raised knee and waited for Nolan to say something.

He stood facing her, hands in the front pockets of his slacks. "I'm sorry."

She waited, but he didn't say anything more. The silence stretched out, as hot and miserable as having to try on winter clothes in August. At last Alex found her voice again, and what poured out of her was rage.

"Sorry for what?" she asked. "Betraying me? Manipulating me?"

"Oh, please, Alexandra, don't you think that's overstating the case just a bit?"

"No. You knew I wasn't ready to make a decision about getting married. You knew I didn't want to get the kids' hopes up. Why did you tell them we'd talked about it?"

He gave a helpless shrug that irritated her no end. "I told you, it sort of…slipped out."

"How?"

Pacing from one end of the tree to the other, he recounted a convoluted conversation he'd had with the kids about her acting and the possibility of her taking off to Hollywood and Rick's pressuring him to marry her in front of Tasha. "It simply…escalated from there. What else could I say?"

"Hell, I don't know," Alex said. "You're the lawyer. You're supposed to be good on your feet."

"It's not the same thing as being in court." He stopped pacing and turned to frown at her. "They're our *children*. The more you try to evade their questions, the more suspicious they get."

"But surely you could have figured out some other way to reassure them than that."

"I did the best I could, but you know how intelligent and intuitive those two are." He pulled his hands out of his pockets and made fists of them. "One tiny mistake and they pounce."

"Isn't it amazing that your tongue should slip in a way that's going to make me be the bad guy?"

Nolan gave her a crooked smile. "Only if you refuse to marry me."

Infuriated, Alex surged to her feet. "That really gives me a lot of choice, doesn't it?"

His smile vanished. "You haven't already decided not to marry me, have you?"

"That isn't the point."

He raised both hands beside his head, fingers spread wide. "Then what is?"

"It isn't just about whether I want to marry *you*. It's about whether I want to be married, *period*. Been there, done that, and frankly, I didn't like it much."

"You were married to a jerk."

Alex laughed at his blunt but accurate description of Brad, then shook her head in exasperation when she realized Nolan thought a marriage to him would automatically be quite different.

"Well, he didn't start out a jerk," she said. "He was actually fairly charming in the beginning. He didn't turn into a jerk until after the wedding."

"So, you're wondering if I'll turn into a jerk after our wedding? Is that what's bothering you?"

Now, it was Alex's turn to pace. "Maybe. That's part of it, anyway. But, Nolan, don't you see? Once a woman gets married, everything changes. I stop being Alex Talbot and become Mrs. Nolan Larson, and I'll be the first to admit that I was a lousy lawyer's wife. I haven't improved those skills one bit."

"You've said that sort of thing before, but I think we

complement each other beautifully. What difference does my being a lawyer make?''

''Your profession is all about laws and rules. The only thing I've ever liked about rules is breaking them. I told you, I'm just not good marriage material.''

''That's ridiculous.''

''It's not.'' Alex paused and looked over her shoulder at him. ''I've seen the pictures of Jennifer. I'm absolutely nothing like her.''

''You think I haven't noticed that already?'' Nolan asked. ''Believe me, Alexandra, I have, and I like you just the way you are.''

Alex gazed at him, miserably helpless to make him understand that he liked who he *thought* she was—the school teacher, the friendly neighbor, the convenient mother for his son. But that was the sanitized, public version of herself, the one she'd invented to give Tasha a ''normal'' mother.

Would he still like her just the way she was, if she allowed the real Alex McBride to come out? The Alex who loved motorcycles and black leather jackets? The Alex who had always wanted a tattoo? The Alex who still longed to dance all night and run naked through a field of wildflowers? Somehow, she doubted that he would.

''So did Brad,'' she said, resuming her pacing. ''At first. Then he and his mother used everything he'd once said that he liked about me against me.''

''I would never do that to you.'' Nolan scowled at her. ''I'm more concerned about what you said at dinner tonight regarding your acting career.''

''What?'' She turned and stared at him. ''Nolan, you're the one who's been encouraging me from the beginning.''

''I know.'' He glanced away from her, clearly uncomfortable. ''It seemed important for you to have the opportunity to try it while they were shooting the movie here. I never thought you'd get into it this much.''

"What exactly did you think would happen?" she asked. "That I'd fail and then that would be the end of my dreams?"

"No." He looked at her again, his eyes beseeching her to believe him. "I knew you'd succeed, Alex. You're a talented actress, there's no doubt about it."

"Then what did you expect?"

"That you wouldn't forget that you're also an extremely gifted teacher. I never imagined you would even think about giving that up for acting." He held one hand out to her. "I know you get tired and frustrated with teaching sometimes, but you bring something special and unique to the kids of Sunshine Gap."

"Oh, right. I just thrill them all to death when I teach them how to diagram a sentence."

"It's more than that." He sat down beside her, bracing his hands behind him. "In fact, I'm not sure it's any particular thing you do, so much as who you are. You're always the one the kids go to when they're really in trouble. You're the one teacher who hasn't forgotten what it feels like to be seventeen. You're the one who treats them with integrity and respect, and they adore you for it. They cry when they say goodbye to you at graduation."

Alex sniffed in dismissal. "Kids always cry at graduation."

Nolan gave her a long, searching look, then said quietly, "It's when they say goodbye to *you* that they *start* crying."

If he was trying to dump a guilt trip on her, it was working. She stood up again, needing to put more distance between them. "So what are you saying? You think I should stay here and be a teacher for the rest of my life, when I might have a chance to go to Hollywood?"

"It's not my choice to make, it's yours," Nolan said. "It's always been your choice. That's why I thought you saw yourself as a teacher first, and the acting as more of a hobby."

"A hobby?" She shook her head in frustration. "But I told you about Mrs. Talbot and what she threatened to do."

"That threat wasn't worth the breath she used to deliver it, and I think deep down, you've always known that." Nolan stretched his legs out in front of him. "After you finished your degree and taught for a couple of years, you could have left and gone to Hollywood or anywhere else you wanted. So why are you still here ten years later if you don't want to be?"

"I'm sure you have a theory," she said. "Let's hear it."

"All right. You've always made a big issue out of wanting to be an actress. I think Mrs. Talbot's threat was a convenient excuse for you to redirect your career plans without having to lose face, if only with yourself. That way, the loss of your big dream was never your fault, was it?"

"No, you're wrong about that, Counselor. I always knew it was my own damn fault," Alex said, thumping her sternum with an index finger, "that I got involved with Brad Talbot in the first place. Once I had Tasha to take care of, there was no way I could go to Hollywood and be the kind of mother I thought she needed. That's why I didn't go after my dream."

"And I applaud that, Alexandra. I honestly do. She wouldn't be the wonderful girl she is today if you hadn't taken your responsibility for raising her so seriously."

Alex rolled her eyes. "Yeah, she's wonderful, all right. She's mouthy and disrespectful, and—"

Smiling, Nolan interrupted. "And she feels safe enough with her mother to say how she really feels about things that are important to her. That's not a common thing in the families I work with. She's delightful, and she still needs you.''

"I have no intention of abandoning her."

"I think we all know that," he said.

"Then why can't I just explore the possibilities with Blair's agent?" Alex tossed both hands up beside her head, then started pacing again. "What is so damn threatening about letting me see how far I can go? That's all I've ever wanted to do, but if I even say the words out loud, everybody around me goes ballistic."

"When you wanted to go to Hollywood before, you were all of what? Eighteen? And you wonder why your parents didn't want you to go? Would you let Tasha go live in L.A. by herself in five years?"

"I don't know. I'd be worried, all right, but I think I'd try to figure out something we both could live with. This isn't about her, though, Nolan. It's about me." She came back to stand in front of him. "When do I get a turn to do what I want?"

"You just did."

"You think two weeks was enough?"

"I guess not."

"But you thought it would be, didn't you?"

"Yes. I thought you'd try it and...well," he shrugged, "get it out of your system."

"Get it out of my system?" She shook her head in disbelief, tried to hold in an enraged shriek, but failed completely. "Ahhhh! Get it out of my system? You don't understand me at all. Not one damn bit."

"I can hear fine," Nolan said. "You don't have to shout."

"Yes, I do." She shrieked again and curled both hands into fists to stop herself from trying to strangle him. "If I don't, I'll explode. Get it out of my system? Acting is the only thing that makes me feel special. Without it, I'm...generic. I'm just another English teacher. Just another single mother. Just another damned McBride.''

''You?'' Nolan reached for her, but she sidestepped him. If he touched her right now, she'd probably hit him. ''I don't believe what I'm hearing. You're not just another anything.''

''You just don't get it.'' She held up her palms in a plea for understanding. ''The only time I really feel alive and whole is when I'm acting. Do you think I'm ever going to get that out of my system? Do you think I even *want* to?''

''Why does it have to be movies? Couldn't you just do more community theater?''

''Would you like to work as a paralegal instead of as a lawyer?'' she asked.

''No, of course not.''

''Well, I loved working with real professionals instead of amateurs for a change,'' Alex said. ''Miz Hannah was right about my needing to try a new challenge. Why do you object to movies?''

''It's not the movies themselves.'' Climbing to his feet, he stuck both hands in his pockets and looked down at his feet. ''At the risk of sounding like Tasha, I really don't want to live in California again. I worked too damn hard to leave it. Of course, that's assuming that you wanted to be with me in the first place, which is beginning to sound like a huge assumption on my part.''

Hearing the hurt in his voice, Alex inhaled a couple of deep breaths, struggling to calm herself down. ''Nolan, you're the one who said this is all hypothetical right now. Couldn't we take a little time and see what happens? What's the big rush on making these decisions?''

He looked up at her then, his eyes distant. ''I don't want to be your fall-back position, Alex.''

"What do you mean?"

"You either want to be with me or you don't. I don't want to be your second choice behind acting. You know, if it doesn't work out for you to go to Hollywood, well, you can always fall back on good old Nolan. That's not what I wanted with you."

"Wanted?" she said softly. "It's already past tense?"

He looked at his feet again. "It's not fair to leave the kids dangling. They're obviously feeling insecure enough about the future."

"If you just hadn't told them—"

"What's done is done." There was anger in his voice now. "Besides, they're not babies. They've had a good idea of what we've been doing. How long did you think we could hide it from them?"

"I don't know. Longer than this."

"Well, I guess that's it, then." He turned as if he intended to leave. Alex grasped his arm and stopped him.

"You can't be serious," she said. "You pushed me into all of this, and then at the first sign of trouble, you say, 'That's it'?"

"What do you want me to do?" He shook off her hand and moved out of reach. "You don't want to marry me, but we have two impressionable children living with us. We have to be responsible about our own conduct if we want them to learn how to be responsible about theirs. If that makes me impossibly stodgy and old-fashioned, so be it."

"Your attitude makes you impossible, that's for sure. Will you listen to yourself? I have to choose between you and acting. I have to do it right now. Everything has to be done on your terms or I'm not being a responsible parent. Oh, yeah, that really makes me want to get married, all right."

"Okay, Alex, fine." He walked to the road, calling back over his shoulder. "Enjoy your sarcasm. Enjoy your life. I won't bother you anymore."

She let him get thirty yards down the road before calling after him. "Hey, Larson, you said either of us could back out at any time with no hard feelings."

He stopped and turned around to face her. "I lied."

When she made no response, he set off toward home again. Alex watched him go, feeling as if she had a boulder sitting on her chest and soap in her eyes. At least he hadn't lied and said he loved her. Nobody who really loved her would treat her this way. Too bad she'd had to go and fall in love with the big jerk. Well, she'd gotten over Brad and she'd get over Nolan, too.

Still, she had to wonder if even a career in Hollywood would ever replace the loss of her very best friend.

Chapter Thirteen

His steps fueled by anger, Nolan hurried toward home, slowing only when he caught sight of Alex's house. It was big, old and a little dilapidated, but it had three times the charm his own modern colonial did. If houses reflected their owners' personalities, then Alexandra was warm, welcoming and colorful, while he was precise, unimaginative and…oh, hell…stodgy.

Funny, whenever she'd talked about their being mismatched as a couple, Alexandra had always made it sound as if she was the one who couldn't live up to some lofty standard of his. He was ready to agree that they were mismatched, but he was the one who suffered in comparison. It was like mating a bright, beautiful butterfly with a plain, dirty brown moth.

Good Lord, he should have seen it before this. Or perhaps he'd always known the truth, but he'd wanted her for so long, he'd finally ignored it, reached out and captured the beautiful butterfly for his own. But he couldn't hold on to her without killing her, or at least maiming the wildest, sweetest part of her that made her so beautiful to begin with. Since he didn't want that on his conscience, he would have to let her go.

"And if that's not the biggest line of bull," he muttered, shaking his head in disgust at his feeble attempt to rationalize what had just happened with Alexandra. "Maybe I should try writing fiction for a living."

The truth was, he'd let her go because he feared that if she went off to Hollywood, she would figure out what a plain, dirty brown moth he was, and he would lose her forever. Here in Sunshine Gap, most of the really handsome men in the area were either her brothers or her first cousins, and a Nolan Larson might seem like a reasonably good catch. In California, however, she could have her pick of guys who were better looking, more exciting and a heck of a lot richer than he was.

How could he ever hope to compete with that? Or with guys who had all of that going for them and they were in the movie business, too, as actors, directors, producers, writers. The possibilities were endless and horrifying. God, he was dying of jealousy here, and she hadn't even left yet.

But it wasn't as if Alex had ever said she was madly in love with him. She would have been a lot more eager to marry him if that were the case. Wouldn't she? Of course she would.

There was nothing left to do now but get on with his own life as gracefully as possible. He almost hoped she would move to Hollywood. He didn't know if he could stand to live next door to her and know he would never be able to touch her, kiss her, make love to her again. Gulping at the sudden lump in his throat, he forced himself to go inside.

The dishwasher was running, but there was no sign of the kids, which was probably just as well. He didn't feel like dealing with their inevitable questions. He didn't feel like doing anything that wasn't a cliché for a man confronted with a broken heart, such as getting drunk or destroying a room. Of course, he was too damn civilized and stodgy to find any satisfaction in doing either one.

Instead, he put on a pair of running shorts and a T-shirt, and went downstairs to use his weight bench. He methodically worked each muscle group, straining to lift more weight and do more reps than he'd ever done before. Sweat poured off him, but the anger and the hurt remained. An hour later, his arms and legs trembling with fatigue, he trudged back upstairs for a shower.

He walked into his bedroom, stripped off the T-shirt and threw it in the hamper, then went to the window and looked out across the hedge. There was a light on in Alex's bedroom, more on downstairs. She must have gotten home by now. He should probably go over there and apologize to her, but he still felt too angry and hurt to trust himself to conduct a rational, productive conversation.

Undoubtedly it would be wiser to stay on his own side of the hedge for a few days and allow both of their tempers to cool. He was sick to death of doing the wiser thing, however. He wondered if the cavemen had known how easy they'd had it when it came to dealing with women.

Deciding the best thing she could do was to get out of Dodge, Alex went home, called her cousin Grace and convinced her to leave for the mountains the next morning. With Tasha, Riley and Steven and one of the movie wrangler's sons in tow, they set off from the Flying M prepared to spend five days checking on the cows and moving the bulls around. Sometimes the bulls got lazy and congregated under a shady tree, expecting the cows to come to them.

Alex thought they looked like a bunch of old men, sitting out in front of the feed store in town, swapping lies, chewing tobacco and playing cards or checkers. She had to admit to taking a perverse pleasure in harassing those bulls into getting out there and earning their keep. She shared more than one good laugh with Grace at the sight of a two-ton bull clambering to his hooves and lumbering off, switching his tail as if the prospect of having to get up and go impregnate a cow or two was a major inconvenience.

After supper the second night out, Grace sent the kids off to catch some fish for breakfast the next morning, then made a pot of cowboy coffee over the campfire. She poured Alex a cup, and one for herself, settling onto a tree stump to drink it.

''Okay, Alex, I brought you along for your entertainment value, but you've hardly said two sentences since we left the ranch,'' Grace said after taking a sip. ''Time to spill your guts. What's goin' on between you and Tash?''

''She's sulking.'' Alex stood, rubbing her aching buns with one hand while she verified the whereabouts of Tasha and Grace's boys, Riley and Steven. The kids were still drowning worms in the creek, definitely out of earshot. ''She's ticked off at me because I decided not to marry Nolan.''

Grace choked on her coffee and sat up straighter, staring at Alex. ''Say what? Nolan proposed?''

Alex nodded. ''Tasha adores him and can't imagine why I wouldn't want to marry him.''

''Neither can I,'' Grace said. ''I thought you two were getting pretty serious there for a while.''

''We were. But I don't want to get married again.''

''Is it still Brad?''

"No, I really don't think so. You know, I really envy you, sometimes, Gracie."

"Me? Good Lord, Alex, you've got no reason to do that."

"Well, I do. You've always enjoyed doing all the things women are supposed to enjoy doing, and you're so good at cooking and sewing and all of that other stuff. And I'm just not. I never have been, and I never will be."

"You don't have to be, hon. You've got your own special talents."

"Right now it sure seems as if having yours would make my life a lot simpler."

"What happened?" Grace said.

Alex inhaled a deep breath, and when she sighed it out, the whole story of her relationship with Nolan tumbled out with it.

Grace listened attentively until Alex ran out of words. Then she got up, refilled both of their cups and glanced around to make sure the kids were still in sight.

Finally she said, "So you're still dreamin' of Hollywood."

"Not the way everybody seems to think I am," Alex said. "It's not the glamorous stuff like the premieres and the parties that turn me on. It's the work, the creating, the being around other people who do the same things I do and don't think I'm strange because I love acting."

"Do you love Nolan?" Grace said.

"Yes," Alex said. "I do. Other than being a pigheaded, misguided dope sometimes, he's a wonderful man."

Grace chuckled. "Do you love acting more than you love Nolan?"

"Hell, I don't know. How do you answer a question like that? I miss him so much, I ache." Alex's eyes filled with tears. "But now that I've had a taste of what acting can really be like…well, if there's any hope at all that I can do it again sometime, I don't want to give that up, either. Even if I gave up the acting now or if it didn't work out for some reason, I don't know if he'd ever believe I wasn't just using him as a 'fall-back position.' Can you believe he came up with that?''

"Yup," Grace said with a wry smile. "God help you if you dent a man's delicate ego."

Alex sniffled and shook her head. "It's just not fair, damn it. Men don't have make these kinds of choices. They choose a profession, and then everybody else in their lives has to work around it. If Nolan was in my position and I was the lawyer, he would expect me to already be packing, but because I'm a woman, I have choose between him and the profession I've always wanted. I hate that. No matter which way I choose, I lose something I really love."

"What you really need is a man who won't make you choose."

"Yeah, right. As if any man that generous exists," Alex said, swiping at her eyes with the back of one hand. "They all consider their own careers and convenience to be way more important than any work a woman might want to do. Especially when the work is something as frivolous as acting."

"A lot of guys are like that, all right, but don't give up hope completely," Grace said. "You never know who you might meet or what might happen next."

"That's what I keep telling myself," Alex said, sniffling again. "But I don't believe me anymore. I just wish Tasha would get off my back. Lately it seems like she almost hates me."

"She's thirteen years old," Grace said with a grin. "She's supposed to start hating you now. In fact, if I remember how it went with you and me and our mothers, she probably won't think you know a blessed thing from now until she has kids of her own.''

"Gee, thanks a lot for cheering me up," Alex said. "I'll be sure to sympathize when Riley and Steven hit puberty."

Grace shuddered, and they both chuckled. Then Grace's expression sobered and she gazed directly into Alex's eyes.

"If Tasha knew she wasn't gonna have to move away, that might ease her resistance to your acting. Anytime you've got a job out of town and you need a place to park her for a few weeks, I'd be glad to have her stay with us."

"Thanks. I appreciate that, but I'm not sure I'd have the nerve to inflict her on you."

"Oh, fiddlesticks. I'm not her mother, so she's not a pain in the rear end when she's with me. Besides, I'm surrounded by males. I'd enjoy havin' a girl in the house for a change."

The kids brought over a string of brook trout, ending any hope of further adult conversation. Everyone went to work securing the campsite for the night, hanging the food high in a tree to avoid attracting bears, checking the horses and banking the fire. When everyone else had gone to sleep, Alex stretched out in her bedroll, listening to the wind rustling in the pines and studying the stars overhead.

When she finally saw a shooting star, she wished for a man who wouldn't make her choose. If only Nolan could be that man, he'd be damn near perfect. A real Mr. Right.

By the time they all rode down out of the mountains three days later, Alex was tired, hot, cranky and in dire need of a shower. It was mid-afternoon, and Dillon still had a couple of stunt men working in the corral. Blair stood just outside the barn, playing with Curly, the orphaned bull calf who thought she was his mama.

Alex, Grace and the kids rode up to the corral fence and

swung out of their saddles. Alex groaned softly at protesting muscles, stretched out her back and looped the little roan mare's reins around a fence rail. She patted the horse's neck, then hooked the stirrup over the saddle horn to get at the cinch.

"Alex!" Blair ran across the barnyard with Curly tagging along behind her. "Alex, great news!"

Tipping back the brim of her Stetson, Alex smiled at her. "What's up?"

"Remember when I told you that I would invite my agent to come to the Flying M for the Fourth of July weekend?" Blair said.

"Yeah. Did you hear from him?"

"Better than that," Blair said. "He's already—"

"Blair, did I hear horses?" A tall, elegantly dressed man who appeared to be in his fifties stepped out of the huge motor home owned by Blair's cousin, Hope DuMaine. He crossed the yard in quick, smooth strides, giving the impression of a man who knew what he wanted and didn't hesitate to go after it.

Blair held out one hand toward the man and finished her sentence. "He's here."

"No." Alex cursed under her breath and tugged her hat down hard over her dirty hair. "Dammit, Blair, I haven't had a shower in five days. I can't meet him looking this. Or smelling like this."

Chuckling, Blair grabbed Alex's hand and dragged her toward the stranger. "Don't worry about it. He's been here for two days, so he's used to the smells and the dirt. And he loved your dailies. Just talk to him. I'll take care of your horse for you."

Still muttering under her breath, Alex stopped walking when Blair did, yanked her hand free and tried to wipe a little of the grime off on the side of her jeans. Blair stepped forward with a huge smile, gave the man a hug and made the introductions.

"Alexandra McBride, may I present my good friend and agent, Creighton Ramsey. Creighton, this is my good friend and fellow actor, Alexandra McBride."

"Ms. McBride," Ramsey said, his voice deep and resonant enough to send a chill skittering the length of Alex's spine, "what a pleasure to meet you."

Alex gazed into his blue eyes and saw a warmth and admiration there that made her forget all about her less-than-pristine state. "Mr. Ramsey," she said, hoping she sounded a great deal cooler and calmer than she felt.

He took her hand, tucked it into the crook of his elbow and set off as if he were planning to escort her to a country club dinner. "I've watched the clips of your work several times now, and I have to tell you that you have a commanding screen presence. Would you be willing to talk with me about your career plans and goals for, say, an hour?"

"Certainly."

Fighting a sense of disbelief that this really could be happening to her, Alex walked along with him to Hope's motor home. Lord, she felt clueless as to the proper protocol in dealing with a Hollywood agent. Blair grinned and gave her a discreet wave, offering no help whatsoever. Alex climbed the steps, but felt a compelling urge to look back toward the corral as she reached the top.

Even from a distance of fifty yards, she could tell Tasha was glaring at her. Damn. She'd tried to talk to the kid several times during their camping trip, but Tasha had brushed her off at every opportunity.

Well, when they got home tonight, she'd have to sit Tasha down and have a real heart-to-heart with her. But first she needed to talk to this guy and find out about her prospects. For all she knew, there might not be any reason for anyone to get excited.

Nolan wrapped up his last appointment early on Wednesday afternoon, drove back to Sunshine Gap and, in response to a sudden but strong desire to avoid going home, stopped in at Cal's Place for a beer. The tavern was cool and dimly lit, a welcome contrast to the fierce sunshine outside. It was also deserted, except for Alex's brother Cal, who stood behind the bar with a stack of papers in front of him.

"Afternoon, Counselor," Cal said with his standard friendly bartender grin. "Surprised to see you in here this early."

Nolan shrugged. "I decided to play hooky."

He climbed onto a bar stool and told Cal what he wanted. Cal delivered his beer, waited until he'd taken a sip and braced one elbow on the bar.

"What's the problem?" Cal asked.

Nolan chuckled, but it sounded weak, even to his own ears. "What makes you think I've got one?"

"Bartender's wisdom. Besides, you're not the type to play hooky," Cal said. "So, what are you really doing in here at this time of day in the middle of the week?"

"I don't want to go home."

Cal scratched his chin and twisted his mouth to one side in a comically thoughtful pose. "Heard a lot of that, lately. But, most of the guys I hear it from have nagging wives, which you don't. Although my sister sure can be a pain in the behind when she wants. No, wait a minute, she's been up in the mountains chasin' cows around for five days, so it can't be her fault. Must be your kid, then. He's a teenager now, isn't he?"

Nolan nodded. "Fourteen."

"He's the one you want to avoid?"

"Just for a little while," Nolan said. "He's mad at me because of your sister."

"No kiddin'?"

Cal turned an interested bartender's smile on him, and, to Nolan's surprise, he found himself laying out a carefully edited version of his relationship with Alexandra. She was the man's sister, after all, and like all of the other McBride men, Cal was big, strong and known to have a temper. He could fill in the blanks in Nolan's story himself if he really wanted to. Cal listened intently, nodding occasional encouragement and pouring himself a cup of coffee while Nolan talked.

When Nolan had finished, Cal picked up a towel and started polishing the section of the bar in front of him. "Well now," he said, "that's an interesting story. Sad one, too. And you know, I wouldn't have minded having you for a brother-in-law."

"Thanks," Nolan said, saluting him with his beer glass. "I wouldn't have minded having you for an in-law, either."

"Of course, if you weren't so damn dumb, that probably could still happen."

"What are you talking about?" Nolan said. "Your sister's going to leave and most likely will become a huge success in Hollywood. Inside of a year, she won't even remember my name."

"Do you love her?" Cal asked. "Really love her?"

His throat too clogged to speak, Nolan nodded.

"Does she love you?"

Again Nolan nodded. "I think so," he said, his voice husky and raw with the pain in his heart.

Cal muttered something about idiots under his breath, then braced both palms flat on the bar and frowned at Nolan. "Well, for God's sake, you're a divorce lawyer. You should know enough to sit her down and figure out some kind of a compromise. I swear, half the divorces in this town happen because of stupid pride and a failure to communicate. By the way, did you ever bother to tell Alex that you love her?''

Had he? Nolan wondered. Surely he had, though he couldn't remember the specific incident. But even if he hadn't, Alex must know how much he cared for her and for Tasha. Didn't she?

His mind racing, Nolan slapped a couple of bills on the bar and drove home. He'd spent this whole week missing Alex and seeing problems instead of solutions. He still didn't want to move back to California, but maybe Cal was right and there were other alternatives. First, however, he would have to get Alex to talk to him again.

He pulled into his driveway, stepped out of the car and heard a loud snort, followed by a crash coming from the backyard. He hurried around the side of the house and found himself facing the rear end of a black horse. Though Rick often went riding with Tasha at the Flying M, and Nolan had gone along a few times when Alex had teased him into it, he didn't fool himself into thinking he knew more about the big animals than he really did. He didn't know much.

He did know enough not to approach one from the rear, especially when it was agitated, as this one appeared to be. Judging from the snorts and grunts it was making, along with the way it kept shaking its head and pulling back on the reins, which were tied to the hedge, Nolan suspected this horse was becoming seriously irritated. After a good look at his backyard, so was Nolan.

There were huge, ugly footprints embedded in the recently watered lawn, two smashed lawn chairs and pulverized flower beds, not to mention several impressive piles of manure. As if to add insult to injury, the horse stopped pulling on the reins, but only long enough to let loose a noisy stream of urine, most of which splashed onto Nolan's patio. When the animal finally finished, it swung its rear end around parallel to the hedge, giving Nolan a clear view of the brand, a large M with two little wings at the points, indicating a Flying M.

That was a McBride horse, which meant Tasha was probably around somewhere close by. And now, Nolan also saw why the horse was getting so riled. The saddle was hanging halfway down its side in what was undoubtedly an uncomfortable position.

To Nolan's amazement and horror, the horse proceeded to lie down and roll around on the grass, hind legs thrashing, hooves flailing at the saddle. At one point, the beast had all four feet pointing skyward and the saddle resting on its belly. Nolan had never seen such equine gymnastics before, but he would've given the horse a perfect score for style and efficiency.

There was a popping sound, then a clank when the cinch's D-ring and buckle hit the ground. The horse scrambled onto its feet minus the saddle, hide shivering all over in obvious relief. Then with what looked like a negligent toss of its head, it ripped a small branch out of the hedge and ran off with it flapping at the end of its reins.

Nolan ran into the house, shouting for Tasha and Rick. They both appeared at the top of the stairs, looking surprised and none too happy to see him. He quickly related the horse's antics. Face stricken, Tasha raced out of the front door, with Rick following close behind.

Shaking his head, Nolan loosened his tie and finished climbing the stairs. A disturbing thought hit him as he reached the top step. Just what had Rick and Tasha been doing up here alone? Granted, they treated each other as buddies, but Tasha was still a girl, and a darn cute one. If any man knew how much trouble a guy could get into with a female friend, Nolan did.

Instead of entering his own room, he walked down the hall to Rick's and looked inside, but didn't see anything disturbed. Not that anyone could really tell if anything had been disturbed in such a mess, but Nolan still had the impression that no one had been in here recently. He shut Rick's door out of habit, turned to go to his own room, then turned back when he realized that farther down the hall the seldom-used guest room's door stood open and the light was on.

Curious, he walked down the hall to investigate. Looking inside the doorway, he felt a sinking sensation in the region of his heart. Tasha's school backpack lay on its side on the desk. A mountain of stuffed animals were piled beside the backpack. The closet doors were open, showing a jumble of clothes hanging from a rod that should be empty. The sofa bed had been pulled out and made up with blue-and-white-striped sheets and a blue blanket.

The front door slammed downstairs. Nolan hurried from the guest room, down the hall and down the stairs, intercepting the kids on their way to the kitchen. He folded his arms across his chest.

"Stop right there," he said.

Both kids turned around to face him, studying him every bit as intently as he studied them. He saw a militant light in Tasha's eyes that reminded him so much of Alexandra, he would have laughed under other circumstances.

"Where's the horse?" Nolan said.

"Probably halfway back to the ranch by now," Tasha said. "We couldn't catch her."

"Is there anything we should do for her?"

"I'll call the ranch and tell them to watch for her. She'll be all right," Tasha said.

"All right," Nolan said. "Go make that call and then come right back here and talk to me."

Eyes filled with reluctance, she nodded, then went into the kitchen. Nolan turned to Rick.

Though he feared he already knew the answer, Nolan asked, "What's going on here, son? What are Tasha's things doing in the guest room?"

"Alex is meeting with Blair DuMaine's agent, and everybody at the ranch is saying she'll be going to Hollywood for sure," Rick said. "Tasha doesn't want to go, so I told her she could move in with us."

"No, this isn't a good idea," Nolan said, remembering Alex's distraught face the night she had told him about her mother-in-law's threat to take Tasha away. "This is between Tasha and her mom. We need to stay out of it."

Tasha stepped back into the hallway from the kitchen, where she'd undoubtedly been eavesdropping. "Please, Nolan, just let me stay here until Mom comes to her senses. Once she figures out I won't ever go to California, she'll give up this crazy idea. I know she will."

Nolan frowned at the girl, knowing she was probably right. Alex had already abandoned her dreams once on Tasha's account, and she most likely would do so again. If he gave Tasha just the right amount of encouragement, he could keep Alex right here in Sunshine Gap. The best part was, the kid would do all of his dirty work for him.

The vision forming in his mind's eye was so clear, he could almost touch it. A dab of guilt here, a bit of emotional blackmail there, and Alex would do exactly what he and Tasha and Rick all wanted her to do—stay here and make all of them feel like a family. She was the glue who held them all together, after all. That's why they were all so terrified of losing her. And perhaps he was the most terrified of them all.

Yes, he wanted Alex to stay. He loved her. He needed her far more than she needed him. But could he use her own daughter against her to get what he wanted?

Sadly shaking his head, he crossed the hallway to Tasha. "I'm sorry, sweetheart, but you can't stay here. You don't want to do this to your mother."

"I'm not doing anything to her," Tasha protested. "She's trying to wreck my whole life."

Nolan put his arm around her shoulders and gently hugged her. "You know better than that, Tash. Your mom adores you, and I'm not going to help you treat her unfairly."

Tasha dug in her heels. "She's the one who's being unfair."

Releasing her shoulders, Nolan turned Tasha to face him. "Lots of kids have to move because of their parents' jobs, Tash. Rick didn't want to come here, but I made him do it. Your mom's the one who has to go out there every single day and earn a living for both of you. Why should you get to choose how she's going to do that?"

"That's not what I'm trying to do."

"Sure it is. She hasn't even made a firm decision and you're already giving her grief about it. She's just talking to the agent right now. At least get all the facts before you have a tantrum."

Tasha's chin quivered, and her eyes filled with tears. "I thought you liked me."

"I do. I love you, Tash, but that doesn't mean I always have to think you're right. Your mom's wanted this opportunity for a long time. Don't you think you should cut her just a little slack?"

Moving away from him, she pulled herself up as tall as she could, hurt pride in every line of her face. "I'll get my things and clean up your yard. I'm sorry to have bothered you.''

"Tasha, I'm glad you felt free to come here for help. It's just that this time, you need to work the problem out with your mom.''

She turned and ran up the stairs, down the hall and slammed a door, presumably the one to the guest room. Scowling at Nolan, Rick shook his head and went after her, muttering, "Way to go, Dad. You sure know how to handle women.''

"Yeah, right,'' Nolan grumbled, turning toward the kitchen. "I'm thinking of joining a monastery any day now.''

With visions of contracts and screen credits dazzling her brain, Alex stepped out of the motor home three hours after she stepped in, just a smidge tipsy from the champagne Creighton had served with their luncheon, and a lot tipsy with the greatest ego boost she had ever known. She was in love with Creighton Ramsey. In love with life. In love with the whole wide wonderful world.

Then Grace came running from the direction of the barn, waving both arms and hollering. "Alex! Alex! Oh, my God, Alex, have you seen Tasha?''

Instantly sober, Alex jumped to the ground and ran to meet her cousin. "No. What is it? What's wrong, Grace?''

"I don't know…for sure.'' Grace panted, struggling to catch her breath. "Her horse…just came running up the drive with no saddle…and no rider. Nobody's seen her…for a couple of…hours at least.''

"Didn't she turn her loose with the rest of them?'' Alex asked.

"Nobody remembers her doing that. When you went in there to talk with that guy, Blair told us some exciting stuff, and we all went in to the house to get cleaned up and find something to eat. There were people comin' and goin' every which way. I'm sorry, I just wasn't payin' attention to her.''

''It's not your fault,'' Alex said. ''You said the horse came up the driveway?''

''Yeah. I'll bet she rode her home. Or tried to.''

Her stomach knotted with anxiety, Alex grabbed Grace's arm and set off toward the ranch house. ''Well, then, let's go call and see if she's there.''

''Blair's already doin' that. Oh, look, here she comes.''

They broke into a jog, veering off when Blair waved them toward her little red rental car.

''What did you find out?'' Alex asked.

''There was no answer,'' Blair said. ''Come on, I'll drive into town, and you two can look out the windows.''

''Did you try Nolan's house?'' Alex asked.

''No,'' Blair said. ''I'm sorry. I didn't think.''

''I'll call him,'' Grace said, starting toward the house again. ''You two get started looking from this end just in case. If I hear anything, I'll come after you.''

Blair and Alex got into the car and took off in a cloud of dust. Alex struggled to breathe slowly and deeply, knowing she would be of no use to Tasha if she panicked. But all she could think was, oh, dear God, please don't let my baby be hurt. Tasha was a good rider, but even the best riders had accidents sometimes. A horse coming home with no saddle was not a good sign.

Never had the eight miles to town seemed longer or more desolate. The trees and pastures and country roads she normally loved took on a sinister cast. What if Tasha was lying just over there in that brush, badly hurt, but hidden from the road? It could take hours to find her. Too long. Way too long.

And it was her fault. All her fault. Tasha had already made it clear she didn't want to go to L.A. Why hadn't she listened to her own child? Was she so selfish she couldn't see beyond her own wants and desires? What kind of a lousy excuse for a mother was she, anyway?

Damn, if this was what so-called success brought into her life, Alex decided she hadn't been a bit crazy to fear it.

Chapter Fourteen

Before Blair could shut off the engine, Alex jumped out of the car and charged for her house. She ripped open the front door and ran inside, shouting Tasha's name.

"Tasha! Tasha, are you here? Tasha!"

A figure stepped out of the kitchen, and when Alex saw that it was Nolan, and his expression was utterly serious, her knees nearly buckled. Oh, God, he was here to deliver bad news. He held up both palms and rushed toward her. She could see his lips moving, but the odd roaring in her ears blocked out the sound of his voice. Then the lights went out.

She came to with a circle of worried faces—Nolan, Grace and Blair—gazing down at her and a throbbing knot on the side of her head. Groaning, she struggled to sit up, but several pairs of hands instantly restrained her.

"Lie still, Alex," Nolan said. "You're hurt."

"Tasha?" Alex said.

"She's fine." Nolan gently stroked her hair out of her eyes. "That's what I was trying to tell you."

"I'm right here, Mom," Tasha said. "I'm okay."

"So am I." Alex pushed the restraining hands away and sat up, swaying a little before her equilibrium returned. Tenderly probing the lump beneath her hair, she grimaced at the pain even the lightest touch provoked. "What did I hit on the way down?"

"The ottoman," Nolan said. "Lucky for you it didn't have any sharp edges."

"I'm sorry, Mom," Tasha said, her voice wavering as if she were fighting tears. "I didn't mean to scare you so bad."

A closer look at Tasha's face told Alex her daughter had already been crying for a while. How long had she been out, for heaven's sake? She held her arms open wide and felt a fierce surge of love when Tasha came close for a long, hard hug.

Lord, was there any more wonderful sensation in the universe than embracing a child you'd thought might be hurt or even dead?

Of course, when the realization that Tasha really was perfectly fine sank in, Alex's next instinct after hugging the stuffing out of the kid was to strangle the little wretch for scaring the devil out of her. Grasping Tasha's shoulders, she held her at arm's length. "What happened? How did the mare get away from you? Did she throw you?"

A pink flush darkened Tasha's cheeks as she slowly shook her head. "I just left her tied up to the hedge too long. I loosened the cinch, and the saddle slipped, you know? I guess she got mad and rolled on it, and when the cinch broke, she ripped the reins free and took off."

"Why didn't you call the ranch? You knew she'd come home, and that we'd all worry."

Tasha nodded. "I started to call as soon as I realized what had happened, but then I got, um…distracted, and I sort of um…just forgot about calling."

"Distracted?" Alex climbed to her feet and promptly plopped back down on the sofa when the room tilted giddily. "What could have distracted you that much?"

Tasha sat on the sofa beside Alex, but shot a scowl at Nolan before answering. "I heard Nolan and Rick talking about me when I went to call the ranch, and I came back and we got into an argument."

"An argument? You and Nolan? About what?"

"About my moving in with him and Rick."

"Moving in with him and Rick?"

"Yes, Mother," Tasha said, impatience creeping into her voice.

Alex knew she probably sounded like a parrot, but none of this made much sense to her. Maybe she'd seriously scrambled her brain when she fell. She glanced around the room then, noting that Tasha's clothes, still wearing their hangers, were draped over various pieces of furniture, and her stuffed animals were piled up at the bottom of the stairs. When at last the picture became clear, she felt nauseated.

"You already did it, didn't you? You moved in over there, I mean," Alex said, her voice becoming faint in her own ears.

"Yes."

"Why?"

"You know why," Tasha said. "Because I don't want to move to L.A. I already told you that, but when you went off with that agent, I knew there wasn't any hope you'd stay here."

"We couldn't even talk about it, Tash?"

"What could I say that I hadn't already said? Everybody

else was so excited for you and so impressed with your success, what I wanted wasn't important to anyone.''

"That's not true," Alex said.

"It is, too." Tasha jumped to her feet, fists clenched at her sides, glaring down at Alex. "The only thing you care about anymore is going to Hollywood and being a big movie star. You've already forgotten all about me."

"No, Tasha, I haven't."

Tasha rolled her eyes and gave one of those disgusted little huffs teenagers do so well. "Oh, pu-lease. You'll just drag me to L.A., where I'll be the stupid hick from Wyoming who doesn't know anyone or anything, and I won't fit in, and I'll be miserable. And you'll be so busy building your damn career, you won't even notice. You don't need me around. Hell, you probably don't even want me around anymore."

"Natasha, I'm ashamed of you," Grace said. "And you should be ashamed of yourself. How can you talk to your mother that way after she just passed out because of—"

Alex held up one hand. "No, Grace, it's all right. Let her say whatever she needs to say."

Tasha's chin quivered, but her glare didn't soften. "I won't go to California. When I came here and told Rick, he said I could move in with them, so I did." Tasha paused and shot Nolan another scowl. "He said I couldn't, so I brought everything back here. But if you try to make me move down there, so help me, I'll run away."

"I see." Feeling as if her heart had shattered, Alex collapsed back against the sofa cushion.

"I didn't realize she hadn't made the phone call," Nolan said. "I was appalled when Grace called, but we didn't get her call right away, because we were helping Tasha bring her things home. Grace tried to catch up with you, but you had too much of a head start."

Alex tried to smile at him to let him know she understood, but her face felt oddly stiff. She cleared her throat and tried to smile again, but knew she hadn't succeeded. Lord, was it possible for a person to bleed to death without any physical wounds? She couldn't bear to have so many people watching it happen to her.

"I, um…I want to have a few minutes…alone," she said.

"I don't think that's a good idea," Grace said.

Alex looked deeply into her cousin's eyes for a second, letting her glimpse her desperate need for privacy. "Please, Gracie. I just want a few minutes."

A worried frown creasing her forehead, Grace slowly nodded. "Okay, but I'll be right outside if you need anything. Come on, everybody. Let's go."

Closing her eyes, Alex listened to the sound of their feet retreating, then the sliding glass door to the patio opening and closing. She just sat there at first, letting a blessed sort of numbness wash over her. She heard each breath, felt each beat of her heart, and yet she knew that a part of herself was dying, and she was deliberately killing it.

Not by choice. In reality, she had no choice, and she'd known that all along. That was why she initially had resisted Nolan's encouragement to take part in the filming of *Against the Wind.*

If only she had listened to her own instincts, she could have saved herself, Tasha, Nolan and Rick a great deal of pain. Nolan would still be her best friend, and they all would still have something that at least resembled a family. She would still be able to tell herself that she really liked teaching just fine; after all, you didn't miss what you'd never really had, and until now, she'd never had a real taste of her one big dream.

A soft, bitter laugh escaped her lips. Some big dream. It

had caused her everything from a vague, general sense of dissatisfaction to a deep, endless yearning, to the raw, visceral pain that was even now, ripping and tearing at her insides. It simply had to end.

No career, no dream, no goal was worth the possible loss of her daughter's love, trust or safety. Alex remembered her own parents telling her time and again—particularly when she'd caused them a night of worry, fury or grief— that they sincerely hoped she would end up having a child just like herself someday. Those hopes had all come true in Tasha.

Natasha was every bit as headstrong as Alex had been at that age, and not for one second would Alex allow herself the luxury of believing that Tasha's threat to run away had been an empty one. The kid could and would do exactly what she'd threatened to do, and Alex had no defenses against the kind of fear she experienced at the thought of her baby living on the streets or God only knew where. Better to kill off her own silly dream than to risk having to watch Tasha self-destruct.

Besides, what did she have to cry about now, anyway? She'd achieved her goal of acting in a movie. At least she'd done it once, and she'd done it fairly well if Blair DuMaine, Patrick Quillen and Creighton Ramsey were telling her the truth. It was more than a lot of wanna-be actors could say. It was probably more than she herself deserved.

From now on, she would concentrate on becoming the best mother and the best high school English teacher she possibly could, and that would be enough to make her happy. If it wasn't, well, maybe she'd get a dog. Or take up belly dancing, or do crafts or learn to play the piano. There had to be something else out there that would fill up the huge, bleeding hole the loss of acting would leave in her life. It was up to her to figure out what that something was.

She would not feel sorry for herself. She would not be bitter or angry or resentful. She would simply bury all of those emotions so deep, they would never see daylight on her face. She would pick herself up and go on with her life, the way any other hardheaded McBride would.

Deeply disturbed by the distraught expression on Alexandra's face, Nolan reluctantly followed Grace, Blair and the kids outdoors to the patio. Tasha and Rick immediately set off for Nolan's house, which was probably a good move on Tasha's part, considering the irritation in Grace's eyes whenever she looked at the girl. Not that Nolan blamed Grace. He wouldn't mind turning Tasha over his knee at the moment, either.

Still, Tasha was Alexandra's child, and she was, after all, doing what any child would do, namely, trying to get her own way. He didn't approve of the way she'd gone about it, but it undoubtedly wasn't his place to tell her so. If she was his daughter, however, he wouldn't want her to believe that she could get away with such behavior.

The three adults sat down at the umbrella table. Nolan glanced at Grace, then at Blair, feeling an enormous sense of guilt and helplessness settling over him. He had never intended to hurt Alexandra when he'd nagged her into going to the cattle call and all of the rest of it, but he obviously had. And now, he didn't have the faintest idea how to go about repairing the damage he'd caused.

"I don't like this," Grace said, glancing back toward the house. "I don't like this at all."

"What do you think she'll do?" Blair asked.

"Think? Shoot, I *know* what she'll do," Grace said.

"She'll do what any mother who loves her daughter would do."

"You mean she'll quit acting?" Blair said.

"Of course she will," Grace said. "It'll just about kill her, but Tasha's all she's got."

"But maybe if we talked to Tasha—"

Grace cut Blair off with a shake of her head. "Won't make any difference to Alex. Damn, this is not fair. I never understood what she meant when she said it before, but I'm sure as hell beginning to."

"When she said what?" Nolan asked.

Grace gave him a long, level look that somehow made him feel extremely small. "When she said that she envied me because I'm good at doing all those female things women are supposed to enjoy doing. Imagine that. A woman as talented and beautiful as Alex envying somebody like me because I just naturally enjoy takin' care of other folks."

"I don't mean to offend you, Grace, because I sincerely admire the job you do at the Flying M," Blair said. "But why would Alex envy that? She has so much to offer."

"Of course she does," Grace said with a smile. "And I'm not at all offended by your question, because Alex envying me doesn't make a lick of sense. Unfortunately what she said was true. A woman who's got a big dream like she does generally has to choose between the work she loves and the people she loves. And men really don't have to make those choices. Not very often, anyway. She's right about that, too."

"I have the impression that you're not just talking about Tasha, now," Nolan said. "What's your point, Grace?"

"I think you know exactly what my point is, Mr. Larson. Alex cares a lot about making the people she loves happy. It just seems to me, that if anybody around here really loved

Alex, they'd care about whether or not she was happy, too.''

"I care if she's happy," Nolan said.

"Do you really? Do you want her to be happy doin' what *she* wants to do? Or do you just want her to be happy doin' what *you* want her to do? Why is Alex's dream—*whatever* it is—any less important than yours or Tasha's or Rick's? Why should she have to give up her chosen profession just to make you three happy and comfortable?''

Before Nolan could come up with an honest answer, Alex slid open the patio door and stepped outside. She had more color in her face and an affectionate smile for her cousin. "Down, girl," she said, patting Grace's shoulder. "I've made a decision, and it has nothing to do with Nolan, so leave the poor man alone.''

Grace placed her own hand on top of Alex's and gave it a squeeze. "Whatever you say, hon.''

Blair stood and looked at Alex. "What did you decide?''

"I'd like you to go back to Creighton and tell him I really appreciate all the kind words he had for me this afternoon, but I can't do what he wants," Alex said. "In fact, I'm not going to do any more acting at all.''

"Alex, you can't do that," Grace said, scrambling to her feet. "We'll figure somethin' else out for Tash.''

"Please, Alex, do think very carefully about this," Blair said. "You wouldn't have to move to Hollywood. A lot of actors don't live there anymore. According to Dillon, they're all coming here to Wyoming and Montana.''

"No, Blair. Listen—''

"No, Alex, *you* listen," Blair said. "You don't have to make movies all the time. One or two a year probably would be enough to keep the door open for you until Tasha's ready to leave home. If you're not the female lead, you wouldn't have to be away from home all that much. A few weeks at most.''

Nolan stood, but none of the women paid any attention to him. His mind was whirling with new ideas and possibilities, but he'd need some time to sort them all out, and he had a terrible feeling he wasn't going to get it done before Alexandra blighted the rest of her life.

"No, Blair," Alex said again, another ten decibels louder this time.

Blair's voice rose to meet Alex's. "Dammit, Alex, don't do this to yourself. You've got a wonderful opportunity here. The door is open and your foot is in it. But if you don't take advantage of it right now, the door will close and it may not open for you again. You don't have to make this decision this very second. Take a few days to think about it.''

Alex inhaled a deep breath, and Nolan could almost hear her mentally counting to ten. Then she gave Blair a patient, yet absolutely final, smile that chilled Nolan to his soul.

"There's nothing for me to think about. Since the day she was born, Natasha has always been the most important thing in my life. She always will be. If you have children of your own someday, maybe you'll understand that.''

"I *do* understand that," Blair said. "But Alex, has it occurred to you that maybe you're giving her too much power over your own life? If you date somebody she doesn't like and she threatens to run away, will you give him up? What else are you going to let her control with emotional blackmail?''

"That's for Tasha and me to work out," Alex said. "Right now, I can't afford to have her doubt how much I care about her. Please tell Creighton that I'm sorry he wasted a trip to see me.''

"All right, Alex," Blair said with obvious reluctance.

"Thank you," Alex said. "Where is Tasha?"

"At my house with Rick," Nolan said. "I think they're still cleaning up the mess they made in the guest room, and they still have some work to do in the yard."

Alex nodded. "Send her home when they're done. If you'll all excuse me now, I really need a shower and then I believe I'll go to bed. I'm exhausted."

"Sure," Grace said, giving her a one-armed hug. "Call me tomorrow when you get up?"

"Will do," Alex said.

Nolan waited until she went back inside the house. Grace and Blair pushed their chairs into the table, but before they could leave, Nolan tapped Blair's shoulder. She turned to face him, her eyebrows arched in a question.

"It really doesn't matter if Alex takes a few days to make a decision about this?"

"I don't see why it would," Blair said. "Creighton's going to be here for the Fourth of July weekend. He'd expect her to think things over. Why do you ask?"

"I really do want Alexandra to be happy doing what *she* wants to do," Nolan said, smiling at Blair and then at Grace. "Will you give me a few days to try to work some things out before you deliver that message for her?"

Blair looked at Grace. Grace studied Nolan with a narrow-eyed intensity that nearly singed his eyebrows, then turned her gaze back to Blair and nodded. Blair looked at Nolan and smiled.

"All right, Nolan. You've got until Creighton Ramsey leaves on the morning of July fifth. That gives you five days."

Nolan smiled back at her. "Thank you. You two might try praying for my success."

"Trust me, we will," Grace said. "'Cause if you hurt

that girl, you'll answer to me, to my brothers and to all of her brothers.''

"The last thing I want to do is hurt her, Grace. I do love her, you know."

"I believe you, Nolan." Grace's stern expression softened into a smile that reminded him of Alex. "Good luck, cowboy. She's not an easy one."

"You've got that right," Nolan said. "But I happen to think she's worth it."

Chapter Fifteen

Nolan entered the back door of his own house, took a beer from the fridge and carried it out onto his patio. The horse's destruction in his backyard was still evident, and while he intended to let the kids clean up the majority of the mess, he couldn't see waiting to hose down the cement where the horse had expressed her displeasure so emphatically. Once that was done, he grabbed one of the chairs the animal hadn't stomped, picked up his beer and sat down to think through his strategy.

It wouldn't do to go at either Tasha or Alexandra too directly. For stubborn people like them, it was usually more productive to hit them sideways at first, so he could get at least a few of his own points across before they lined up all of their reasons for resisting what he wanted them to do. Therefore, the question was, what was the best line of attack for a thirteen-year-old girl? Or, to be more accurate, a defensive, upset thirteen-year-old girl.

By the time he'd finished his beer, the answer had come to him. Smiling to himself, he stood, turned to face Alexandra's bedroom window and thought about how much fun he was going to have telling her all about this someday. Preferably while sharing that very bed up there with her. Damn, but he was good.

He carried the empty bottle back inside. Realizing he was hungry, he decided to lure the kids down from the upstairs with food. Even if they were still upset, they were probably as hungry as a couple of starving wolves. Though nachos weren't high on the list of nutritious dinners, they were great kid bait. Sometimes a man simply did what he had to do.

Whistling softly, he put together a huge tray of tortilla chips, throwing on plenty of extra cheese, refried beans, olives and salsa. While it was heating in the microwave, he called the kids, poured them all a glass of milk and set the table. He heard their feet pounding down the stairs and reminded himself to play it low-keyed and very, very cool.

Rick entered the kitchen with his usual eager gait, his eyes glowing with delight at the sight of the gooey platter in the center of the table. Tasha hung back in the doorway, as if she had doubts about her welcome. Nolan smiled and motioned for her to come in.

"It's all ready," he said. "Dig in while it's hot."

She gave him a hesitant smile and slid into the booth beside Rick. "Is my mom coming?"

"No, she said she just wanted a shower and then she planned to go to bed. I guess she was pretty tired after all of the riding and camping you guys did. Was it a fun trip?"

"It was more fun when Rick came along, but it was all right," Tasha said. She scooped a pile of tortilla chips onto her plate. "Mom's okay, isn't she?"

"Oh, sure," Nolan said, hoping that wasn't the biggest

lie he'd ever told. For all he knew, Alex was over there sobbing her heart out, but he needed to get to Tasha while he still could. "By the way, Tash, I've got some good news for you."

"Yeah? What's that?"

"You're not going to have to move to California."

"Really?" Her eyebrows shot up under her bangs. "Cool. How do you know that?"

"Your mom told Blair to tell that agent to take a hike. She's giving up acting."

Rick stopped shoveling food into his mouth long enough to frown. "No way. Alex wouldn't do that."

"Well, she did. I was standing right there and heard the whole thing. Blair warned her she wouldn't get another shot at Hollywood, but Alex said she didn't care." Nolan smiled at Tasha, who was starting to look just the slightest bit uncomfortable. Not much, but enough, he thought. "She must love you a bunch to give up something she loves as much as she's always loved acting. You're a lucky girl."

Tasha nodded, but didn't say anything. Rick frowned at her. She looked up, saw his expression and frowned right back at him.

"What's your problem?" she said.

"I'm not the one with the problem," Rick said. "You are."

"Oh, yeah?"

"Yeah," Rick said. "I don't even have a mom and you've got the greatest mom I've ever seen, but you treat her like dirt. I can't believe you'd let her give up acting."

"Come on, Rick, you know she won't really quit. She'll still do the community theater thing and drag us all along with her just like always."

"I don't think so, Tasha," Nolan said. "She told me that wouldn't be much fun for her after she's worked with professionals. But, you know, she'll find something else to do with herself, I'm sure.''

"That's right," Tasha said, making a so-there face at Rick. "Mom always finds something weird and different to do. God, I hope she doesn't start in-line skating all over town like Mrs. Bishop does. That would be so-o-o embarrassing, I would die.''

"God, Tasha, I can't believe you," Rick said. "You are totally selfish and self-centered—"

"Rick," Nolan said, though he actually felt extremely proud that his son had developed so much empathy for Alexandra. "I wouldn't worry about her in-line skating too much, Tasha. I think she'll probably start spending a lot more time with you.''

"Why?"

"You made it perfectly clear today that you want all of her attention. Now that she's giving up acting, you're all she's got. She's going to build her whole life around you.''

Tasha set down the tortilla chip she'd just loaded as if she'd suddenly lost her appetite. "Well, I don't want *all* of her attention. I mean, jeez, I don't want her hanging around me all the time. Ick.''

Nolan turned his face toward Rick and winked. Rick nodded his head slightly, and Nolan had to clear his throat to stifle a chuckle.

"That could be a problem for you, Tasha. You'll be leaving for college in only five years. If your mom doesn't have some strong interest of her own, well…it'll be awfully hard for her to let you go. Since she doesn't have any other children or a husband, she'll really be lonely for you.''

"She'll be all right.''

"Of course she will. She'll just call you all the time and visit you a lot. I'm sure your friends in the dorm will get a kick out of Alexandra. She's such a character, who wouldn't?''

"She'll have a job," Tasha said, as if reassuring herself. "She'll still be a teacher."

"That's true," Nolan said. "But that means she'll have summers off and all those vacations to spend with you. She'll even be able to share spring break with you every year."

Tasha scrunched up one side of her mouth and studied him through narrowed eyes. After a moment a wry smile tugged at the corners of her mouth.

"Nice try, Nolan," she said. "I know what you're trying to do, but it won't work. If Mom and I stay here in Sunshine Gap, one of these days you two will kiss and make up, and she'll probably even marry you. She'll be your headache. Not mine."

"I wish that was true," Nolan said. "But I'm sorry to say that's not likely to happen now."

"Why not?" Rick asked. "You love her, don't you?"

"Yes, I do," Nolan said. "I love her and I need her, but I've really let her down."

"What did you do?" Tasha said.

"I was too greedy and selfish. I wanted her to be here for me all the time, but I forgot that it goes both ways."

"What do you mean?" Rick said.

Nolan hesitated, searching for the right words, choosing the ones that had finally helped him understand where he'd gone wrong. "When you really love somebody, you're supposed to want their happiness as much as your own. When Alex wanted to explore her new career opportunities, I flipped out and told her I wouldn't go back to California. I didn't even try to find a compromise so that maybe we could both have what we want."

"How do you compromise moving?" Tasha said.

"Sometimes you can't," Nolan said. "But I think in this instance, there were other things we could have done. She wouldn't have to live right in L.A., for one thing. There are lots of nice little towns in California she could commute from. Or, we could have lived in Nevada or even right here. I'd just have to be willing to do without her for a few days or a few weeks sometimes."

"Yeah, that's right," Rick said. "Most actors don't work all the time. It wouldn't be a whole lot different from when you've got a big trial, Dad. When that's going on, sometimes I don't see you for days."

"That's true," Nolan said. "The point is, we could've worked something out, I'm sure, but I didn't even try. I expected her to give up something she's wanted her whole life and do what I wanted her to do. And then I wouldn't listen to her when she tried to talk to me about it. I imagine she resents me like hell for that, and frankly, I don't blame her."

Tasha drew in a shuddering breath, and when she exhaled, a sob came with it. "Then she must resent me, too, because I did the same thing to her. I've been a selfish brat, haven't I?"

"I'll say," Rick said. "If Alex was my mom, I wouldn't care what she wanted to do. I'd try to help her."

"God, I'm a terrible person." Tasha buried her face in her hands and sobbed in earnest.

"No worse than me, honey." Nolan reached across the table and stroked Tasha's hair in what he hoped was a comforting gesture. "I practically dangled an acting career in front of her and then yanked it away when she succeeded. I don't think she'll ever be able to forgive me, but I know she'll forgive you."

Tasha looked up at him, swiping at her eyes with the backs of her knuckles. "You think so?"

"No doubt about it. You're her baby. She'd do anything for you. Even give up acting."

"No. She can't do that," Tasha said, determinedly shaking her head. "But I don't know if she'll believe me if I just tell her I've changed my mind."

"Yeah, that bit about running away was harsh," Rick said. "Your mom totally freaked when you said that."

"Well, there's got to be some way to convince her." Tasha looked at Nolan. "And we've got to get her to forgive you, too. Then we can be a family again."

"Alexandra is the one who makes us all feel like a family," Nolan said. "I think that's why it was so hard for us to imagine getting along without her, even once in a while."

"Could be," Rick said. "But what are we going to do now? Once she's made up her mind, it's not easy to change it."

"I think I've got an idea," Nolan said. "But first, I want your word that you will never threaten your mother with running away again, Tasha. That really was a lousy thing to do."

"I know. And I won't do it again, I promise."

Nolan smiled. "All right. I'll need help from you two." Both kids nodded eagerly, then leaned closer while he outlined his plan.

Alex wandered around her house for the next three days, feeling as if she'd been gutted. She didn't cry or rage. She didn't go anywhere or do anything. She couldn't concentrate on a book or a television program. She couldn't sleep. She wasn't hungry. If she had a purpose for living, she couldn't name it.

Tasha, the one person Alex wouldn't have minded talking to, was making herself extremely scarce. There was some kind of activity going on over at Nolan's house, but Alex couldn't figure out what it was. Nor could she bring herself to care enough to find out.

Fearing she would lose what little was left of her mind if she didn't find something to do with herself, Alex decided to clean the basement. A project of that magnitude would give her something to focus on for days, perhaps even weeks. She pulled all of the boxes off the shelves in the storage room and dragged them into the laundry room.

She'd barely opened the first box, however, when she heard a knock at the back door. Ignoring it, she dumped the contents of the first box onto the cement floor and moved on to open the second one. The knock came again. She straightened up and put her hands on her waist, waiting to see if whoever was up there intended to take the hint or be persistent.

The knock came again. Cursing under her breath, Alex dodged around the pile of stuff she'd created and climbed the stairs. She wasn't ready to talk to Grace or any other McBride, and she wouldn't hesitate to tell them so. But it wasn't a McBride on her back steps. It was Rick Larson.

She opened the door. "Hi, Rick."

"Hi, Alex." Rick stuffed his hands into his front jeans pockets and shifted his weight from one foot to the other, giving her a tight, nervous-looking smile. "How are you?"

"I'm okay," she said. "How are you?"

"Okay, I guess. But I haven't seen you in a while, and I, well…I really miss you, Alex."

Alex's heart instantly became as soft and gooey as a melted candy bar. "I miss you, too," she said. "You want to come in and have some cookies or a soda? Or both?"

"That sounds good," he said, "but do you think we could sit outside? It's, uh…really nice out tonight."

"Sure, I suppose we could."

"Need some help?" Rick asked.

"No. Sit down and I'll be right there."

She poked through the cupboards and the fridge, appalled at how little food there was in the house. She really had to get her grocery shopping more organized. No wonder Tasha was making herself scarce; she'd starve if she stayed at home. The best Alex could come up with was a box of crackers, peanut butter and a can of frozen lemonade. Loading a tray, she carried it out to the patio.

Rick jumped up and took it from her, then held her chair for her with the innate good manners and charm of his father. The thought gave Alex a sharp pang, but she quickly suppressed it. She hadn't heard from Nolan since the day Tasha's horse had gone back to the ranch alone. Alex figured that was a definite sign that he didn't want anything more to do with her.

"Help yourself," she said, indicating the tray with a rueful laugh. "I couldn't find any cookies, I'm afraid."

"I'm really not hungry," Rick said. He poured them each a glass of the lemonade, however, and sat back with a sigh. "So, what've you been doing, Alex?"

"Not much," she said. "You?"

He shrugged. "The usual summer stuff. Swimming. Hiking. Fishing with my dad."

"That's nice," Alex said.

"It's okay." He drank from his glass, then shot a glance over his shoulder toward his own house. "This is good lemonade."

"Thanks," Alex said. "I can measure those cans of water with the best of them."

Rick laughed more than her feeble joke deserved and shot another glance toward home. "You do ice cubes well too, Alex."

"Is there something wrong, Rick?"

He whipped his head back around to look at her, a too-bright smile on his face. "Wrong? Oh...no, nothing's wrong. Everything's just fine. Why do you ask?"

"You seem a little nervous," Alex said.

"Nervous?" His face flushed a painful shade of embarrassment. "Why would I be nervous with you? You're practically my...well, you know, I sort of think of you as my...mom. I know you're really not, and maybe you don't want to be now that you and Dad aren't friends anymore, but that's how I feel about you, anyway."

Alex reached across the table and laid her hand over his. "Rick, it's okay. I think of you as the son I would choose if I could. No matter what happens between me and your dad, you'll always own a piece of my heart."

Though she hadn't thought it was possible, his flush actually deepened. He cleared his throat. Shot another glance toward home. Cleared his throat again. Wondering what on earth was the matter with the boy who had always been so poised and mature for his age, she poured him another glass of lemonade.

And then came the voice.

"She don't beat ya. She don't hardly ever ground ya or yell at ya. She gives ya food to eat, clothes to wear and a roof over your head. Honey, what more do ya want in a mom?"

Alex froze, one hand still on the lemonade pitcher. That was Nolan's voice coming from the other side of the hedge. What in the world was he doing over there?

"I want her to be happy," Tasha's voice said. "She ain't happy at all, Nolan. She just wanders around the house all day like a sad, sad ghost. And it's all my fault."

"Your fault?" Nolan said. "But you're such a sweet little gal, darlin'. How can that be?"

"I wasn't sweet at all to my mama," Tasha said, her

voice filled with what sounded very much like genuine regret. "I was selfish and spoilt, and I stomped on my mama's dreams and broke 'em. And I don't know how to make it right with her again."

"That sounds awful dang serious," Nolan said.

"It is," Tasha said. "Her heart's breakin', I can tell. And my heart's breakin', too 'cause I love her a whole, big bunch. I really wish I'd listened to her when she tried to talk to me. She must think I'm a terrible daughter and a real bad person."

"Well, you're not the only one, darlin'," Nolan said. "I didn't listen to her, either, and I love her as much as you do. I just didn't understand what she needed, you know? I was too busy thinkin' about what I wanted, to ask her what she wanted. Now, I don't reckon she'll ever forgive me, but if she would, why, I'd find a way for that wonderful woman to have all her dreams come true."

"Wouldja Nolan?" Tasha said. "How wouldja do that?"

"I don't rightly know for sure," Nolan said. "Maybe I'd just buy her a hundred tickets on one o' them newfangled airplanes, so she could go work wherever and whenever she wanted while I stayed home with the younguns."

Alex snorted with laughter at his horrible Western drawl as well as his dialogue, although the content of his words sounded fairly...interesting. It was all so corny, so dopey, so absolutely wonderful—only people who loved her one hell of a lot could have brought themselves to deliver such dreadful lines without completely cracking up. She didn't realize tears were streaming down her face until Rick stuffed a wad of tissues into her hand. She blotted her eyes and tried to smile at him. He winked and tilted his head toward the hedge.

"Well, we ain't too young anymore, ya know," Tasha

said. "I can even cook some. So can Rick. I reckon we could get along without her once in a while, if she didn't stay away too awful long."

"Sure we could, darlin'," Nolan said. "And maybe sometimes we could go along with her. All I know is I'd sure rather have her around sometimes than not have her around at all. I got a great big ol' diamond ring here for her, anytime she's ready to marry me. Dang, but I miss that woman. She was the best friend a man could ever ask for. Better even than a golden retriever."

Alex smiled at Rick. "He's going to pay for that one."

Grinning wickedly, Rick whispered, "You drag the hose over to the hedge. I'll turn it on when you're ready."

"But what can we do to make her smile again?" Tasha asked. "I've just gotta see my mama smile and hear her laugh one more time."

"We'll think of something, darlin'. I promise ya that."

Feeling truly alive for the first time in days, Alex attached the trigger sprayer to the end of the hose, then dragged it to the gap in the hedge, gave Rick a thumbs-up sign and tucked the hose behind her back as she stepped into Nolan's yard. Nolan and Tasha stood in the middle of the yard, facing her house, each clutching a dog-eared script. They'd obviously put a lot of thought and effort into what they wanted to say for her benefit.

When they looked up at her, their eyes wide and hopeful, if a bit apprehensive, Alex's heart turned all soft and gooey again. But Nolan was still going to pay for that line about the golden retriever. She adjusted her grip around the nozzle's trigger, getting ready to shoot.

"Hi, there," she said.

"Hi, Mom," Tasha said.

"Hi," Nolan said.

"Cute idea," Alex said, "sending Rick over to lure me out of the house, I mean. Your, uh…play was cute, too."

"Thanks," Tasha said. "I think."

"It was a compliment," Alex assured her. "Did you mean what you said?"

"Yes, Mom, I really did," Tasha said. "I love you."

"I love you, too, sweetie," Alex said.

"I meant everything I said, too, Alex," Nolan said. "Every single word."

Alex smiled then. "Really, Nolan? Every single word?"

"Of course. I've loved you for a long, long time."

"Well, good. I love you, too. Especially when you compare me to a big, furry dog."

With that, she whipped the hose out from behind her back, squeezed the trigger hard and let him have it full force. Tasha shrieked and jumped back from the cold water spraying off Nolan's chest onto her. Nolan held one hand in front of him, trying to direct the heaviest stream away from his face as he advanced on Alex. Rick whooped with laughter from the other side of the hedge.

"Turn it off, Rick," Nolan called.

"No way," Rick called back. "I got her out here to listen to you. Now you're on your own."

"A golden retriever, Larson?" Alex shouted. "Is that your idea of being romantic?"

Dancing around and moving the hose to her best advantage, she laughed maniacally. Nolan bravely battled on, getting closer and closer to her in spite of the continuous soaking she gave him. He finally wrestled the nozzle out of her grasp, drenching her almost as much as she'd already drenched him. Tossing the hose back through the gap in the hedge, he grabbed Alex around the waist, jerked her against him and kissed her breathless.

"No, *that's* my idea of being romantic," he said against her lips. Then he kissed her again.

Alex wrapped both arms around his neck and clung with every bit of strength she possessed. She didn't care that her hair was a mass of dripping rat's tails or that her shirt had probably gone nearly transparent wherever it was wet or that her shorts felt cold and soggy. She only cared that Nolan's arms were around her, his heart was pounding out the same frantic rhythm as hers and his mouth was devouring hers with the same fierce hunger and desperation she felt.

God, but she had missed him, missed holding him, missed loving him.

To her amazement, a boisterous cheer sounded from inside Nolan's house, and a moment later, her entire family and half of the movie's cast and crew came through the back door, most of them carrying food or something to drink. A boombox appeared from somewhere, and the next thing she knew, a full-fledged party had sprung up in the backyard.

Nolan danced her to the far end of the patio, both arms clasped possessively around her waist. "I went about this all wrong before," he said.

"Went about what all wrong?"

"Asking you to marry me."

"Oh, that," she said. "What do you think you did wrong?"

"I didn't start with telling you how much I love you. We've always been so in tune with each other, I guess I just expected you to know how I felt by instinct. It occurred to me later that you may have thought I simply viewed our relationship as being convenient, and perhaps not much more."

"I'm not sure what I thought," Alex said, smiling up at him. "I like the words I'm hearing now, though."

"You can hear them as often as you want. I love you, Alex."

"I love you, too, Nolan."

"Will you marry me?"

"Yes."

"No conditions about careers or where we'll live?" he asked.

"No. I've got myself an urban cowboy, who writes awful scripts and organizes parties for me, and two great kids who love me. That's all I really need to be happy. The rest will work out somehow."

Nolan turned around and hollered to the crowd. "Hey, everybody, she said yes!"

There was another boisterous cheer, then everyone filed by, shook Nolan's hand or pounded him on the back, hugged and kissed Alex, picked up whatever they had brought and left the same way they had come. Within fifteen minutes the party had vanished, and Cal had taken Tasha and Rick to spend the night at his place.

After the last vehicle drove away, Nolan found the sudden quiet a bit...unnerving. He'd spent so much time and energy focusing on convincing Alex to accept his proposal, he hadn't planned any strategy beyond that moment. Damn. He should have a bottle of champagne on ice and flowers for when he gave her the ring and maybe some scented candles for the bedroom.

She turned to him with a soft, sultry smile, and the rest of his worries flitted off into the night. This was Alexandra. His very best friend. His woman. His mate. He didn't need strategies or sophisticated moves to impress her.

The only thing he needed, he already had in abundance— love for Alexandra. Taking her hand, he led her inside and upstairs to his bedroom, where he proceeded to at least try to show her how very much she meant to him. Afterward, they cuddled in his bed, talking and laughing and making plans for the future.

At last the spaces between words became longer and longer, and a lazy, sleepy sense of well-being settled over him. Alex snuggled against his side, providing a sweet warmth he enjoyed even on a hot summer night. Suddenly his mind flashed back to the instant when she'd whipped the hose out from behind her back and blasted him with it, and he couldn't hold in a chuckle.

"What's so funny?" she asked with a yawn.

"I was just thinking about the moment when I finally knew everything was going to be all right," he said.

"Oh, yeah? When I said I'd marry you?"

"No, it was when you let me have it with the hose."

She raised herself up on one elbow, a worried frown wrinkling her forehead. "Oh, Nolan, that was an awfully juvenile thing for me to do. I really should apologize—"

"I loved it," he said, pulling her down for a long, satisfying kiss. "That's when I knew my Alex was back."

"Your Alex?"

"Yeah." Nolan smiled and slid his fingers into her hair. "You know the one I mean. She's kind of a wild woman who continually reminds me that life is too short to waste it being stodgy all the time. Please, don't ever lose her, Alexandra. Without her, life's not half as much fun."

* * * * *